KU-406-223

What Are the Bugles
Blowing for ?

NICOLAS FREELING

What are the Bugles
Blowing for?

Heinemann: London

William Heinemann Ltd
15 Queen Street, Mayfair, London W1X 8BE
LONDON   MELBOURNE   TORONTO
JOHANNESBURG   AUCKLAND

First published 1975
© Nicolas Freeling 1975

434 27180 2

Made and printed in Great Britain by
Morrison & Gibb Ltd, London and Edinburgh

'What are the bugles blowing for?' asked
  Files-on-Parade.
'To turn you out, to turn you out'
  the Colour-Sergeant said.

        .   .   .   .   .

'What makes the rear-rank breathe so hard?' said
  Files-on-Parade.
'It's bitter cold, it's bitter cold'
  the Colour-Sergeant said.
'What makes that front-rank man fall down?' says
  Files-on-Parade.
'A touch of sun, a touch of sun'
  the Colour-Sergeant said.
They are hanging Danny Deever, they are marching
  of him round,
They have halted Danny Deever by his coffin on
  the ground,
And he'll swing in half a minute for a sneaking
  shooting hound.
—O, they're hanging Danny Deever in the morning!

A 'BARRACKROOM BALLAD', BY RUDYARD KIPLING.
(quoted by permission of Mrs George Bambridge and Eyre Methven Ltd.)

Kipling's dropped aspirates in his 'soldier talk' now appear dated. Anway, as George Orwell remarked several years ago, to restore them strengthens. On the other hand, the sentiments expressed do not date, and need no strengthening. Such was also the opinion of T. S. Eliot, an officially approved poet, highly thought of by all civil servants.

N. F.

THE FIRST MAGISTRATE REVIEWS
A DOSSIER

The President of the Republic had had supper with his family, in his flat. He did this once a week, on average, and when he could, which was rarer, he spent the rest of the evening with them. Even if he had official business after, he did not discuss it, since like any trained thinker he could switch off compartments of his mind. Tonight, though he had made jokes, eaten as usual simply, a fish salad, and drunk a glass or two of his favourite country wine (unpretentious, shipped for him in a barrel from the village and served in a jug), all who knew him had seen that he was not comfortable: this was unusual but nobody had commented.

Now he was walking with his quick nervous stride, for he was a man of scarcely fifty, and liked to correct the deskbound stoop by simple exercise; a thing rarely possible in his good city because of being recognised and, too, one so rarely had the time. In chilly drizzling autumn rain most eyes were downcast or masked by umbrellas, and paid no heed to the passer. If they had, and perchance been importunate, there were two secret-service men (no longer known as gorillas), one walking a little in front. He must have had eyes in the back of his head though, for when the President looked at his watch and decided sadly to get on with it, he dropped back at once and as the car drew up the three men got into it as smoothly, perhaps, as for a scene in a gangster movie.

The President took all this for granted: he was well served. The guards were a burden of his office, and a heavy one, and a daily one. There were other burdens heavier yet, but not, thank Heaven, daily.

The car whisked through the wet shiny streets, turned in at the gate of the official residence, drew up at the portal: he jumped out, handed his hat and damp raincoat to a valet, went straight to his private office, switched on his reading-lamp and sat down. There was only one file on his desk: here too he was well served. The ordinary cloth-bound files were marked with a simple code showing the department where they originated. Ministry of Justice. This evening the President was not economist, administrator or diplomat, but magistrate.

To be First Magistrate is in general an empty title, but in this country there is one decision which is taken by the President alone: it is too important to be left to the Minister of the Interior or the Keeper of the Seals. The legalist and juridical problems have been examined by those competent to do so. What is left is a human, personal problem, for it is nothing more or less than a man's life. In the case of a man condemned to death for a capital crime by the Assize Court, in the Republic, the prerogative of mercy belongs to the President solely. The death penalty in this country still exists, untouched on the statute book. It is rarely demanded by the Public Prosecutor, and still more rarely passed by the Court. As for the President, he had never met this problem before. There is a tradition and a good one that he takes this particular function very seriously, dating from Vincent Auriol, the first president of the Fourth Republic and followed by all his successors. The file on the President's desk was a man's personal dossier.

It was unusually thick: this was no banal criminal, no man made brutish by hardship or unbalanced by illness. The lawyers, and the doctors, were quite clear upon this subject. No mental disease, no psychosis or by any definition disabling neurosis. No legal or juridical flaw in procedure. No doubt, in fact, anywhere. The authorship of the crime had never even been questioned. And here it all was, neatly typed abstracts of everything from the preliminary police enquiry down to the Court of Appeals. But there had been— still was—a political element. It had been examined by the political police, considered by the President's personal assistants. Conclusion: nothing there to justify interference with due process of law.

Politics. . . . The President was a skilled and adroit politician; he would hardly have been elected otherwise. His mind, his training and formation, his experience as a state servant: all had bent this man towards a habit of seeing things in abstract terms. In religion, philosophy, in political and economic science, he rationalised as far as he could, as far as was consistent, as far as he dared. One could and did consider even such things as his family life, his health, his pleasures and enjoyments as abstract matters. There were limits to this—luckily.

At the end of the dossier were the usual letters. Relatives, the usual requests for personal interviews, the defence counsel, the elderly gentleman who was a judge at the Court of Human Rights, the notable criminal advocate who was the leading pleader against capital punishment. Last there was a letter still sealed, unopened by his secretariat, marked 'Uncensored' and the envelope stamped with a prison visa. A plain white envelope of good quality, addressed by hand to 'The President of the Republic. Personal.' Black ink from a real pen, firm upright handwriting of character and intelligence. No need of a graphologist's report to tell the President that, nor the multiplied psychiatric experts which were in the dossier, which he had read attentively.

The letter had been respected. One did not fabricate letter bombs from condemned cells. The President reached for his letter knife, part of a simple and very beautiful desk set given him by the People's Republic of China. What form of death penalty did they have in China? It was not he thought a problem they allowed to worry them. Did they shoot people? If one admitted the idea at all a bullet was perhaps as dignified—and honest—a method as any. Talk of barbarity was cant. Whether one broke or severed a neck by traditional methods, or adopted the clumsier techniques of the chemically minded, who imagined that gas, electricity or a pharmaceutical poison were more hygienic—tidier as it were—than blood, it was cant: the whole thing was barbaric. One took life; there was an executioner, and a victim. Whether the one be doctor or butcher, be the other dressed in formal evening clothes or rags, be the procedure public or secret, the fact remained unaltered. The firing squad was in any case reserved in this country as a military punishment.

The President permitted himself a formal meditation on death, such as took place when he entered the crypt of the Monument to the Resistance on Fort Mount Valérien—there were also other occasions, some private.

He opened and read the letter. It did not help him much. The man asked, in simple and formal language, to be put to death. That

3

was all. He thought for only a moment or two longer before deciding that his Yes or his No was not yet ripe. He put the letter back in the envelope and this back in the file, closed it, pushed it to one side, took a sheet of memo paper and uncapped his pen, thought a moment before putting it to the paper, then wrote rapidly.

'I will not pronounce on this matter before an element which in my view is missing has been supplied. Pray instruct that the officer conducting the original police enquiry be brought here and given an interview with me. This will be done immediately.' He initialled, attached the half sheet to the clip outside the file, drank a little Vittel water and went to bed, where he slept as soundly as the man in the cell.

II

THE DUTY OFFICER IN HOT WEATHER

Henri Castang was sitting on the base of his spine, on a hard wooden chair in front of the open window, in the Police Judiciaire offices on a flaming hot August day, and a Sunday at that, whistling to himself, drearily enough.

'Memphis in June.' Sounded good, sung by Mister Carmichael in that blurry, whisky-laden voice. Even whistled by himself it had a nice tune, which he could do with one finger on the piano. The words had a pretty irony. Cousin Amanda making a rhubarb pie. He didn't know much about Memphis, but getting it slung in your eye was nearer the mark at a rough guess.

Half the country was on holiday, and the other half wasn't doing more than it had to, because the thermometer marked thirty degrees, and being the weekend had gone off to look for the sweet oleander in the surrounding countryside. He didn't know about perfume but guessed that the acrid stench of recently doused forest fires would be close enough. There was nobody in the office but him, and a duty agent asleep somewhere, and a switchboard operator doing a crossword, and this here shady verandah. He nearly split himself yawning. Narrow Frankish face. All of a muddle, like the rest of him. If he saw the back of his head when getting a haircut it was a Mediterranean bullet, round and Gaulish. The features were not straightforward Slav, the way his wife's were, but vaguely Bohemian in cast, and the short wiry black hair going prematurely grey in bits. He wished he were in Memphis: it would make a change.

Probably not much of one. Cities were all the same. If Castang had woken up in Bremen or Palermo he would have gone to the office just the same, and soon picked up the local accent. This was just a provincial capital. Half a million souls say, counting the out-lying suburbs, counting the Portuguese and the Turks, and the Brits, and a few Americans all doubtless in C.I.A.

As a cop you'd see no difference. You'd be filling in the same forms in Malmo or Barcelona, with Martin Beck or Van der Valk as a boss instead of Commissaire Richard, who was less eccentric but what odds did that make?

Richard wasn't on holiday but had taken the weekend off. Out somewhere playing golf he supposed. Or something.

You could only express the difference in clichés. In Memphis he supposed there'd be more blacks, and here the cops wore képis so you were in France, but in the long run it was all McKeesport, Pennsylvania, and the smell would be just the same.

Work was languid. He'd been there all morning and caught up on the paper. And now it was midafternoon and hot, even though this old barrack was solidly built with thick walls. Plain-clothes cops had a gun problem. Castang was wearing a loose overshirt of rough towel material which absorbed sweat and came low enough to conceal the belt holster on his right hip. It gave his stocky body an oddly squat look but he didn't care. What you lost in dignity you gained in comfort.

He looked out at the horsechestnut trees, in full leaf but rusty already: they didn't much care for their diet of salt in winter and sulphur dioxide in summer. In the branches hung a paper dart. The last duty dogsbody had been engaged in aeronautical research.

The telephone rang while he was in midyawn.

'I wish to speak to the Commissaire.' It was a peremptory voice, used to prompt obedience.

'Not here at present, I'm afraid.'

'Away?'

'Just out. Sunday, you know.'

'Ah. Yes, of course.'

'Duty officer speaking; can I help you?'

'I require your presence,' abruptly.

'You'd like to explain your difficulty?'

'I am a murderer.' Type with loose screws, further loosened by the heat.

'Yes?' in a deadish voice. 'Who of?'

'My wife. My daughter. A man.' Brisk and factual, but the

6

dotties often were; had it all worked out, most detailed and plausible.

'Where?'

'Here. My home, I'm speaking from my home address. Number seven, Rue des Ecrivains.' Not in Memphis. Here.

'When?'

'Now. Ten, no, roughly twenty minutes ago.'

'What with?' These bald questions were the only quick way of detecting a real emergency. The dotties sometimes replied to this one with 'an atom bomb' or 'the evil eye'.

'A gun. My gun. I keep it in the bedside table. It is my legitimate property.' This insistence on legitimacy struck Castang: a pointer too that he was not dealing with loose screws.

'And your name is . . .?'

'La Touche. Gilbert La Touche.' Something familiar too about this name: rang a bell somewhere, but dim. Castang pulled a message pad towards him with the phone tucked in his collarbone, picking up a ballpoint and glancing at his watch. Message received 16.37. Dog watch in dog day, while in doldrum, but this might be a squall, for a small black cloud had appeared upon the brassy and boring horizon.

'Right, I'm taking notes, Mr Gilbert La Touche, seven Rue des Ecrivains, you think you may have killed one or more persons with a pistol, that's all correct? Have you rung a doctor?'

'No. No use.'

'Or Police Secours?'

'No. I am aware that the criminal police is needed; it was logical to ring you.'

Logical . . . legitimate . . . He wrote 'appears collected' on the scratch pad, and said 'You've a family doctor?'

'Serves no purpose,' with a sort of polite irritability.

'People sometimes look dead and aren't.'

'There is no mistake,' primly, a man unaccustomed to his judgment being called into question.

'If for no one else then for you. You may not realise it but you're suffering from shock.'

'Nonsense. In the absence of the Commissaire, nobody is needed but yourself—and talk less, man.'

'Are you alone in the house?'

'Yes—the servants . . .'

'Never mind. I'll be with you in a few minutes—about five. Do nothing at all. Don't touch anything—remain where you are.'

Pure routine—Castang clicked the receiver bar.

'Switchboard—that was an emergency. Hold and record incoming calls. I'll check back when I know what's in it: may be serious.' The duty agent, a handsome boy from Nice with wavy black hair and pale skin—rather a silly boy—was typing languidly in the outer office.

'Come on,' said Castang briefly. 'Emergency.' The keys of the wagon, a small Renault with no markings. The boy put on his gunbelt. Castang slipped and checked his own pistol, leaving it cocked. If the fellow really had a gun . . . maniacs were sometimes unpredictable.

The Rue des Ecrivains was in the oldest part of the town, a quarter where streets were medievally narrow and some houses, however patched and repatched, had bones many hundreds of years old. One-way streets, with no parking permitted. Here it was really hot. At the corner was a tiny fountain with a trio of plane trees grouped around it, at which Castang made a face, it looked so fresh and peaceful. They'd have to park on the pavement in the grilling afternoon heat funnelled and pinned down by these high narrow walls.

III

UNMOVED CALM OF AN INSPECTOR
OF FINANCE

It came as a surprise. Number seven was an archway with over it a coat of arms in carved stone, crumbled by time. Double doors stood open, of three-inch oak iron-knopped and barred. They drove through into a little cobbled courtyard: a car was parked but there was room for a second. It was shady and pleasant, with a vine growing on the sunny wall and boxes of geraniums, and decorated with its original furnishings of wrought iron, things for attaching horses, holding torches, scraping mud off one's boots. Behind, chiselled stone, white plaster, wrought-iron balconies—a small town house of the seventeenth century.

Castang looked at it and said 'Nice house.' There wasn't any more to say: homicides can happen anywhere. He did not know, though Vera could have told him, that it was one of the showpieces of the city, a 'hôtel particulier' classed as a historic monument. It meant to the police only that the people inside, dead or otherwise, were rich.

More wrought iron, like black lace, with a monogram worked into it. A bell handle, which pulled produced a faint musical jangle like falling water far away. Then complete silence. Siesta time for the rich. A prolonged siesta, a big sleep.

The door opened; a man stood there, a man of fifty, perfectly tranquil. Neatly dressed in a summer suit, Legion of Honour in buttonhole. In no sense disarranged or abnormal, no twitching or grimacing, but the controlled voice of authority that had spoken on the telephone.

'You are the police?'

'Castang. I am an officer of Police Judiciaire; this is Agent Lucciani.' A hand invited entry, courteously.

'We'll go upstairs.' Floor marble, black and white chessboard. Stairs white marble, wrought-iron balustrade. Portraits in gilt frames; florid fatfaced persons in lace and watered silk, men in wigs, women in complicated and insanitary-looking hairstyles. Landing of pale parquet with geometric patterns of paler marquetry. Doors open to a suite of drawing-rooms.

Stairs continuing, narrower. Second landing, like the first, but bedrooms and—a lot more recently—bathrooms. The stairs went on to another storey, but in plain wood, to children and servants.

A door stood open. Castang could see part of a bed padded in dull yellow silk. The fresh blood made a colour contrast.

As the man said. Three bodies. Unmistakably dead. Two women, one middle aged, one young. A man, large, massive, hairy. All naked. Flagrant; a crime of passion. The man lay on the floor, on his back; several entry wounds in the big belly. The women on the bed, executed with a single shot in the head. A small-calibre pistol; Castang looked for it. It was there on the floor, a little six thirty-five Colt. Automatic, six shot. Now empty; the man had four wounds. Castang picked it up with a ball-point through the trigger-guard. Pretty little gun, walnut-gripped, a woman's handbag model: the work it had done meant it was no toy after all. He wrapped it in a paper tissue and put it away. The three were very dead indeed and the man calm and, one would say, perfectly sane. But rules were rules.

'We'll need this doctor.'

'As you like,' indifferently.

'One who knows you preferably. Use your phone? You'll show Monsieur Lucciani? Doctor straight away, Jacques, then switchboard. Photographer, technicians and message through to Richard at his home if you can, no hurry for ambulances, dead on arrival, notify the path lab three customers. Official notification to the Proc for a homicide. Monsieur La Touche?'

'Yes.' Standing there so tranquil, with a slight smile, as though appreciative of efficiency in others. So much calm was abnormal.

'You told me that you were the author of these deaths. You maintain that? Very well. The doctor is for you; it's a rule. I want you now to understand this clearly. This is a homicide, it has the appearance of a crime. I am an officer of police. Pending the arrival of the Commissaire, or the Procureur, or another legal officer, I assume the responsibility for everything here. I will be bound shortly to put certain questions to you. You are free not to answer them, or indeed not to say anything at all if you think it would incriminate you to do so. Do you understand that?'

'Perfectly. I am neither shocked nor confused, and in complete possession of all my faculties.'

'You have no right to say that, and I take no note of it: it is simply untrue. I may not in any case question you till the doctor's had a look at you. Till then I want you to stay downstairs with Monsieur Lucciani: he has to keep an eye on you. All right?'

'I understand,' still with that slight ironic smile.

'Very well. Don't drink any alcohol.'

'I never do,' simply.

Castang was alone. There would be the usual thorough technical examination. Everything would be photographed from every angle. It was unnecessary—perhaps. It was obvious what had happened— perhaps. Only one thing was obvious to him that minute; that this was going to be less simple than it looked, if only because inevitably the Press was going to jump upon this. It was important in the extreme that all the formalities should be most carefully observed, that it should be cut and dried. No margin for error whatever. He wished that Richard were here. He wasn't, and the likelihood was he wouldn't be. Very well, pending the arrival of an officer of the law, which he himself wasn't, being a simple police officer, he was going to see that everything was carried out as the law dictated. Meant no more really than having things tidy. The human element came later.

Looked at in this mechanical light the thing was easy. The man had arrived unexpectedly, unheard. He had taken his wife in flagrant adultery—and his daughter. Castang frowned at that. Outside his experience, this detail. And outside most people's too—no? But there it was. Surprised, the trio had been more or less paralysed. The man had walked over to the bedside table, taken the pistol he knew to be there—it mattered little whether it were his or his wife's; it was there: the drawer still stood open. The big man, the lover, and a fine big hunk of flesh he had been, even if a little too fat (but all that flesh was grass now) had tried to react. A mistake; four bullets in that big target. And then, quite coolly, and that was a thing which would have a legal meaning later on, the man had shot the two women, with one well-aimed shot each. So no self-defence, no struggle or accidental discharge. A straightforward assassination.

Two well-made women. A cop felt no emotion of any sort whatever looking at the two still beautiful naked bodies. With a small-size pistol, the bullets had stayed in the heads. No mess. Little blood. Even the features were scarcely distorted. But grass, grass, grass.

A crime of passion by a husband is not, whatever the public believes, a legal argument. But temporary insanity, of course, is. It would not be a difficult affair, if there was no mistake in the preliminary enquiry. And that was his, Henri Castang's, job.

The windows were open but in the hot windless air the smell of perfume, smokeless powder and fresh blood hung overpoweringly, like honeysuckle. He stared out at a stone-flagged terrace where the upper classes had been drinking tea, and a formal walled garden beyond, with box hedge and flowers, box hedge and vegetables, the usual herbs round a sundial and a strip of grass to finish with, and fruit trees espaliered against the walls. Lovingly cared for, probably by some Portuguese footman.

The dim memory of why the name La Touche meant something had come swimming back. . . . Paper . . . a yearly report of some sort: the fellow was a financier. It hadn't interested Castang, who knew nothing of finance. A bank; an insurance company? No, something governmental—the Accounts Tribunal, that was it: the controlling body on public spending—the fellow was an Inspector of Finance! Absolutely the top of the basket. But he'd killed people just the same as a factory hand at Renault. The difference was that this one would have highly placed friends. No wonder he was calm. Castang's nose twitched as he turned back to the room. The smell, above all, was of money. Not that it bothered him: he'd be off this case in twenty-four hours, as soon as the preliminaries were accomplished.

The doorbell rang.

The doctor was a bloodless secretive one who thinks a word, let alone a smile, diminishes his capital and amounts to an act of recklessness. And look where that leads to. He examined his patient in the study downstairs, was brief about it, rejoined Castang, who was smoking in the hall, with downcast eyes and a nun-like glide which conveyed distaste for the police. Giving any information

12

whatever was a grave infringement of ethics, and it took a struggle.

'If you refuse to answer I'll have the police doctor go over him, that's all.'

'Unnecessary,' prim.

'No disabling malady, such as might cause abnormal behaviour?'

'Such as what?'

'Like epilepsy,' sighing, 'or diabetes or migraine.'

'No.'

'Physical symptoms of nervous trouble, a depression, or over-tension?'

'This was a superficial examination,' contemptuously.

'Quite. I'm forced to remind you of the legal obligations. He's in possession of his faculties?'

'Meaningless.'

'Meaning that he can see, hear, speak and understand clearly, and is able to return an answer to simple questions.'

'You mean bullying.' Castang was used to it. Every cop is.

'Doctor,' agreeably, 'you should commit a murder.'

'How dare you?'

'You would discover just how many safeguards there are for a presumed author—neither accused, charged nor condemned—of a criminal act.'

'Do you wish me to complain to your superiors?'

'The Public Prosecutor will be here shortly.'

'You are ignoble,' signing his name bitterly, tearing sheets off his memo and prescription pads, handing them over with hatred.

'You will be reimbursed by the State, Doctor,' making it sound insulting. 'Have you given him a sedative or other medicament?'

'No. There is an aid, prescribed there, for the restoration of neurophysical balance. To withhold it might constitute failure in coming to the aid of a person in danger. A criminal offence—as you are doubtless aware. I would so testify.' Snap, as of jaws of crocodile: the man headed for the door. Castang didn't stop him.

'Lucciani—a cop to stand in front of the gate. And find a chemist that's open.'

La Touche was sitting in a stiff little armchair, maintaining his air of polite indifference.

'How do you feel?' asked Castang.

'Tired. It's nothing. Quite in touch. Able to answer your questions.'

'Very few for the present. I should like to have a formal identification of these persons. Your wife?'

'Yes.'

'And your daughter?'

'Yes.'

'Is the man known to you?'

'Yes.'

'There may, you see, be relatives to notify.'

'He's a painter. His name is Davids. He lives in Paris. I forget the address. There's probably a card in his wallet.'

'Thank you. Has he a wife?'

'I believe so.'

Castang did not pursue it.

IV

DUE PROCESS OF LAW

An ancient prescription in French criminal law is that in grave crimes 'The Parquet shall descend' upon the scene. It is jargon for the legal authorities; the Public Prosecutor, known as the Proc, or his substitute, and one of the judges of instruction attached to the local tribunal. In former days these grave gentlemen were obliged to visit in person, accompanied by their clerks, the theatre of affairs. It was not at all a stupid idea. Lawyers are ridiculously divorced from any sense of reality at all times.

However, nowadays the 'visit' has become a formality. A police officer of the rank of Commissaire is by definition an officer of justice, and his presence ensures that the law has been respected. It is rare nowadays that the Proc appears in person.

Castang was not a Commissaire, though he held a law degree, which is a condition, and with a bit more seniority and by passing an examination he might expect to become one. He was an officer of police, with several powers conferred by the Code of Criminal Procedure—he could for example interrogate witnesses. But there was a lot he couldn't do. He was waiting in consequence for a Substitute, one of the half-dozen or more bright young men attached, in a major city, to the Prosecutor's office.

It came as a slight shock to see the Proc in person. Though to think of it, the surprise was lessened. An Inspector of Finance is a highly-placed personage. To see the occasion treated as a social call was a foretaste, doubtless, of things to come.

'Hallo Castang,' cordially, 'how are you then?' offering a legal hand, large, dry and chalky. 'Not been on holiday yet? Well,

Gilbert,' imperturbable as though invited for cocktails, 'this is a sorry matter. My condolences are nonetheless sincere for my being obliged to undertake a melancholy duty, as you will understand: I heard of this with consternation. Well, Castang, where's Richard?'

'I don't know, sir. He will have been notified I should hope by now.'

'Well well, we'll manage without him. Tell me briefly, then.'

'Monsieur La Touche himself notified me by telephone of what had happened. I have taken the usual steps. The technicians will be here shortly—here they are, in fact—for verification, though at first sight there is—well, let's say it seems straightforward. Monsieur La Touche has made the necessary identifications, and has been kind enough to give me his complete co-operation.' It takes more than that to embarrass a cop, but Castang did feel a slight oppression at La Touche just standing there, in a casual social attitude of someone receiving guests at a large boring party where a lot of people are just there to grease the wheels of business. A bit glassy of eye.

'Ah, Mr Ergh. So good of you to come.'

'The doctor has just been,' added Castang colourlessly. 'Monsieur La Touche feels able to tell me whatever I need to know.'

The Proc nodded: it was what he needed to know.

'Would you have the goodness to show me, Gilbert? Castang accompanies us with your permission.' The technical squad were holding back politely, waiting for the Proc to pass in front of them. He was a bit like the parish priest, thought Castang irreverently, come to say the rosary at a wake. He walked on heavy feet to the bedroom, looked imperturbable at the scene offered, came back downstairs with a nod to the photographer to go ahead, slowly drew out a cigarette-case; blew out the first puff of smoke with a noisy, stolid heave of the lungs. La Touche might have been showing the house to a prospective buyer. No no, no damp anywhere.

'Very well, Castang, in Richard's absence you'll continue with your preliminary enquiry. Gilbert.'

'Yes?'

'I'll be leaving. This goes forward with no further intervention on my part. A question of form: have you an advocate here in the town with any penal experience?'

'Dieudonné is my usual man of affairs. His practice is commercial. His brains, I suppose, would supply the lack of habit in the penal code. I imagine he'd be competent.'

'He'll know what to do, at least. I'll get on to him, unless he's away. Jérome's away. Let's see; Szymanowski will be senior judge in that case—you don't know him personally do you?'

'No.'

'Very well. I'll designate him accordingly to instruct this affair. You'll be all right with Castang here. He's an able chap: he'll see that matters are handled correctly.'

'The Press,' said Castang, 'will I suspect be here very shortly.'

'Not while I'm here they won't,' said the Proc sharply. It gave him leverage to get his big body moving. 'I'm going,' abruptly.

Castang watched him go, walking heavily through the courtyard looking neither right nor left. At the gate he was accosted by a familiar, slightly cheap figure. Like dogs, thought Castang; they know it all and understand nothing. They rush wildly, eagerly at anything, perpetually bringing back sticks with an air of vast importance, and when faced by a master-figure, they cringe. The Proc paid no attention to the questions and just rumbled ahead like a tank. There was already a clown there with a microphone.

'Lucciani,' said Castang, 'Press. There'll be more. Tell them Richard—' no. Useless; they had to be given bones, however bare. No cop can afford to be high-hat with the Press. They can be bellowed at but if sulky they bite. 'Let them as far as the hall and no further—and make sure of that. Tell them nothing else because of the technicians—Monsieur La Touche,' surprised to find himself so deferent, 'you realise your privacy is going to get pretty badly invaded. We'll keep your house guarded but right now it's run the gauntlet. You may as well get it over with. There's paperwork to do so I have to ferry you down to the office. I don't want to put handcuffs on you, but just for you to accompany me in a friendly informal way. Have I your word for that?'

'Certainly,' vague. 'Sorry; I mean yes, of course. I feel rather sleepy, I'm afraid.'

'We'll have some coffee—or to be accurate, Nes. Let's shove, shall we?'

'Lucciani,' bringing up at the bottom of the stairs with an expressionless face for the photo-flash, 'see that the house remains guarded and that the cop is relayed, and that you in person lock up after the ambulance has been, and that you in person bring me the keys . . . Castang, Inspector, P.J. This is Monsieur La Touche, the owner of the house, who has for the moment nothing to tell you.'

'What is this?' interrupted a journalist tartly. 'Suicide, homicide or what?'

'The appearance is homicide. The Procureur has authorised me to make a preliminary enquiry. Since that's all I know it's all I can tell you.'

'This the suspect?'

'As you can see he is not under restraint. He is doing his best to shed light upon the circumstances. The rest remains to be seen. That is why an enquiry has been ordered.'

'How many dead are there?'

'Three; two women and a man. Madame and Mademoiselle La Touche and a man so far identified only as a Monsieur Davids. All have died as a result of gunshot wounds, whose authorship the technical examination in progress should determine. The Procureur authorises nothing further at this time, and no photographs in other parts of the house. This evening at the office Monsieur Richard may be able to make a fuller statement. That's all.'

As they got into the car a movie camera filmed them for that evening's television news. They got through the obstacle of some fifty curious onlookers and headed for 'the office'. Not the administrative office from which he had been called, but the urban police headquarters, an extremely ugly building, of the mid-nineteenth century and of massive discomfort, but at least cool. The interrogation rooms used by the P.J. were at the back: Castang found a cop and sent him for paper cups. The result was hot and strong, anyway.

'We have to keep you—you realise? Detention cells here at the back. Tomorrow some time you'll be presented as we call it to the instructing judge—you aren't familiar as I imagine with these procedures. I realise you're tired but we have some work this evening. Not a great deal. I'm allowed to question you for only so long. There are intervals laid down for rest, meals and so on. Then a bit more work before bed. Tomorrow with any luck we'll be finished with these preliminaries, and the judge decides what happens further, and your lawyer will be present and it will be explained to you. Sorry about this stuff, it's the best we can do. All set? This is called a *procès-verbal*,' as though to a child. Castang was repeating a lesson long learned by heart. 'It's a typed paraphrase in abbreviation of the question-and-answer process. You have the right to alter or obliterate anything you disagree with before signing it. It serves to give the judge a broad outline, and as basis for further enquiry should that prove necessary.'

V

THE RIGHTS OF A SUSPECT
ARE SAFEGUARDED

La Touche seemed to be waking up a little. Shock wearing off, or the stimulus of Nescafé, a thaw at finding the cops a little less like orang-outangs than previously supposed: perhaps a little of all three.

Castang was hammering at bureaucracy: date of father's birth.

'Lord. 1894 I do believe. Am I accused?—I've forgotten this branch of law, I'm afraid.'

'You aren't even a suspect. You're a presumed.' Inspector of Finances: Master of the Rolls—lawyers loved these antique titles. 'Judge makes an act of accusation if he sees fit. It's to be expected that he will. And you're—were—married to Hélène de la . . . that's a mouthful; spell it, would you?' These names of the nobility, as encountered in the births-deaths-and-marriages of the *Figaro*—all orthographical death-traps. 'Sounds very grand.'

'It is,' agreed La Touche. 'Like Oriane de Guermantes; all the duchesses are her cousins. Since I admit everything, this statement will be rather bald, despite the imposing preamble. The judge will be disappointed because his dossier will remain meagre. I suppose I'll be expected to plead insanity.'

'Don't let your mind run ahead. You've two daughters, Charlotte and Patricia. Which is the dead girl?' without inflection.

'Charlotte,' likewise. 'The younger. Seventeen.'

'All right, that's finished with. So now a brief sketch of events. You came home. Unexpectedly?'

When it is all written down some people become confused. Often they make long rambling explanations to alleviate guilt, when it cannot be obviated. They become immensely loquacious. The uneducated may take refuge in stout denial, saying 'You lie' to the most unimpeachable fact. The bourgeois, with some training in logic, see every piece of evidence as incontrovertible but embroider, interminably. The professional criminal of course is like a politician: when he cannot lie he prevaricates. Experience teaches the investigating officer how to produce a clear and if possible consequent narrative, with helpful remarks ranging from 'For God's sake say something I can believe' down to 'I wouldn't put it quite that way if I were you' to a misery quite unaware how shatteringly he is incriminating himself. He does this as much in self-defence as in sympathy. He will be accused anyway by a defending counsel of fabricating evidence and extorting admissions by threat, if no worse.

La Touche, befitting a man with legal training, used spare manageable sentences easy to transcribe literally; thought before he spoke; weighed his words. What presented difficulty was that he seemed deliberately to paint himself in as black a light as possible. Castang found himself—almost 'offering inducements' to make the statement less bald, 'behaving improperly'—but there were no tape recorders running.

'Had you remembered that the servants were away? Would it be a thing you would ordinarily recall?'

'Made no difference whether they were there or not. The servants all knew perfectly. They always do.'

'Since this painter was making a portrait, there was nothing unusual or striking in his being there that afternoon?'

'Davids can't resist any woman.' Present tense. Is the man really aware that he has killed these people?

'But there are plenty of women who would find him resistible; who would in fact resist him.'

'Not my wife.' Which was as bald as you could wish it.

'You suspected, then, infidelities. But it would still come as a violent shock.'

'I didn't have to suspect. Even knowledge I took for granted. She was notorious.'

'Come now.'

'If not widely known then deeply. Thoroughly, if you prefer.'

'Were you intent upon stopping scandal?'

'She made no scandal. Well brought up. A sense of what is becoming. Occasionally reckless, but took pains not to compromise me—at work, say. Not that I am in the least a public figure.'

You are now though.

'The presence of your daughter would have been to you a guarantee, wouldn't it?'

'Not in the slightest. Corrupt. Always has been.'

'Come—no all right, leave that. Despite everything, when you stumbled upon this scene—isn't it fair to say you had a violent reaction?'

'By no means.'

'Think carefully. Anger, humiliation, even envy. One may act in what appears a calm fashion—or some people can—but there is a violent interior tempest.'

'No.'

'I am not trying to suggest you were incapacitated. That would be going beyond my brief, which is just to get at facts. Then no emotion at all?'

'I said, Monsieur Castang, no violent emotions. I felt many things, in a controlled fashion. I decided to finish with all that.' The man would be saying in a moment that his act was premeditated! He did . . .

This won't do, thought Castang to himself. Man can't have forgotten all his penal law. Must surely realise that if he confesses to homicide with premeditation he is technically an assassin, and risks the death penalty. He stopped and lit a cigarette, making a performance of searching for a light. He reflected that the psychiatrists would pounce on all this. Rigidity, overwhelming need of tidy patterns, rejection of wounding and disabling images, castration right and left: the shrink would make hay.

'I can guess,' said La Touche amiably, 'what is passing through your mind.'

Castang changed the subject.

'Could we have a brief résumé of your studies and qualifications, and perhaps in broad outline your career?'

'Certainly.'

Co-operative, conscientious. That is surely relevant and must be noted. And doesn't it show a sense of remorse? The pill, too, was relevant—it is likely quite a strong sedative. The man had not

23

wished to take it. On being urged he shrugged, said he'd make no fuss.

Uncanny the way he picked up one's thought.

'I should like to say that I'm aware everyone is going to ask me whether I feel remorse. Down to the President of the Assize Court. I'd better make myself clear right from the start. I'd like you to note it.'

The manner of authority comes from the tranquil certainty of being obeyed. A wish is a command. But you haven't—have you?—lived twenty years of marriage without realising that family life is played according to different rules.

'What I'm here for.'

'Pity, I feel,' said the man accustomed to dictating memos, 'and consciousness of an irrevocable action. I have though learned to take decisions and to carry them out without useless doubts and scruples after the event. We thus separate the notion of remorse from that of regret or a useless longing that what is, should not be. It is done and I did it.'

Castang typed obediently word for word. To feel a sort of moral superiority in the man sitting in the other chair gave him a start. He smoked quietly and wrote a note in the book beside him. La Touche paid no attention.

Dignified; undiminished. It came from generations of ease and assurance. From being used to universal respect. From being good at his job. Surely, too, from a sort of integrity. The man would never allow himself to commit, or be cognisant of, a dishonest action. Large sums of public money were accounted for with minute exactitude. The detachment of the senior civil servant. One was perfectly aware of vast and shocking scandals, daily. Incompetence and mismanagement. Upon a vast scale. Equally, enormous corruption and public feather-bedding. The gloriously bland silky hypocrisy of government where arms sales were concerned, or the misapplication of a gigantic sum for electoral purposes. The stranglehold of the middlemen—the ten, twenty, thirty bandits standing between the ridiculously low price to the producer, and the outrageous sum demanded of the consumer. This man saw them all, with detached distaste, and did nothing. That was rather like a policeman—wasn't it?

Long practice in the flexible and civilised manner, everything left unsaid, in which these senior officials reach compromise. An interesting lot. Much like the syndicate making up that English insurance group—Lloyds, wasn't it? Trust: word is bond: a signature on a scrap of paper a gold ingot.

They all knew each other. Many were related; all shared the same background. Frequently they had been in this world for two three or more generations. Gone to the same schools and training grounds. Known personally to half the professors, quite a few of whom came to dine at the house. Birth, wealth, security, honour. A Rolls-Royce mind. Marriage, after graduation into an important department of government, to a suitable young woman. And wherever one went, everyone—from ministers down—got up from behind their desk in acknowledgment of this effortless domination.

What was a man like this doing in a squalid interrogation room with a provincial cop? What could they possibly have in common? Was it the same blunting of moral sensibility, a sort of detached and even cynical indifference to human folly, greed, avarice? This man too was a policeman. On a vaster scale. Yes, there was a lot in common. More, with an urbane and polished person like Commissaire Richard.

Castang felt a momentary sort of rage. This, surely, was all drawing-room comedy. The Proc had come in person. Richard would be getting unspoken instructions. He himself had been left to conduct a preliminary homicide enquiry because it had no importance. He was regarded as a reasonably house-broken cop, able to go through the forms without making a balls of it. It wouldn't matter what he wrote provided he got it in the right language. The judge would pay no heed.

Shrinks would appear in numbers, making low-key remarks about pressure and the wife's instability, with parentheses addressed to the daughter about too much intermarriage in old families.

A trial, respecting all forms. An advocate-general prosecuting who was somebody's cousin and would speak with studied moderation. A formal sentence suspended and replaced at discretion by voluntary treatment in a clinic. Retirement, not too premature. Memories of this tragic accident effaced. Dear Gilbert had lost his wife and daughter in a ski disaster. Avalanche, yes; road accidents are vulgar.

'Once more,' said La Touche a little diffidently, 'I think I might guess what is passing through your mind. I shall hope that we come to know one another better.'

The summer suit, and shirt, in good taste like the tie and the cufflinks and the effaced English shoes. No crocodile there, any more than the wife would have dreamed of wearing panther. Such things were for the nouveaux riches, vulgar. Shit.

'I simply do my job,' he said, hoping not to sound servile. 'No efforts of understanding or any such things are required from me. Above all, no conclusions. I marshal events in a fairly lucid précis, and ensure that the procedures are respected.'

'I think you may be mistaken,' urbane.

The door opened, and Richard came in, unfamiliar in his weekend sports shirt.

'This pistol,' said Castang, 'is your property? And you kept it habitually in the drawer of the bedside table? As is the convention. Was it usually loaded? I mean the cartridges in the magazine? The magazine in place in the butt of the pistol? You are familiar with the mechanism? Did you leave the thing there with a vague idea of security, or did you sometimes take it out to clean? You practised with it, from time to time?'

Richard sat quietly down with a sign to pay no attention.

'This is Commissaire Richard,' cross, and deliberately misunderstanding. 'He is the head of the regional service. He will doubtless have things to ask you.'

'Not for the moment.' Despite the sports shirt, Richard looked smart: never windblown or ruffled. Tall, thin, handsome, quiet. Now slightly disconcerted, since La Touche got up at the introduction, held his hand out courteously, and said 'Delighted to know you, Commissaire, but I'm afraid I'm causing you trouble.' For two pins he would have said 'How was golf?' thought Castang sourly.

'There are worse things,' laconically.

As frequently with remarks of Richard's, one was not certain whether this was a snub or not. La Touche took it to be one: two red spots showed for a moment on his cheekbones. With Richard's entry the temperature had dropped: the atmosphere of understanding and almost a certain friendliness slipped away. Castang studied his notes and lit another cigarette.

'We have covered most of the facts,' he said.

'There are so few,' said La Touche. 'Death of two women and a good man.'

'You loved your wife and daughter?'

'I think I did. Badly, as is evident. Not enough, as is obvious.'

'And they loved you?'

26

'I should have thought so. You may think I don't know the meaning of the word. You might very likely be right.'

'You used the word "good" in speaking of Davids. You admired him? He was a good painter?'

'He was a remarkable human being. One seldom meets a person of such quality. His talent—yes, also: exceptional.'

'Are you doing yourself justice in these answers?'

'I see no occasion to concern myself about that.'

Richard was sitting immobile, with no flicker of the eye. His mouth had a sardonic turn, as though silently saying 'theatrical performance'. His face, ordinarily a healthy pink colour, looked grey in the evening light, as though made of aluminium; the skin dull, polished here and there by much handling, daily usage through many years. He has a very considerable experience, Castang was thinking, a great deal more than me. He is a good and unbureaucratic cop.

'Would it be fair to suggest that you felt envy for this man? Perhaps on account of qualities inspiring affections?'

'Yes it would. I did. And more—hatred, fury. Laughter—he was extremely funny. Sometimes contempt. I qualify that. An unjustified contempt because the man was astoundingly simple and open, like a child. I don't mean childish; I mean an unaffected naiveté. On the other hand he was, occasionally, contemptible.'

'I see. I don't think we need go any further at present. I'll give you this to read over and sign if you will,' typing the final phrases of official formula concerning time, place and circumstances. His eyes slid across to Richard, who shrugged very slightly.

'Thank you. We'll have more to talk about, but that will be in the morning, after certain verifications. I'm going to have to lock you up now. I should explain that you are as yet officially not charged with anything at all. You are held at disposal as it is known, for twenty-four hours, after which the instructing judge decides whether to order your detention.'

'I understand. It is unnecessary. I admit openly all possible accusations.'

'That may be so. We respect various safeguards the law insists upon.'

'Are you always so punctilious?' murmured La Touche.

'Where crimes against the person are concerned, yes,' rather more acidly than was needed. 'Will you come with me?'

The jail was behind police headquarters, along a covered alleyway

like a railroad tunnel, approximately whitewashed. Castang, who
was used to it, felt an unexpected prick of shame at the air of
dilapidated antiquity. La Touche seemed unconcerned. The warder
had to fill in lengthy and tedious forms. La Touche glanced
indifferently at drawings on the walls, did not even wrinkle his nose
at a smell of stale cabbage soup, disinfectant and ingrained dirt,
which did little ordinarily for the detainee's self-respect. He was
carrying no personal property at all bar a handkerchief. Didn't
smoke; no money or address book. Like royalty, who leave such
matters to ladies-in-waiting. Castang went along with the incurious
warder, thinking he'd better do something: the man had no idea.
Richard would have made a face. What d'you want to do—tuck
him in?

'Never been in prison before? Like during the war, say?'

'I have lived a sheltered life.'

'I see. I have to have your tie. And the shoelaces. Are you wearing
a belt, or braces?'

'I have no suicidal urges.'

'It's the regulation. However, if you like to tell me I can find
you some things at home. Tide you over the emergency, say.'

'I need nothing.'

'Nonsense.'

'You are humane.'

'I have to go back to the house anyway.'

VI

CZECH INSISTENCE ON BEING CONTRARY

'I'll be late for supper,' said Castang on the telephone. 'Got a homicide. Shouldn't be long though: maybe an hour.'

'Cold soup anyway,' said Vera's voice. 'I'll expect you when I see you.' That was that. He went to wash off sticky grime with kitchen soap and a police roller towel.

Even after sunset it was still fearfully hot in the Rue des Ecrivains. Smell of baked dust; car smelt of ovens, baked enamelled metal. Castang felt fatigue, an empty reverberation in the head, sounding noisy and busy, though the street was now still and empty. Everyone had headed for the supper table, switching on the television. Local news, before the national news: he wondered whether that camera man had got his film ready in time.

The black and white marble of the hallway—there was something startling in the mixture of grandeur and simplicity here: the house was quite small really, but all the rooms looked large, perhaps because they were so well proportioned—was deliciously cool and clean. The technicians had finished.

'No problem there,' said Lucciani. 'Waste of time really. Clear as the Blue Lagoon. Here's the keys.'

Simple as daylight, simple as champagne. All the simplicity bothered Castang.

Richard had said the same when Castang had got back from locking La Touche up. He was in his office, smoking a cigar, tidying papers his secretary had left to be signed. He hadn't even looked up; the step of his subordinate was familiar.

'So simple it stinks. I've read your report. It's all right, hits quite a good note in fact. Not that it matters very much. Without interest, all this.'

'You think so? I thought him interesting.'

'Naturally,' dry. 'He's anxious to be interesting. Been a bore all his life—now's his chance. He's posing. He knows he's perfectly safe—how indeed could he be anything else?'

'Good, insanity plea, yes of course—but is he insane?'

'What a silly question. Are you insane? They are and they aren't, as you very well know. At moments convenient to themselves they are. Kills the man. All right, that's insane—in an Inspector of Finance it is, anyhow. Killing a couple more puts him on the safe side. Make him that much more insane. Take off that wiseacre look; stick to the facts. He could, or I'm much mistaken. Sick of those two women: been a bloody nuisance for some time. Admirable opportunity for getting rid of them. There'll be much sympathy no doubt for his point of view. Premeditation doesn't have to be something laboriously planned and thought out over weeks: it can take two seconds. This situation is much too complex, thinks a trained mind: he simplifies it.'

'What happens now?' asked Castang stupidly, feeling fatigue in the bridge of his nose, stiffness in the back of the neck.

'Szymanowski will call for expert opinions. Nothing left to chance —if the first doesn't find the man is bonkers the second will. A bit of humming and hawing over what constitutes bonkers, but a formula gets hammered out which the Proc will accept. He'll make a show at the trial, but any good defence lawyer will find a bargain for the courtroom. Plea of diminished responsibility accepted—two quiet years in a clinic with woods around and a tennis court, where the director gets called warden and has bars on his windows but wears a white coat and invites the inmates to play bridge. Yah. Just see to it that the papers are clean though: Szymanowski likes to call attention to sloppy procedure.'

'There's no technical hitch?'

'I've just phoned the house,' said Richard simply. 'The rich, my boy, are never interesting.'

'I wouldn't know,' said Castang. 'I'm going over there to fetch the man his pyjamas.'

'Don't steal any little silver boxes.'

Hitch? asked the technical squad—you're as bad as Richard.

What hitch? Painter's been having a fine time, screwing these two bitches crosseyed. Isn't it nice to be rich?

In the kitchen he found a thin woman with glasses, Portuguese, voluble, distraught. Everyone was on holiday, she was the cook's cousin, the family had been in the country, she just came in to air the rooms—oh, what to do now, oh dear, such a quiet gentleman, so considerate, never gave trouble.

He went through the house again. Kitchen much modernised, pantry with china cupboards and stuff, a dining-room, a dark study full of lawbooks. In the suite of drawing-rooms on the first floor there were a lot of pictures hanging. In the bedrooms the technicians had done a thorough job. He found an overnight bag, male pyjamas and slippers, added a couple of sets of underclothes and socks. If the man got a toothbrush belonging to his wife, well—she had no further use for it. A track suit, yes; sensible thing to wear in jail.

Tacking across the landing he found two girls' bedrooms, one very disorderly. This presumably was the girl who had died, for the other looked as though it had been unoccupied for some time, although aired and dusted by the excellent servants. It was conventional, with little traces of individual personality. He wondered where the second daughter had got to. This old satyr Davids must have been a fine figure of a bull, but three together would impose a strain, surely. The things people got up to . . .

He went back downstairs. On one side of the drawing-room was a library. He took a few books at random for La Touche. More pictures, including a very cleverly composed and intricately painted still life. In a classical, Dutch sort of style—he wondered whether it was any good. Vera would know but she wasn't here. It was only interesting to him because it was signed 'Davids'. Some of the things in the drawing-room he didn't understand at all. One might, eventually, after a lot of time and study which, sorry, he hadn't time for.

On the other side of the drawing-room was a morning-room; he supposed that was what it was called. A smell of fresh oil paint: the man had worked here. He really had been painting a picture!

The room was oddly conventional. Business room for upper-class lady, the competent and well-trained mistress of an upper-class establishment. He looked at the bureau—letters, invitation cards, appointments book. Phone directories, address books, household accounts, menu cards, cookery books for planning parties. . . . The room was decorated with photographs of family relations and several horses. And two large portraits in crayon of two little girls, ten and eight, all most delightful and roguish but they had travelled some distance further, since then.

The picture hung over the carved stone chimney piece, still unframed, perhaps unfinished. Hung to see how it would look, perhaps, or because the paint had been wet. He touched the surface gingerly: a scrap tacky. The man might have been working on it that day: how long did this stuff take to dry? Vera would know.

The painter's easel stood where it would get a good light. On the chair behind it hung his linen jacket, shapeless and bulging. He had been a big man. It could well have taken four bullets from that popgun to stop him. Castang wondered whether there could be a self-defence plea there, and shrugged: what did he care? He was interested though in this jacket—the technicians hadn't been fiddling at that. An uninterfered-with witness, so to speak. Lord, it was more full of junk than a pedlar's basket.

This man at least had been real; a life lived intensely. Breast pocket, spectacles, and a handkerchief, silk but paint-stained. Side pocket, handkerchief, cotton, paint-stained. Crumpled packet of horrible menthol cigarettes. Bottle of pills. Other side—more hand-kerchiefs, of paper! Another bottle of pills! A little plastic bottle with a spray, for throat or sinus. And a handful of toffees wrapped in silver paper. The inside pocket held a heavy worn wallet full of cards, papers, money, and assorted rubbish.

Trouble with his sinus and a liking for sweets. Castang was pleased. It was a life. The first homicide he had ever been on had been put together by Richard from the starting point of an uneaten meal. Richard had shown him how to construct an unknown man, identify him, and arrest him. From a liking for overdone meat, sugar in all the vegetables, and German mineral water.

So far it had all been empty, staged, void of meaning. Brothel scene, lit with glaring, gaudy, but artificial lights. Depersonalised—there had been something, too, very irritating in the attitude of La Touche. One had to agree with Richard: it did look like comedy. Consider; man walking in, discovering this absurd great weltering sex scene. Calmly going to bedside table while the trio, presumably, stood about fixed in consternation. Taking the pistol and loading it

—a most important legal point, proving co-ordination and pre-paration, prerequisites for a homicide to be termed premeditated, and the author an assassin.

And La Touche had behaved in a very stagy way afterwards, also. Ringing up the P.J. like that (not just the *Police Secours*) and saying 'I admit everything' with a phony sort of flourish. He must have been aware, and well aware, that he was going in three useful American monosyllables to cop a plea. His answers too to questions were lucid and connected, but unsatisfactory.

One would have liked to ask the others questions. It was most annoying that they were all dead.

They'd been, though, human beings. Now carcasses; shapeless lumps of flesh. Might as well have been knocked to pieces by one of those huge bullets that tore the entire bones off your face, so that it flew asunder like a smashed porcelain vase.

Castang looked at the occasional table. Laid with a coffee service. Three used cups. Nobody had bothered much about it. There had been a little dish holding chocolates. The dish was still there, but the technicians had eaten all the chocolates.

The painter had been a real man. A man who liked to have sweet things within reach to pop into his mouth from time to time: a toffee, a girl, a biscuit. A humble small earthworm of doubt had come crawling into Castang's well-drilled subordinate's mind. He wasn't sure any more that Richard was automatically right, that this was no more than a formal exercise in legal technology. It must have been an unconscious revolt against everything being kept so smooth and pat and well-oiled, because he committed an illegal act. He unhooked the canvas on its stretcher from the wall and walked off with it. Illegal act because this, technically, was theft. Also because in a homicide case the disposal of all property is frozen, and nothing may be moved without the authority of the examining magistrate.

He locked up, made sure that the grille to the street entrance was closed and that there was a cop on patrol, and drove home. Two or three small knots of morbid sightseers were chattering and pointing, breaking off to stare at him. There wasn't much to see. Plain-clothes cop with a flat object wrapped in old newspaper and an overnight bag. He left this at the wicket-gate of the jail and went on home. Not really late. Ten past eight. In four hours both a great deal, and singularly little, had happened.

Castang lived on the second floor of a house with no lift, in a quiet bourgeois street facing an old disused canal. Not an apartment block, but a smallish house: only four storeys, and two flats on each floor. The street was inhabited by prosperous folk, and the rents were high: much too high really for an officer of police. Vera, his wife, who was slightly crippled by an accident, found the getting up and down a slow hobbly business: she was not good on stairs. Finding an apartment on a ground floor, or in a block with a lift, had often been discussed, and as often turned down. She was too deeply attached to her poplar trees on the pavement opposite, to the grass-grown canal bank and the water which gave the view some distancing and perspective. For nearly three years she had been stuck in a wheelchair and this view had been all she had. She could take exercise now—laboriously. The half kilometre of towing path, where other people walked their dogs, was a constantly-renewed delight. They had no children, and no animals.

The summer evening, despite the early twilight of Central Europe, was torrid, windless, sultry. How was it in Memphis? People were lounging on balconies or at windowsills in sweaty undervests, scratching irritably. The canal water was not stagnant, but sluggish, and there were plenty of insects. The cafés were doing all their business on their pavements, and the streets smelt of ice-cream, warmly sickly.

The people paid no attention to Castang and his parcel. Even without the protecting fold of newspaper they would not have looked: folk are not trained to look at pictures. You could walk all the way down Fifth Avenue carrying a Rembrandt self-portrait without anybody noticing, save to wonder why you didn't take a cab.

Vera had seen him arrive, sitting on her little balcony. Characteristically, nothing naked or sweaty there: she took a lot of warming-up at the best of times, addicted to cardigans and electric blankets when everybody else was puffing. This evening it was warm enough even for her, but she looked as cool as a freshly drawn beer, and as welcome, in a bou-bou, a wide enveloping cotton shift in a bright primitive print. Far from naked underneath either; both Czech, and strictly brought-up, about cotton underclothes. Castang thought she looked good. Naked women are to any cop considerably devalued objects at any time: there were far too many of them around, even if he had not just had two—and dead at that—on his plate.

34

Vera looked at the canvas he was carrying. Characteristically too, she said nothing. Castang poured out the beer she had been keeping cold and had a draft to fortify him while undressing. Walked off into the shower, leaving clothes scattered. This annoyed Vera: men were incapable of being tidy. He came out rinsed, walked about still plastered and tousled, climbed into clean shirt and trousers, finished the beer, looked appreciatively at cold soup, bread, cos lettuce and cheese which was supper waiting, lit a cigarette and was ready for a domestic chat.

Vera had the picture up on her working table. Herself a draughtsman, an illustrator in indian-ink of some originality, she was looking at it with professional attention. This was the chief reason why he had brought it home.

Vera looked at the picture; he looked at Vera. A bell of fair hair cut short; Slav features rather exaggerated, cheekbones pulling her eyes apart and squeezing them narrow. She was not in the least pretty. Beauty was something else altogether. He knew nothing whatever about pictures, but knew you had to look at them. He looked at his wife, and sometimes thought he understood art. She scooted her wheelchair across the room—this was still in daily use because she was expert at it, and it was much quicker than getting up and sitting down again—took one of his cigarettes—it was characteristic again that she should do this instead of asking him to throw her one—and went back to the picture. Smoking in the awkward fashion of a woman who takes two or three a day, just to be sociable; not eating it or drinking it.

'Where d'you get this?'

'Is it any good?'

'Have you bought it or something?'

'Would that be a mistake?' This question-game was stopped by her turning around and looking forbidding. A picture was serious: she did not want to be teased.

'Not at all a mistake. But it's unfinished in several places, and he was working on it this afternoon. Do you mean to say he let you take it like that?'

'He wasn't asked. He's dead. The thing is—or will be—an exhibit in a homicide. The subject is dead too.'

'Extraordinary.' She didn't mean the homicide. Vera was used to homicides, having been married some years to a criminal-brigade cop. She had decided at the start to be detached about them, the way she was detached about danger, or his wearing a gun. The thing was lying, on its belt, upon her sofa. Even weird, or horrible events do not bother artists. The subject of a picture, however gruesome—the 'Raft of the Medusa' say, all about cannibalism—does not greatly interest them. It is the picture's being good—or bad —that has importance.

'You know who the painter is?'

'His name is Davids: mean anything to you?'

'Did he kill her?'

'The husband killed both of them.'

'I'm not surprised. Let's have supper.'

Typical. She would not talk about something serious without time and space. To think, but above all to stand back, to look again, to put herself at a distance. She had always been like this, even as a gymnast, before breaking her spine. It had slowed him down in a valuable way. Earlier, he had been too impetuous to make a good cop. Nowadays, he knew better how to look more, and think less. All cops of experience are stolid, and lack zeal. Only some are stupid. Looking stupid, being phlegmatic, and laconic, belongs to cops all over the world, and wasn't invented by Scotland Yard.

The soup had yoghurt in it, and sorrel, and a clean bitter taste. Vera grew chives in a windowbox, as well as geraniums.

There was also a rule, much like the rule on small yachts: no drinking, and no smoking, before the washing-up is done. The flat was small, and like a boat in many ways. Vera had even a few ropes rigged at strategic points, to help her round the deck in stormy weather.

'How's Richard?' polishing furiously with a tea-towel. She didn't mind being poor, but hated mustard-glasses. A glass, that one drank out of, had to be crystal. Castang said that this was just Czech salesmanship.

'Being rather cynical about the fellow we've got. He's one of these obscure big wheels in the administration—Cour des Comptes or something. An Inspector of Finance, no less, the bugger is, so naturally one thinks there'll be a careful beautiful legal whitewash.'

'And will there?'

'It's early days yet. The instructing judge is Szymanowski. Polish, you know. Conscientious. Likes to give the dirty French a slap over the knuckles.' There hadn't been much said over supper;

36

a complaint about the bread. Vera sometimes baked her own, but only at weekends. 'I've better things to do than worry about my belly' was one of her phrases. 'All these amateur cooks with their endless chi-chi make me shit' was another. Sometimes she cooked well and sometimes badly. There were few dogmas. One was that he should make the salad-dressing, because she tended to be too heavy-handed with the vinegar.

During the washing-up she tacked off to write 'scouring-powder' on her shopping list. Finally she sat down and started looking again at the picture.

'Is it any good?' They were back again to square one.

'What do you think?'

'I thought it was. Balanced, stable. The fellow isn't sugary. Liked sweet things though—reach out and crunch a praline, while working.' Vera started to laugh.

'Of course it's good. You don't have to be so diffident.'

'How should I know?'

'You don't have to pretend to be so cretinous. For a start the technique is tremendous. Hardly anybody knows how to do that nowadays, even if they find it valid. It will last. Extremely accomplished. Fellow knows his old masters backwards. Painting is at a very high level of technical dexterity, but look, it's beautifully composed. Static, highly worked and poised, but a fine movement and passion in it. What was his name?'

'Davids.'

'It doesn't mean anything to me,' said Vera, 'but there's no reason why it should. I can easily enough find out more. Lovely painting. Good portrait. Is it any way like her?'

'I've only seen her dead with no clothes on.'

She was alert and vivacious, with great charm and determination. The face was accustomed to getting its own way, and when it did took on an expression of gaiety and delight. The portrait did not show what happened when the woman failed to get her way.

'I can understand shooting her,' said Vera. 'Shooting that good a painter is less forgiveable.'

'A toffee-eating girl-tumbler.'

'As though that mattered!' For her he was welcome to crunch up all the girls he had a mind to. To get shot by some dim Calvinist lawyer was a great waste.

'So to you it's not a boring story,' suggested Castang.

'Not in the least. The trial might be boring; they generally are. But not the instruction. Pity it's Szymanowski—Polish old maid,' irreverently.

'You're just being Czech,' said Castang with some truth.

VII

GOD-GIVEN APPEARANCE OF A DEFENCE . ATTORNEY

Castang was a bit slow in getting out of bed; lay in fact five good minutes longer than he should have. For no particular reason, unless it was a private presentiment that it was going to be an extremely tiresome day and therefore to be put off as long as one could. He told himself he had a car, and would therefore get to the office quicker than by bicycling as he usually did. This was against all logic: he still got caught in the traffic jam. It was going to be another hot day. The streets were still fresh from having been hosed down from the fire hydrants, but only in the gutters was there any moisture left: the roadways smelt already of dust. He arrived a good three minutes late; and was unsurprised to be told at once 'Richard's waiting for you. In none too good a mood. Seen the morning paper?'

'No.' He hadn't had time to open it. The sense of foreboding had obviously been accurate.

Richard's office was large and bare, with a big desk over by the window and nothing else, seeming a long way from the door, so that nervous trainees bowed three times on their way over to it, as though at the court of a Hapsburg emperor. He didn't look up when Castang came in, being busy reading the papers. They were all strewn about the desk.

'We'll have to start employing a clipping agency,' said Castang. Richard banged irritably at a page which crinkled in the middle instead of turning over properly.

'A whole campaign already,' in a lifeless tone. Castang came round the table to read over his shoulder.

'Where do they get all this? That lawyer? What's his name—
Dieudonné?'

'God-given in more than name.' A snort. 'Doesn't let the grass
grow under his feet. Must have phoned the Paris papers after the
television flash.'

'I didn't see it, I got home too late.'

'Nicely timed, to commit a triple homicide at four in the afternoon
in August when there's no news. It was a dead evening and they fell
upon it—God-given is the word. This is going to build.'

The local paper was the usual gas-filled balloon, with a flaring
headline saying 'Drama of Jealousy' and the bad pictures taken the
evening before: himself, unrecognisable he was glad to say, escorting
La Touche—full-face, inscrutable and dignified—to the car, and
blow-ups of the courtyard and windows. Richard's face, so blank as
to appear mentally deficient, and the text of his Press release, bald
and free from comment, but an excited footnote saying 'Turn to
Page Seven'.

Dieudonné must have gone straight to the newspaper office, and
they had given him space. Oh, nothing really prejudicial: on the
contrary, full of prudent reservations about 'When the judge is in
full possession of the facts', but a lot of hairy innuendo about artists
who destroyed domestic tranquillity, and the rights of respectable
householders to do justice upon the thieves of their honour.

Monsieur Szymanowski would be reading these effusions right
now, and his lip would be lengthening.

So far, all this was banal, and no more than they were used to.
But at the bottom was the source of Commissaire Richard's knitted
brow; a subheading in small print saying 'Zionist influence?'.

'A reliable source in the person of a close business associate of
Monsieur La Touche gave a hint last night which arouses specula-
tion. "This painter Davids was of course Jewish," he told our
reporter. "Frankly, I have been wondering whether Israeli intelligence might not be involved." Questioned about this apparently
enigmatic remark, he disclosed that La Touche has recently been
acting as financial adviser to petrochemical interests in Near-Eastern
countries with very considerable funds to be invested in selected
fields of European property and industrial markets.'

'Just the kind of meaningless innuendo that does harm,' said
Richard, crossly for him.

The Paris papers had small paragraphs on the diverse-happenings page. These ranged from the sober 'A provincial tragedy' in a serious paper to the sensational 'Bloodbath after orgy' of the gutter Press. But they all had something. It was as though they had all been warned that this one had untold potential and could easily be 'the-start-of-something-big' they all thirsted for.

The two policemen looked at each other, both wondering about the country's big evening paper. Coming on the street at lunch-time, it had missed a sensation timed for television. It might decide to make up for that by creating a splurge today. They were always hard-up for an orgy, and this afternoon's edition might well begin with a five-column headline. 'Parisian Satyr Wrecks Provincial Peace.' They both shrugged. There is not a lot cops can do about the Press . . .

'Stuff about the painter, of unholy morals and dissolute existence, whose career has been abruptly terminated,' said Richard, 'is one thing. Antisemitic crap about Israeli intelligence is another.'

'He looked so Jewish,' said Castang. 'You know—big nose and curly lips—just like a cartoon in the *Völkische Beobachter*.' It had been Doctor Goebbels' newspaper. 'Unfortunate for Jews, that now and then they do look like Fagin.'

'Virtually certain to be a canard,' said Richard. 'A dirty tactic but a normal one, for a defence lawyer. La Touche behaved so level-headed and logical that the insanity plea, to the public, might look weak. So he throws up a smokescreen. We don't have to pay it any heed. I'll make a few phone calls.' Richard was, being a sensible man, fairly friendly with the local political police, DST, who if one is to believe their carefully innocuous title 'survey the territory'. It all sounded sensible. Castang knew that however silly it was it might do harm. There is always a small and dotty current of antisemitism. It is exacerbated by an equally small and dotty band of friends-of-Arabs. Governments, who are officially very tender towards oil-producing countries, and sensitive to their caprices, dislike being embarrassed by fantasies of this nature. And, one must admit, Israeli intelligence exists. It has even been known to make a fool of governments. Homicides to the criminal brigade are bread-and-butter. Nobody though wants a homicide for a political motive.

Officially, to be sure, the Commissaire of the criminal brigade and his investigating officer couldn't care an old franc about the Press. They had the author of the crime in a box, at the disposal of

justice, fresh and dewy as a sheaf of gladioli. They had a full statement admitting responsibility, and no defence lawyers were going
to set up a loud quack about extorted confessions, tortured suspects
jumping out of windows, or suchlike gauds. Experience, too,
gave them no exalted opinion of the Press. Justice in this country
is deliberate, and purposely so: one good reason is that the dust dies
down. The Press has a perfect horror of being a bore, and justice
always is a bore. By the time—months later—an affair comes up
for trial the effervescence has ceased and the sediment has settled.
The Press itself is quite cynical about this, and feels free to contradict earlier wild fantasies; taking advantage of its own chatterbox
superficiality.

The Great Public, whichever country it may belong to, forgets
and forgives nearly anything, for deep down at the bottom of itself,
where it keeps its conscience, there is an ashamed admission that
the way down into the pit is steep and slippery.

Nearly any criminal, however base, can arouse sympathy. The
most abject can arouse pity. When the appalling Christie, who killed
women, raped the dead bodies, and in an effort to cover himself
sent an innocent man to execution, came himself to be judged, it
was noticed that the judge who pronounced sentence of death was
in tears. For that handful of wretched women: for the man who had
been hanged, an illiterate boy on the borderline of mental deficiency
with a fondness for fine-sounding lies: for the police, the lawyers
and the judge who had killed this boy with every respect for legal
form: for this ghastly object who was still, somehow, a man: for
mankind.

The public does not like its conscience to be awakened in this
way. It is not grateful to be reminded for whom the bell tolls. The
police, on an everyday level the repository of mankind's conscience,
makes a damned fine whipping boy. The cop therefore is little
better, in the eye of the public, than the common hangman. Worse;
he is suspected of doing favours. Of pulling, stifling, blinding justice
for favour.

The cop knows this. Not wiser, but perhaps humbler, he lives
with it. He grows a protective skin, and accused of cynicism as well
as brutality he becomes, with fatal ease, both brutal and cynical.

And the best of cops—Commissaire Richard was a very good one
indeed—quails at the thought of a case covered by political protection, be this real, or purely imagined. Once imagined, the public

42

will persist in the delusion that it is real. The crooked cop is one of the favourite myths of mankind.

Mankind has always dodged its own responsibilities, and always will. The crooked cop is like the fornicating priest or the immoral artist. Does he not preach morality? Be sure then that he does not practise it.

Patient reader, forgive the rhetoric.

Not even Castang felt indifference; even knowing that whatever happened he would be covered by his boss. Commissaire Richard ran an efficient service because he was trusted by his subordinates. This, in turn, because he did not try to dodge responsibilities.

Monsieur Dieudonné timed his appearance well. Castang had only just got to the foot of page seven when Richard's secretary entered to announce his arrival. Fausta was an enigma to the most experienced of detectives. Richard himself pretended to an immense bland complacency at having so efficient, so pretty and so heartless (one assumed . . .) a secretary. Quite as though he were Svengali, and she Trilby. For no one else would she sing in tune. She had superb teeth, and brown hair she could sit on, though nobody had ever seen her doing so. Everyone claimed he had; he, only he.

A pushing man, this Dieudonné. Shameless as any cop. Just walked in, not waiting to be invited, a thing Richard detested. He got a cold glassy look and no bonjour. A thing Fausta detested still more. At the best of times she had a lack of sympathy for pettifogging attorneys.

'I asked you to be kind enough to wait.'

'Oh come now, this is nonsense. We can dispense with formalities surely.'

'The Commissaire is engaged, and I do not tell lies.'

'Yes yes, my dear, you do your job; I realise,' indulgently.

'I will let you know,' said Fausta, cold as the circle of Dante, where attorneys among others are buried to the neck in ice.

Castang was repressing a grin like a sneeze, with a pain in the bridge of his nose. That Fausta had an infallible instinct. And do Richard credit, little as he wished to cause offence to a lawyer, and especially this one, the principle of loyalty (and vanity . . . 'My Fausta' . . .) gained the upper hand.

'Give me five minutes, would you be so good?' with perfect urbanity. Some people will never give up tugging.

'My dear Commissaire—'

'I don't think you had an appointment, did you?'

'One would think oneself at the dentist's.' An offensive laugh. And Fausta with a beaming smile, showing her lovely teeth as much as to say 'We'll pull all yours out'.

'Would you like to read the Paris paper?' A poisoned arrow that. How did she know? She always did know, the cow.

Lawyers are never snubbed, or they would not be lawyers. Insubmersible like a water-polo ball. He popped in again five minutes later as though for the first time.

'Well well, Commissaire. Just thought I'd make my number. How naval that does sound. Battleships firing broadsides. Rather old-fashioned of them.'

Round bustling man with an actor's face. Frivolous expression to mask the shrewdness. Fiftyish, sparse dark hair slicked back over a large round skull; much intelligence; merry twinkle in alert little eyes, amused indulgent folds round talkative, clever, tight little mouth beautifully shaved.

'This is Monsieur Castang, who is conducting the investigation.'

'What investigation? As far as I know there isn't any—am I wrong? No factual doubt, surely? You've got your author, and a pistol, and measurements and prints and chalkmarks, all according to rule, all lovely. All my eye too, of course, but that's a different question. You've no worries surely, my dear man?'

'None whatever,' said Castang politely.

'Have you?' asked Richard, interested.

'Me?' astonished, 'I'm not a criminal lawyer. Abler hands than mine will pick up the reins. I am simply a man of affairs. I look after the family and financial interests of my clients. Monsieur La Touche is in fact an old and valued friend. Nothing astonishing in that.'

'Such dynamism,' said Richard.

'Ach,' in a deep bass voice, 'my dear Monsieur Richard. . . . We're between us men of the world. We understand each other. You are aware—none better—that if one does happen by misfortune to get involved in a fight, a good rule, the best of rules . . . get in first. Avoid haste, avoid precipitation, avoid litigation—like the plague—be mild-mannered, be circumspect. But if you have to hit somebody, hit him hard. And make sure—of course you'll agree —to get it in first.' And all the wrinkles twinkled, together, in enjoyment.

44

'Good,' said Richard. 'So no shillyshally; there's the defence, all mapped out. No hesitation at all. Regardless of what the preliminary enquiry may show, or the judge may conclude, or the instruction may bring to light. You've it all buttoned up; a campaign to blacken a dead man.'

'Quite right. Dirty old lecher. Satyr. Lousy artist. I can't afford to hesitate, my dear man. There'll be a crew of worthy people clamouring, no doubt, that he was a hero of the Resistance and heaven knows what. An emotional smokescreen. Natural enough. Legitimate, too. Some of it even true, maybe?'

'Was he a Resistance hero then?' asked Richard.

'Ribbon in his jacket lapel,' said Castang.

'There you are—I'm simply anticipating the tactic. To be sure Monsieur Castang here, whose acquaintance I am delighted to make, will uncover further facts. Some may be seized upon. I won't say distorted, but perhaps exaggerated in a manner prejudicial to my client. Not by the police; heaven forbid,' piously. 'It can happen though, can't it. I forestall,' turning out the palms of his hands.

'You invite,' said Richard. 'Attack promotes counter-attack.'

'Possibly. But I will have been first. I play quite fair with you, you'll notice. I'll be seeing the examining magistrate this afternoon. I may or may not decide to call a Press conference. He is bound to inculpate my client formally, as the admitted author of these acts, which are criminal within the meaning of the Code. No question of hearing him as a witness. From that moment the defence has every right to protect our client. You can't quarrel with that attitude. No move of mine could be seen, by any stretch of the imagination, as a criticism of the police.'

Richard's quiet voice contrasted with this volubility.

'Very well. Nobody in this office is under any pressure to discredit a suspected or accused person. The facts are beyond dispute. There's a man in custody. He'll stay there until a judge decides otherwise. I don't myself call Press conferences much—they generally call me.'

'Quite so, my dear man, quite so.'

'Nor do we know anything yet about this painter, until the judge calls for a supplement of information. Nor about his relationship with this oh-so-respectable bourgeois family.'

'Oh come, Commissaire—sarcasm . . .'

'Monsieur Castang will look for facts to replace suppositions.'

'Splendid,' said Dieudonné, imperturbably happy.

'Thank you for calling, Maître.'

'My privilege,' beaming like an emblem of the Sun King.

'Overkill,' said Richard after the door had finished closing. 'What should he be so anxious for?—we weren't going to do anything. But he's scared of something discreditable.'

'He was just a little too god-given.'

'You'll be going to Paris, my boy.'

'Oh. What a god-send.'

'We want to know a little more now, don't we? About artists, and also about these harridans of daughters.'

'But the judge will send a commission. Paris can do the leg work.'

'I think I'd like you to find out for yourself.'

'Oh,' groaned Castang. 'It's much too hot.'

VIII

POLISH INTRANSIGENCE OF THE JUDGE
OF INSTRUCTION

The telephone had rung neatly on its cue. This often happened for Richard. Some drivers are like that: as the auto goes down the avenue all the green lights come on for them.

'You're to go over to the Palais,' said Richard, 'and see Monsieur Szymanowski.'

It generally presaged a tiresome moment for police officers. This judge had a reputation for being severe with the police, fussy about detail and having a biting tongue; being in general a ghastly-Pole from the barbarian-north.

Castang was unalarmed because to him, at least, the judge was oddly mild. He didn't explain this: it might be due to a number of things. Castang himself had a Slav look, wasn't quite 'properly French' and had not, perhaps, an automatic assumption of superiority. And Vera; being Czech, being named for the national gymnastics team: her running away had created a small diplomatic nuisance. Marrying Castang had put him—ever so slightly—on the shit list. And though Monsieur Szymanowski had been French all his life he would always be 'that bloody Pole' to too many people.

And he had come up from nowhere, through sheer determination and coming top in examinations. He hadn't married any Hélènes or important persons' cousins. It had made him an acid person, but not in the least neurotic. His wife was fat, plain, nice—and Belgian. Worse than being Czech or even Polish in some eyes. His house smelt of red cabbage rather. And she played Chopin badly but lovingly on the piano. And their daughter had unfortunately

47

inherited her father's looks, being a bony, flat-chested young woman with no eyelashes. She was unmarried, lived at home, did social work (and was extremely good at this thankless job) and had generally a tendency to sanctity. They were very Catholic, and the house was full of Black Virgins.

How did Castang know all this? He had never been in the house, and couldn't possibly have known about the icons and the red cabbage. But Colette Delavigne, a friend of Vera's, the junior of the examining magistrates and the 'children's judge' had been there on social occasions.

The man's looks were against him too: he was thin and sharp-featured, with colourless, silky-thin fair hair, and gold-rimmed glasses which caught the light and reflected acrid glitters. And he spoke the hard French of the north, Béthune or Valenciennes, where he had grown up.

'Good morning, Castang: sit down. I wanted to see you before I look at this man. I know nothing about him at all. It could turn out a nasty mess.'

Castang didn't have a yes or a no to that.

'The Proc just goes pooh-pooh. He doesn't see anything in it but the habitual sensationalism and the inevitable publicity. Not really a public figure, he points out. No technical muddle—still, I'm a little less sanguine. A racial smell, and remember that appalling muddle up in Douai, a football match, bourgeois against the miners. I suppose you'll think I see Béthune everywhere.'

'No; I think you might be right,' said Castang.

'La Touche—what's that, Huguenot? And this wife, de la something du something else. Huguenot dukes, eh?'

'I'm not well up on dukes. I'll find out.'

'I'll handle the dukes,' said Monsieur Szymanowski, 'but the fact is that France still hasn't got over the revocation of the Edict of Nantes, to this day. A lot of magistrates tend to be tiresomely allied to these old Protestant families: I'm being indiscreet but you see . . .?' Castang did. 'There'll be a lot of sympathy for this man. Since the woman's dead they can black-sheep her quite safely. . . . What worries me more is this Jew.'

A tiny trace of Polish antisemitism? Proper Poles don't know any Jews. One admits their existence, and they are part of Poland, and it wasn't Poles that staffed Treblinka—lot of filthy Latvian barbarians —but one somehow doesn't *know* any.

48

'You're thinking I see Poles under every bed too,' gloomily. 'I can smell them a league off, it's true. This painter has a smell of backwoods villages in Galicia—I'm being frivolous, of course: I simply want to find out.' Down it went in the notebook.

Dukes.

Jews.

'The political slant is doubtless irresponsible invention.'

'Richard is looking into it.'

'Now this daughter—well. . . .' Her behaviour had not been what the judge expected of daughters. 'The Proc has some acquaintance with this family and tells me the daughter was a tedious child, running away to Paris to be liberated. But there's another—he may have got them mixed up.'

Daughters.

'I've had Maître Dieudonné on the telephone, wanting of course access to his client. Behaving very stiff—doesn't impress me, but he may know the answers to a lot of these things. You'd better try to get La Touche to fill in what he can before they build a hedge round him.'

Parlour, Castang wrote last, but that had to come first. The point of legal delay is a sore one. The Code says clearly that a suspect may be held by the police for no more than twenty-four hours before being seen by the examining magistrate, and a further twenty-four hours with the authorisation of the Public Prosecutor. The police get accused of breaking this rule more often than most, and it is obeyed with a punctilious ostentation.

'The Press is making a considerable fuss,' said the judge out of the blue.

'Yes, Monsieur le Juge.'

'Well . . . I'll give them to understand that I'll be treating this affair with exactly the same severity that any Algerian immigrant would have to expect. No more, and no less. They'll find me quite intransigent on this point.' And so would the cops.

'Quite so, Monsieur le Juge.'

IX

AN INTERVIEW IN THE CONVENT PARLOUR

It is the jargon term for the dingy little room in the 'house of arrest' where detainees, for they may not be called prisoners before their trial, may talk to their lawyers, or the cops, without a guardian being present. It is remarkably like the 'little parlour' in a convent. Not of course the real parlour, be-waxed and be-flowered, where Reverend Mother receives *monsignori*, such as the Director-General of Penal Establishments, but an airless, badly lit, and horribly depressing small room, sporting no decoration but an oleograph of the 'little' Saint Teresa in a shower of roses, here replaced by a forbidding portrait of the General, with a rectangular mouth, telling the populace that liberty is within their grasp, which detainees find an inept observation. Here unimportant curates get given breakfast after an early Mass: here poor relations are left to stew while a nun is sought ('dear Mother is just saying a prayer in the chapel'): and sometimes unwashed persons seeking charity get 'stood', so that there is always a slight but unmistakable smell. There is here a bare table and four bentwood chairs, and that's it.

Nobody could look less like a detainee than La Touche.

He was spotless, with a shaved, brushed, showered look, wearing the carefully-pressed track suit that Castang had left for him. This gave him the look of a distinguished middle-aged artist who has been engaged in strenuous physical activity: an orchestral conductor, let us say, just after rehearsal.

'Comfortable?' asked Castang, more or less without irony.

'Very,' with no irony at all.

'Your Portuguese lady can leave parcels of laundry and stuff.'

'Thank you.'

'The food, of course, tends to be constipating. One can get fresh oranges from the canteen.'

'Good.'

'Nothing's a problem, really, when one has money.'

'My dear Castang,' smiling broadly, 'you don't say!'

It was no more than the buttering-up which is frequent when the cops wish to gain someone's confidence. There are several corny old gags, like Would you want me to get the doctor to give you a sleeping pill? 'Inmates' have always the right to see the doctor, and distract themselves with the pleasures of hypochondria.

All this guff was not needed here. Castang was relieved, because he was only a hypocrite really when the job demanded it—frequently though this happened.

'You'll be seeing the judge this evening. All fixed up. Your lawyer's been in touch—dropped in to see us.' La Touche made a polite gesture of refusal to the automatically proffered cigarette. The cops always offer their cigarettes. It is their way of saying 'No hard feelings, you know. Nothing personal.'

'But you didn't come just to make these polite enquiries.'

'No. But no interrogation. Background, on a pretty general scale. Things we need to get straight.'

'I'll be happy to help in any way I can.'

'Your wife's relatives, for instance . . .'

'You don't have to bother about them. They'll make a funereal fuss but you can safely leave Dieudonné to cope. It's what he's for,' with some aristocratic hauteur towards 'attorneys'.

'They'll doubtless be visiting you.'

'They may feel that convention dictates a show of sympathy, if not solidarity. You think they may cause you trouble.' At his game of good guesses again. 'Don't be perturbed: they've no love for me —never have had. Too frightened to budge, one way or the other. In any case I've no wish for any visitors. You can forget too the idea of highly placed personages intervening on my behalf. When I see the judge, I've no doubt I'll be able to put the matter in its true light. They are essentially unimportant people, making an effort to persuade themselves that they may upon occasion have important roles to play.'

So much for dukes. Castang decided to leave it at that, until somebody challenged him to a duel.

'I'd like to talk about your daughters.'

'Yes, that's more complicated.'

The impersonal tone caused a sudden intense irritation.

'Yes, well, one of them at least won't be worrying you any further.' La Touche said nothing, slowly raised his eyes to the level of Castang's and lowered them again.

'Sorry,' suddenly ashamed of a piece of police brutality which was a commonplace.

'You don't have to be. I deserve it. Nor will you be the last.'

'No, but I didn't have to be the first.'

'No more than I merit—but don't take that as a vulgar parade of remorse, designed to impress you. I feel little—too little. I tell myself she got what would in any case have been coming to her. She may have been beyond a better remedy. A nasty little thing. She was only a child, but she was old enough too to know better. She may have been badly brought up, but the debate would be futile. Her mother was not a bad woman. I was not a bad man, nor even a neglectful parent. They were brought up with some firmness, and plenty of affection. And showed themselves a pair of corrupt little cows.' A crudity designed to prod Castang, and it did.

'What does that mean?' asked Castang shrugging.

'Rubbing themselves against men, and if it succeeded, screaming,' with a flat, cold clarity. 'To giggle at male discomfiture and the abrupt subsidence of an uncomfortably erected penis gave pleasure. A vicious pleasure. And I did nothing about it. Inhibited, I suppose.'

He wasn't mincing his words now. A little late in the day.

'I'll leave that to the experts.'

'I've handled these experts before now.' Not contemptuously, but like a man under no illusions. Castang was taken aback. He had himself a vague respect for the 'expert', but prisoners cling to them as to life rafts. 'Bombing the judge with my experts' is a favourite jail pastime and fantasy.

'Come now, Castang; you're an officer of experience.'

'Let's stick to daughters,' he suggested.

'Yes,' said La Touche. 'One clings to bonds; blood, love, life shared. It's not to be written off like a bad debt. To cut is to cut into your own bone and sinew. I can't talk about it yet.'

'You'll have time, with the judge. Still . . .' The wife was one thing, the daughter another. 'I'm interested at present in your surviving daughter.'

'Patricia?' as though speaking of an acquaintance one has not seen for some months, 'she's a vagabond. She's an expert black-mailer among other things. If she has not yet been arrested and indicted for numerous offences it is because so far she has known how to acquire a steady supply of money. It won't last. You're wrong to say she survives: she's on borrowed time.'

'On dope?'

'Yes. She has been weaned a couple of times but it never lasts. Curiously, she was once rescued by Davids, who picked her up off the pavement in Paris. It was my first meeting with him. He per-suaded me to take her back. Getting her to come back was perhaps harder.'

'You said he was a good man.'

'Right, and there's a proof. He did not—I should make this clear —worm himself into my house. I myself asked him to stay. I myself commissioned the portrait of Hélène. He made some drawings of Charlotte. It was stupid of me to throw her at his head like that.'

'And Patricia?'

'Oh—she went off again. They find food, shelter, sympathy any-where. There is a sort of grapevine across all frontiers. A sort of, by the way, which is one of their favourite phrases, illustrates the confusion of their thought. They have a horror of anything precise. Now I,' said La Touche a bit sarcastically, 'am the contrary. Obsessive. Not on that account a maniac.'

'So an anarchist group of sorts. Any political aims or definitions to your knowledge?'

'None whatever,' said La Touche, plainly bored with the subject.

X

THE HEAT OF THE DAY

To do any work in the month of August is ridiculous. This is a civilised notion, rooted in antiquity. The governor of a town being besieged by King Louis XIV, hearing that His Majesty was short of ice, promptly sent him some, with a courteous message: the thought of any gentleman going short of ice was a disturbing notion. How on earth did war manage to get declared in 1914? There was a cipher clerk left in the Foreign Office, eating three gigantic meals a day in the intervals of stupefying yawns, but anyone who was Anyone had gone to Scotland upon serious business. Grouse got shot in August: people didn't. For anarchists to go shooting an Archduke was preposterous; just like them, somehow. Only anarchists would be so energetic.

As for the Law, and all to do with it, it is the Long Vacation. Dickens left a picture, vivid as always, of London dead in a heat-wave, of Mr Snagsby the law-stationer having a picnic in Cook Court, Cursitor Street, and the holy Mr Chadband ingurgitating.

Somehow it is the emphasis that has changed, in our democratic times. Especially in France. Try to get a spare part. There may be a few factories open, and they may be—probably are—on strike, but no one pays any notice. It is, though, The People that is on holiday. The Establishment no longer withdraws to its country seat, there to fan itself in the shade while the merry merry peasantry gets the harvest in. Ministers and governments rush about, snatching the odd weekend, perhaps, but having to be brought back by helicopter because there is a crisis somewhere. As for the Law, it trots about, business as usual. It may be forgiven, perhaps, for taking roundabout ways on its errands, by keeping to the shady side of the street.

It was hotter even than yesterday. Thirty-five: this is really hot. Castang took his time going back to the P.J. offices. Here the Law was at work. Languidly. So lucky that it was all so exceptionally straightforward.

Technical report on the pistol. Nothing wrong with it: it worked in a normal fashion; not rusty or anything. Short-barrelled pistols were wildly inaccurate at anything beyond breathing distance, and a mixture of dust and congealed oil in the chamber made this one more inaccurate still, but that fact had played no part. The cartridges were old, but the thing still went off. If you had wanted it to go off for some serious purpose—you were being fallen upon, let's say, by some rabid dog—it probably would have refused to fire at all. Notoriously chancy weapons, pistols.

Medical reports: no autopsies or pathological skill needed. These people had died of gunshot wounds in themselves mortal: that was enough, surely. The subjects appeared to be in rude health, apart from this unimportant detail.

Funerals had to be arranged. Contact had been made with relatives. No problem meanwhile in our progressive days: the Medico-Legal Institute possesses efficient refrigeration equipment. One no longer has to wait till the frosts of December, to do a bit of pig-killing. Decomposition can be arrested, just like criminals.

Richard's man from DST hadn't been in the least excited by mention of the painter Davids. Briefly, he had said Israeli-Intelligence-my-foot. He knew nothing whatever about La Touche. Ask the Economics Squad. Nothing illegal as far as he knew about giving investment advice to people with a lot of money.

The Economics Squad asked irritably whether there was any suggestion of something fraudulent. Had any regulation concerning exchange control been contravened? No? Why were they being bothered then? If the judge ordered an enquiry, well, they supposed that could be done. It would take a Very Long Time.

The Paris police was too busy changing its sweaty shirt and saluting tourists to be bothered with missing girls. Nobody had reported her missing. True enough, a year ago there had been a complaint. It was true that information had been received—some café waiter, concluded Commissaire Richard—that the subject Patricia La Touche, aged then seventeen, was being sheltered by a painter named Davids, who might thereby have been contributing to the delinquency of a minor. The complaint, however, had been withdrawn by the said minor's legal guardian. Affair classified: file would have gone to archives. If the judge really wanted . . . etcetera.

The painter Davids was a bona fide person. No criminal record. Polish in origin, naturalised French many years since. Had been deported, during the war that was now a dim and unimportant memory, to an extermination camp. Fellow was a Jew. Had somehow avoided extermination. Man was a perfectly good citizen with various military and civilian decorations. Nothing known against him. No report that he was engaged in any subversive political activity.

All these people were keeping to the shady side of the street. And so was Castang. He went home to lunch.

Vera had made stuffed tomatoes, roasted them, let them get cold, and made a kind of aspic jelly with fresh tarragon leaves. So far, so good. But she too was keeping to the shady side of the street, and was in a tiresome frame of mind: what Castang called her talent for Invincible Ignorance. Saying things like 'I fail to understand why women commit adultery'. He wasn't going to argue. It was too hot. It was too hot, today, for adultery even. There were peaches for dessert, with a purée of fresh raspberries that were no longer fresh. The skins of the peaches were tough, so she had blanched and skinned them. And so *Pêche Melba* got invented. With decidedly dragging footsteps, Castang went back to the office. This damned bore La Touche had to be brought up before the judge, formally inculpated with homicide, remanded into the custody of the House of Detention while the legal arguments got prepared, the Experts called for, and the Instruction generally set creaking upon its tramlines in a smell of hot softened asphalt. The thermometer in the concierge's office now marked thirty-*six*.

Richard wasn't even back before the telephone was ringing.

'Castang?' The judge. 'There's some kind of demonstration afoot outside the Palais. I notify you because it looks as though, possibly, it might have something to do with our man. I've told headquarters to deal with it. Take a look, though, before you bring your man over.'

Central Commissaire Fabre, the head of the Urban Police, was on holiday. His replacement was another person with no ambition to go frying eggs on pavements.

'I had a cop take a look. Nothing to it. A few hippies carrying banners—I don't know; something Zionist, or maybe anti-Zionist: does it matter? Too hot for demonstrations. The judge is an old woman. What does he want me to do—turn a fire hose on them? They'd love that. Free window-wash. Could do with a rinse, myself.'

Richard, looking offensively cool, as though himself in aspic with fresh tarragon leaves, arrived at this moment.

'What's the fuss?'

'Judge says there's a demo outside the Palais.'

'Well, go and look.'

The Palace of Justice is a building of unparalleled ugliness covered in statues of a vaguely mythological nature. Nothing, that he could see, to do with justice. Orpheus in the Underworld or something. Some were naked with beards; others swathed in flowing garments in which they had got caught out in the rain: in France called 'draperie mouillée'. The group outside looked as though strayed off the façade.

Anarchists, in the sense that they were mad dogs and Englishmen: they seemed to enjoy the heat. Not, though, serious anarchists, who would not be exposing themselves to identification in this way. The public has the right, of course, peaceably to assemble and to appeal for the redress of its grievances, and the police are careful to respect this. If they interfere they are being provocative. Even if there is a disturbance of public tranquillity the police does little, because there is little it can do, short of the riot squad and the water cannon.

The placards said 'Justice has already BEEN done', 'Liberate La Touche', and 'One Zionist Spy Less'. There were no more than forty odd. He didn't think they were to be taken seriously. Certainly no call for the usual technique—the only one there is, short of fire hoses—of taking ringleaders down to the station 'to have their identity verified'. There was no need to do anything at all. They wanted to be noticed, so he wouldn't notice them.

They noticed him, though. In the forecourt of the Palais a cop was strolling up and down, to whom they paid no attention, but at sight of himself a catcall went up. Damn that photograph in last night's paper.

'P.J. cop. Castang, Castang.' And in chorus 'Rat Poison'.

He went away again. A shuffle of the banners across the gateway told him what to expect. The Palais was only a hundred metres across and down the road from the back door of the jail. It was the practice to take prisoners on their way to see the judge on foot, simply handcuffed to a cop. It saved trouble, and gave everyone a pleasant stroll. If they now let La Touche be seen he would be recognised and there would be a scuffle. But if they put him in a police van, salad-basket or black maria, there was a barrier to force. Drive slowly and you risked being blocked in a humiliating position. Drive fast and you risked some lunatic being knocked over, and then you were in real trouble. He went back and reported things to Richard. Who simply said 'Use your judgment.'

He took a plain-clothes cop, and an unmarked car, handcuffed La Touche to the first and drove the second himself.

'They want to liberate you,' he said to La Touche. 'Make you a martyr.'

'Really?'

'Maître Dieudonné will of course disclaim all responsibility.'

'That is deplorable. I will accept it.'

'You can't. You see, we are now responsible for you. Just leave it to me.'

At the sight of the car there was a scuttle. A dozen assorted tritons and nereids sat down across the gateway. The uniformed cop on the steps came down them.

'Now—none of that. Out of it, I tell you.'

'One moment,' said Castang getting out of the car. 'You realise that by obstructing this gateway you are committing an offence.'

'Rat Poison.'

He appeared to see the banners for the first time. He read them gravely.

'Ah. I see. You wish Mr La Touche to be freed. Can't be done, as you know perfectly well. Nor will it be done, by means like these.'

'Hiding behind the judge.' 'Fuck the judge.' 'He's got the key—take it off him.'

'Unfortunately, you're completely in error. Monsieur La Touche has no wish whatever to be freed. What's more, he'll tell you so himself. Here.' La Touche leaned forward, polite and controlled.

'Would you be kind enough to clear the way,' he said. The fellow with the wreathèd horn hung about, disconcerted.

'Do hurry up,' said La Touche, 'it's damned hot in this car.'

'Look, don't you realise you're being framed?'

59

'So are you. And I'm in a position to know more about it than you do. Drive on, Castang. Get that stupid girl out of the way or she'll be doing herself an injury. It's too hot, you know, for this sort of thing.'

'Keep an eye on the car,' said Castang to the cop, 'and whatever you do, make no threats.'

'One might add,' said La Touche mildly, 'never explain anything, and never argue. I'm sorry, Castang. I'm not at all pleased. I'll tell that ass Dieudonné as much.'

'It was well planned,' said Castang appreciatively.

'An effort to subvert the due process of law. That is not in the least what I want. Nice and cool it is, in here.'

'Has Maître Dieudonné arrived?' Castang asked the concierge, who was pretending not to have noticed anything, not being paid to defend the Palais with his life's blood: what did they think?

'Ten minutes ago. That's his auto—the green one. In the robing room probably, having a fag. I'll let him know you've come.'

Monsieur Szymanowski, who went in rather for the dignity of his office, had not been looking out of the window. His clerk had though, and so had the typists.

'Sit down then, gentlemen. . . . Ah, Monsieur Dieudonné. We were waiting for you. Have you been here long?'

'No more than a few minutes,' quite as brazen-faced as he had been that morning, in Richard's office.

'And you had no difficulty getting in?'

'Oh, you mean the demonstrators? Oh, I paid them no attention.'

'And they paid no attention to you. I take note.'

'I hope I do not understand the inference, Monsieur le Juge.'

'I make no inference, Maître. Since the only inference possible is that a member of the Bar should have been in collusion with persons attempting to interfere with justice, I take care not to draw it.'

'That is quite unwarrantable and I protest. These people are manifesting their support of and encouragement for my client, as is their right, and having no interest in my humble self they let me pass.'

'I take note of your declaration, Maître,' said the judge, lighting a cigarette.

'May I say a word, Monsieur le Juge?' asked La Touche.

'Do.'

'Dieudonné.'

'My dear Gilbert.'

'Four words—five. Don't. Or I'll sack you.'

Castang admired the man: he didn't turn a hair.

'Quite so, Gilbert. Would you like to recall too that in matters regarding the law you would be well advised to allow your adviser to use his own judgment, and that this would be the advice given by any lawyer? Any one at all.'

'Shall we get down to business?' asked the judge, moving his ashtray a fraction closer.

XI

THE COOL OF THE EVENING

It took some time, but it was no more than formality. The judge, who had no choice in the matter, pronounced a formal inculpation for wilful homicide. Since, as he remarked, the legal responsibility appeared to turn upon a possible temporary unsoundness of mind, he proposed to remand the detainee into the custody of the House of Detention—provisional liberty being of course impossible—and to commit a panel of psychiatric experts, who would formulate an opinion and in the fullness of time make their findings known to him.

Despite various suggestions put forward, he saw no reason for accepting a political involvement, nor need to impound business papers. Doubtless—since Maître Dieudonné here present was empowered to pursue business matters—these papers would be at the disposal of justice if need arose. In the meantime, the Police Judiciaire in the person of Inspector Castang or such other officer as Commissaire Richard saw fit to designate would be empowered to pursue the enquiry, and to endeavour to produce such witnesses as might have germane information, such as this young woman Patricia La Touche. A series of formal interrogations would also be pursued upon the details surrounding this grave crime. That would be all for today, gentlemen: the clerk would now produce the record of this examination for agreement and signature.

It is all very ponderous and bureaucratic, and to the Anglo-Saxon eye ludicrously like the notice regulating the Behaviour of the Public, as pinned up in pubs or buses. The Code Napoléon is like that.

However, the sniggering at pomposity tends to die away once a few myths have been punctured. Chief, and most persistent, of these myths is that under the Code a man is presumed guilty until he can prove himself innocent, or the exact contrary of Anglo-Saxon law. This notion is, of course, rubbish. The truth is that unless the judge is convinced, after exhaustive enquiries, that there is a strong case for the accused to answer, he will never go to trial at all.

There are two further very strong safeguards. One is that the defence lawyers are present at every interrogation, have access to every paper (and every word must be consigned to paper, for only the written word has weight) and can question every witness. The other is that the judge of instruction does not appear in the trial court, where he has no function, and no status. He merely forwards his recommendations. All pressure upon the accused person is thus removed.

The great disadvantage of this system is the immense amount of time it consumes, and the vast paperwork involved.

The great advantage is that shocking miscarriages of justice, such as have been far too frequent under the Anglo-Saxon system, are avoided. Nor are there any expensive and elaborate farces, such as the trial of the Moors Murderers, where the question of their sanity was never raised.

Nor is there the squalid trickery, a commonplace in the United States, about the admissibility of evidence. Once the judge of instruction (or examining magistrate as he is sometimes known) has raised the point, and he realises, and raises them all, for he is a most painstaking person, all evidence is admissible to the trial court.

The system is of course open to abuse. First and foremost the time involved. A perfectly innocent man, submitted to the sadly leisurely processes of instruction, can sit in jail for two years. And the caution—or hesitancy—of instructing judges has frequently meant that men and women have been kept imprisoned, on relatively trivial charges, for longer than the time of detention to which they would have been condemned, by a court of trial, for the offences they have committed.

Inspector Castang knew all this. It wasn't any of his business. He went home. And was bored, because his wife made a tirade against 'justice'. She was far too sensible to do such things ordinarily. To get her dislodged from these barren complaints he told her about the confrontation that afternoon.

'I don't understand these people—what do they hope to gain?'

She was fiddling about with scrambled eggs, and watercress, and some left-over rice, and a couple more fragments, out of which she could produce one of her 'something borrowed and something blue' salads that were strangely good.

'A crowd like that is like your cooking. Mostly bland enough. You can find people to demonstrate for nearly anything out of a hazy kind of do-goodery. Being kind to poor down-trodden Arabs. Some are a bit more crunchy, and will seize on a pretext to embarrass authority. Much the same to them whether it's the cops or the Rector of the University. Whatever seems authoritarian or paternalistic, they're agin it. And you might find a couple who are pure hot peppers and who are real professional agitators. We've a file on them, and so has DST. Fabre had a man down from Paris who gave a lecture on crowd control and had some of the best-known ones on film clips, but I was on duty and missed it.'

'But did they really think they could prevent you taking the man in to the judge?'

'Of course not—come to that one can get in the back way through the courtyard. One provokes them a wee bit to see what comes into the open. I mean finding out who's the cook. Hardly likely that a lawyer like Dieudonné would go to trouble like that on his own. He might have stirred it up, but he might have instructions from someone. But not, in any case, La Touche. Unless he's playing a pretty subtle game: lots of ostentatious collaboration with the Law while quietly building up a big system of making it politically inexpedient to condemn him.'

'Oh, it all revolts me,' said Vera unhappily. 'Bring it back to something I can understand.'

'I wish I could,' said Castang. 'I wonder where that watercress comes from. If you ate wild cress, nowadays, you'd quite likely catch typhoid.'

'Better not ask,' she said with a snap. 'If you start looking too closely at things like that you'd never eat anything.'

'Good rule for a cop,' said Castang with his mouth full.

The demonstrators had been gone when the group left the Palais. Because the heat had got the better of them? Or because they had made their point—or hadn't made it, since La Touche had refused to let himself be identified with these would-be saviours?

Nobody knew, and since Richard wasn't worried, or said he wasn't, there was nothing for Castang. He'd made his arrest and got his man booked for homicide, and from now on the police had no more than a subordinate role, of interviewing a few witnesses and observing a few reactions.

Richard had been right enough about one thing. The judge had had no hesitation about sending him on errands.

'I've got to go to Paris tomorrow—no, don't worry: only for the day. I can take the plane: back for supper.'

'Why can't they do it there, whatever it is?'

'Because—you'll be pleased—the judge thinks the painter important. He wants me to interview the wife.'

'What about the picture?' looking across the room to where it stood.

'I mentioned it to La Touche. Not interested. Says he hasn't paid for it and isn't going to. So it's the widow's property. She can apply to the judge to have it back. It's not an exhibit or anything. We've photos of it.'

'Did you see the evening paper?' asked Vera.

He had forgotten all about it, but came back to the office to find it lying on Richard's desk. There was nothing to worry about. Quite a lot of space had been given to the 'Drama of the Hôtel Particulier' but as Richard said, they'd a lot of space to fill each day. The reporter had been lazy, or not very well briefed, and hadn't made a big thing of the Arab connection, or the Jewish artist. Colour stuff. Photos of the pretty house in the Rue des Ecrivains. Photos of the country house out in the foothills; the 'château' as they called it. An interview with some Viscount or other who was the deceased lady's elder brother, who had been decidedly prim and tight-lipped. They hadn't gone to town on it. Their real offering of the day was 'Family Swept Away by Wave' in some Atlantic beach resort, and the fact that the rescue helicopter had been diverted at the crucial moment by a frivolous alarm for an overturned sailing dinghy.

Perhaps it had been an alert sub-editor who had added what ginger there was.

'Where is Patricia?' ran the subheading, quite small.

'La Touche has a second daughter, who has not been seen since the tragedy. She is, officially, a student in Paris. Less officially, an active figure in the forefront of various liberation movements. She was also, which makes her non-appearance the more surprising, a friend of the painter Davids. "She was with Lou for quite a time," a well-known personage in the art world told us. "One used to see them on

66

the terrace at Lipp." When we asked whether this domestic set-up had led to further acquaintance with a bourgeois family which on the surface at least seemed too prim to encourage such a relationship our informant laughed. "Lou was always irrepressible. He must have wanted to make it a perfect score." We might conclude by remarking that if this was the case he was not well inspired. It would be the last "perfect score" Ludwig Davids was to make.'

'The judge doesn't want to issue a warrant before he knows where he's going,' said Richard, tapping the paragraph with a fingernail.

'I had him on the phone. He wants you to find out what you can, while you're on the spot, and perhaps see if you could have a word discreetly with the cops in the district. You know how it is when they're on dope; they don't react like ordinary people. She might just not be in the least interested. Davids had a wife, though—let's hear her first, eh?'

Vera cried a little quietly.

'I find it miserable. Everyone so callous. A good painter. And the one idea everyone has is to make sure that this ghastly La Touche person isn't punished for it. Yes yes, I know; don't tell me. But I'm just a private individual. I am allowed to find it lamentable.'

'I'm not at all sure that I agree that he's a lamentable person or at all ghastly. And I think he might still surprise us.'

'To me he seems quite unreal.'

XII

LIFE CLASS FOR THE INVESTIGATING OFFICER

Castang took the morning express to Paris with a sense of novelty. There was precious little novelty about Paris, a city he had grown up in, but 'artists' were new to him, despite Vera. It often happens too that men who are highly specialised, narrowly and even excessively sophisticated within their speciality, are not just ignorant but strangely innocent concerning phenomena outside their experience. To Castang, who had lost both his parents at quite an early age and had been brought up by an aunt, a pious and narrow woman who kept a small shop selling paint and wallpaper near the Lachaise cemetery, artists still tended to be 'Montmartre and all that jazz', and despite Vera he had never learned differently. Education at a classical *lycée*, reading law at the university, and many hours spent in the cemetery, had given him plenty of information about the romantic movement. But his notions were still absurdly close to a stereotype, like those of most people. The broad-brimmed hat and the flowing beard, given to taking opium, writing sonnets, and catching syphilis from models. To be sure, Vera was not like this. But she was his wife and therefore quite different.

All this rubbishy folklore was swept out of existence in a moment. To begin with, Davids had not lived in any picturesque squalor, in the Rue Mouffetard say, but in a modern apartment block of primly genteel nature, well patronised by 'middle management', in a street of no character whatever near the Val de Grace. Everything clean and well-lit; plastic tiles well-mopped, a lift that did not smell. Eighty square metres on the ninth floor, with ten more on a balcony outside the living-room, described by house-agents as a patio. . . . And no smell of cabbage soup around here.

Madame Davids opened the door to him, and again it wasn't what he had expected. The features could he supposed be called Jewish, but not strikingly so. A tallish statuesque woman of middle age, plainly and conventionally dressed in a cotton shirt and trousers. Pale auburn hair, opaque creamy skin, large fine eyes. Voice quiet, movements still, obvious misery under perfect control.

'Come in,' she said. 'Would you like some tea?'

She left him alone in the living-room while she put the kettle on. Even for Paris it was conventional, and in Israel, probably, would be still more so. Light, simple furniture in pale varnished rattan, plain cream-coloured linen curtains and Tunisian rugs, off-white with deep maroon flowers. Plenty of pictures but nothing excessive.

The room was cool, shaded by venetian blinds. It was very tidy and peaceful; harmonious. There was nothing unusual in it but an old-fashioned parlour organ or harmonium in nineteenth-century walnut with a lot of sheet music on its top.

She brought the tea in a padded basket. China tea in thin handle-less cups, good on a hot day, unsweetened. She sat quietly down opposite him and refused a cigarette.

'Just tell me,' she said, 'anything you can. I know nothing.'

He did, disjointedly and as it sounded to him badly. Bald, anyhow.

'I see,' she said at last. 'And you are puzzled. There is too much as you remark that you do not understand.'

'Yes. If we knew more about Davids we might get closer to grasping this other man's situation.'

'There is not much to know about Davids. That you need, or wish, to be told.' Her voice stayed even, and quiet. 'An artist—it is a vocation for unhappiness. Very few things are important. Fewer still that the modern world holds important. This leads to much tension, and little content.'

'Yes.'

'The other thing is that people who have survived death-camps . . .' She trailed off hesitantly. She was not sure that he could grasp. Decided then that she did not care. 'Death has no longer much meaning. Nor have the affairs of this world. We believe, you see, in another world.'

'Yes.'

'That is important. But I have thought, sometimes, that to treat

70

life here with contempt is an error. Even when it appears contemptible. It was given to us: to despise it is surely a fault of pride.'

He sipped the scalding, unsweetened tea.

'So why were we spared? If we were given a new lease of life—
as I was when no more than a child, as Davids was when already
a man, it was because we had something still to do?' She got up
to bring him an ashtray.

'Artists try to heighten, and not to add to baseness.' Now he was
on more familiar ground. 'Mammon is a glorification of greed.
Vulgarity is a glorification of baseness, and what is baseness?'

Yes; Vera, upon occasion . . .

'Everything, isn't it, that we fall into all day? You, as a policeman,
should know something of that. Much—envy and vanity, callousness
and cruelty, hypocrisy and crowd-pleasing. Petty meanness, time-
serving and shallow flattery. But the artist doesn't exist to combat
that, as a policeman combats crime. It is what he makes that counts.
By his fruits you know him. Being what we are,' she spread her
hands out and looked at them, 'one can't get them clean. Always
in the dirt.'

'Some people are obsessive handwashers,' he suggested, 'always
scrubbing away.' She smiled.

'Good. I was afraid you might think me mentally deranged.'

'Not by any means.'

'He suffers, then, and he falls. He suffers to be sure the hatred
of the base, the contempt of the vulgar, the envy of false artists.
And his own baseness. He falls, often, into gross squalor. I have
thought that this may be a search for relief.'

'Perhaps.' She poured him some more tea.

'Davids suffered much,' she said simply. 'Hunger, for a start.
Have you suffered hunger?'

'No.'

'Can you imagine it?'

'No.'

'And very great misery. I am not, you know, trying to justify him.
Nor anything that he has done.'

'I realise.'

'Do you, I wonder?' She fell into a silence. Castang felt a kind
of shame. A cop is an unimaginative animal, but sees much misery,
and even, sometimes, hunger.

'Maybe I can give you an illustration,' she said at last. 'You know, we Jews are fond of little stories. *Hagada* we call them. Parables and little legends. Davids told often this story. It threw light, he said, upon artists.'

'Good. Go on.'

'In England there was a poet. A great poet. For some of the reasons I have touched on he was often a great drunk, and surrounded by whores. He was friends with another poet, because of what they had in common. That one was an old lady, from an ancient family. Grand and aristocratic, and terrifying too, from this age and grandeur. You follow? While this one was a rough, crude, peasant boy. You follow?'

'Yes. Like Davids when he was young?'

'A little. Good. They were going to have dinner together, and this one, who had been upon a big batter, arrived very late, and much stained and dishevelled, stinking of drink and whores, and feeling great shame. So he said "I am so sorry, I am very late and I smell revolting. You understand, it is the fault of the seaside; I have been to the seaside." And she answered "Yes, my dear boy, of course it is the seaside."'

'And what happened to them?' asked Castang, who always wanted to know the end of stories.

'Oh, they died. He was only thirty-two.'

'Yes,' said Castang. 'I should like to ask you how Davids came to meet this family.' If he had really sheltered the girl Patricia for months this woman must know. Or would she have more little stories?

'Ah, you find that important?' Her voice was so soft that it could not be called harsh. 'He deserved to be exterminated, no? A gypsy, a dirty Bohemian. Nobody can blame Monsieur La Touche for exterminating such.'

'Monsieur La Touche will have ample opportunity for explaining himself. Davids no longer has.'

She looked at him saying nothing. She leaned forward and took a cigarette from a box, studied him through the thin veil of smoke.

'Come,' she said at last, stubbing it out quarter-smoked. 'I will show you the studio.'

It was upstairs one flight, the fire stairs quicker than taking the lift. In the European sense a studio is only a one-roomed flat, a bed-sitter with a bathroom and a little kitchen. This one obeyed both definitions. It was summarily furnished, with curtains but no

72

carpet. There was a divan bed with a corduroy cover, a bare wooden table, a few kitchen chairs. Little else. Some canvases, and surprisingly few, were stacked against the walls. There was no mess. Castang had only been in one studio in his life, a sculptor, an acquaintance of Vera's. He had a barn, in the country; a museum of old cigar butts and rusty razorblades, of broken furniture and old locks and tools for everything from bricklaying to watch-repairing. He was certainly learning.

'You kept it clean?'

'Davids. I never set foot here unless invited.'

'May I look around?'

'You are free.'

The clothes cupboard held some lengths of furnishing fabrics neatly folded; for backgrounds he supposed, or to alter lighting. Some old sweaters for the cold, shirts one could wipe a brush on, being no longer fit for society, an odd variety of hats. The kitchen shelves held some paints and mediums, and the sink had been used to clean brushes. There was a teapot, a coffeepot, and cups, but no food. Everything was wiped clean. The bathroom was spotless too.

When he turned back the woman had taken a canvas and set it on the easel, and was wiping dust off her hands with a paint-rag. She turned the easel so that he got a good light.

It was a large canvas, placed horizontally. The subject was a naked girl, lying on a bed or sofa, her arms crossed behind her head. She was striking. She had a stylised pose, similar to that familiar from postcards—the hieratic, oriental woman of Manet's called 'Olympia', or Goya's Duchess of Alba known as the *maja desnuda*. Even Castang could see that she was very well painted. Having looked at the other picture, and been shown by Vera some of the things to look for, helped. Sexy she was, disturbingly so, and wonderfully vivid: she was too enchantingly serene. Nothing there was jarring or violent, but the calm and harmony of a madonna. And this skin and flesh would not decay, these bones never become dusty. He was astonished to find himself so excited.

'And that's Patricia?'

'Yes. She lived here, in this room, for nearly six months.'

'I've heard this story. So it's true? That he fed her, cared for her, got her off heroin?'

'He was good to her,' simply.

'He slept with her of course.'

'Of course,' said the woman with simplicity. To that one could only say 'No further questions' like the District Attorney. There were too many, altogether. Monsieur Szymanowski might choose to ask a few.

'Shall we go down again?'

'Is the picture for sale?'

'It is. Davids refused several buyers. I will be obliged to sell it.'

'There seem few pictures.'

'There were never many.'

'They command a high price?'

'Yes. They are good, you see. I shall have to hope that his death puts the prices up,' still simply, without bitterness. I'd buy her myself, he thought, and even wondered for a lunatic moment whether he could.

Back in the street he had to remind himself that it was the real Patricia—but which was the real one?—that the cop had interest in. He went and had two Pernods in a pub, which didn't bring him any closer the answer.

It was not so hot, today, in Paris: it was just a perfect summer's day. The tourists everywhere were strolling, in a momentary perfection of content at owning Paris. A beautiful day: one they always recall with bliss. The day they had laid aside all care and misery: the day they had felt that a sunsoaked Paris lay before them like *la maja desnuda*. Crowding into the Louvre to see the Venuses and Dianas. Like most of the inhabitants, Castang had never set foot there.

The famous 'empty Paris' of the month of August, with no traffic jams and no neuroses, has acquired its own folklore, but it has its points: the cops are for once not overworked. A lot of them are on holiday too and the ones that are left say they'll think about it tomorrow. Castang found a narcotics squad cop he knew enough to get invited out to lunch, in a 'little place where the wine was still honest' up a flight of stairs and pleasantly like a nineteenth-century brothel.

Patricia was known, but not well.

'She got off the sauce for nearly a year. Prolonged her life.'

'How'd she pay for it?'

'How do you think?'

She'd been lost sight of. Not altogether, but she had slipped outside the orbit.

'Got in with one of these political gangs. Anarchists. It's a mystery where they get their money. The Serious-Crimes boys were interested because they had a notion that this lot, sloppy as it seems, had done a few slickish post-office jobs, but it didn't hold up. I wouldn't know really. Their security's tight enough—they wouldn't put up with Patricia, not at least unless she was pretty stabilised. Try DST.'

'They never tell anybody anything.'

Correct: hereabouts the reception was chillier. One had frequently the impression that they told one nothing because they didn't know themselves.

Castang had known one or two in days gone by, jovial types who got the giggles at things like anarchists. Perhaps things had changed. Perhaps it was just bad luck. These people had always a tendency towards airs and graces with plain stumblebum cops. They came neither under the Ministry of the Interior, like urban police forces, nor under Defence like the *gendarmerie*, and quite certainly not under Justice, but were attached to the Prime Minister's office, where the Intellectuals came from.

He was received in an office with a hush upon it, as though talk would interfere with the Extra-Sensory Perceptions. When the immobile man behind the desk condescended to speak at all the voice was extremely slow and barely audible. He might have been put there to convince suspicious Americans that the French were neither noisy nor indiscreet. He was convinced that Castang was a very stupid person, and that this stupidity would lead to irresponsibility.

'I know nothing of this girl you describe.'

'I am told she knocks around with the group in the Rue Delambre.'

'What do you know of this group?'

'Nothing at all, which is why I come to you.'

'Who is the source of your information?'

'A cop.'

'I do not wish this group to be tampered with.'

'I've no idea of any such thing,' refusing to be insulted. 'The girl has to be interviewed as a witness in a homicide.'

'Show me your mandate. . . . It is most unlikely that a girl with the habits you ascribe should be affiliated to this group. Of which, it is plain, you know nothing.'

'What I said. They may be using her for purposes of their own.'

'If that were so, the more reason not to interfere. Until I know what these purposes are. I repeat. As a matter of policy, I wish for no meddling with this group, for however well-meant a purpose.'

'Look,' said Castang gently. 'If there is no possibility, as you claim, that this girl is in their confidence, it can't compromise them or you if I ask her a few questions on a totally unrelated subject.' If this worthy knew nothing about rumours that Davids had played some political role, Castang wasn't going to mention them.

'You fail to understand,' bleakly. 'If—and I say if—this girl has been used in some minor role, your appearance may be interpreted as a manoeuvre originating in this office.'

'I feel sure you know how to avoid being compromised. I'm sure too that you prefer to avoid even the appearance of obstructing a matter of justice that is purely internal and domestic.'

The man thought for a while. Then he opened his desk drawer, took out a visiting card, turned it over, and wrote something with a green felt pen.

'If you meet,' staring at Castang, 'anyone in the Rue Delambre who can give you any information regarding your enquiry, show him this. Since by so doing I am helping you, more than you may realise, I should be obliged if you will then bring it back to me, and make known any information you may gather. Is that understood?'

'I'll agree to that.'

'One thing more. You wish to do well, in your career?'

Castang took the card with a wooden face and left.

Artists are not the same as ordinary people, Madame Davids tells me. I'm learning a lot about art, today.

XIII

THE UNLUCKY NUMBERS OF THE
RUE DELAMBRE

A small sober flat in a building neither clean nor dirty. The flaked grey paint showed no affluence, nor poverty. The door was of solid hardwood, the brass plate carefully engraved and recently polished. 'Christian Bonnet' it said. 'Expert in Questioned Documents.' The bellpush was polished too. The man who answered it was thirty, slim and light on his feet, with an open, friendly expression and a pleasant smile.

'Monsieur Bonnet? Himself? I have a paper I'd like authenticated.'

'Please come in.' A room furnished simply as an office. 'Do sit down. How can I serve you?'

'It is not in my interest to tell any lies, nor to prevaricate. Turn the recorder on if you wish. I'm not going to compromise you, or myself, or anybody else. I'm an inspector of police from the provinces, I'm looking for a witness in a criminal case, I'm told you may be acquainted with her; it's a very simple matter. I hope I'm not troubling you.'

'By no means,' politely. 'But you spoke of a paper. Am I to understand that this was simply a pretext to gain entrance?'

'No, not at all. I have a written authorisation from the judge of instruction concerned with this affair. No doubt you can tell at a glance that it's authentic.'

'I'll be glad to oblige you. I must charge you, naturally, my professional fee.'

'Sure,' said Castang perfectly serious. 'Here too to save you trouble is my own identification. No fee on that, I think.'

'Certainly not,' laughing. 'Thank you, Monsieur Castang. Yes, these papers are certainly genuine. "Patricia La Touche." No, I know nobody of that name; thereabouts there may have been some error. Is there anything further I can be of use in?'

'You haven't any trapdoors round here? You know, like Sweeney Todd? Push a button and I disappear through the floor.'

'What a lovely idea,' tickled. 'Like Catherine de Medicis in the Louvre—zip, down the oubliette all the boring customers. But what on earth would one do with the bodies? Catsmeat factory.'

'I thought Patricia might have gone down the oubliette: out of sight, out of mind. I really do want to see her—she used to know this chap who got killed. Painter chap—you might have read about it in the paper. I've no curiosity about anything else: I'd hoped you might know where I could get in touch with her. Don't pay attention to the gutter Press by the way—this affair isn't sensational at all.'

'Well, Monsieur Castang, as to that, one would like a few guarantees. Nobody likes to get into the gutter Press. Unwelcome publicity is harming to anybody in the professional way, of however humble a description.'

'I think I can manage that. I've an introduction from a friend. Don't tear it up though: he'd like to have it back.'

'Good. That's certainly a serious recommendation. Now this girl —to be businesslike—no, I don't know her, truly. The name is sufficiently unusual; I'd recall it.'

'Perhaps a nickname. One meets girls at parties. Here's a photo of her that her father gave me.'

'Something vaguely familiar about the face. One can't be sure— these wretched girls change their hair and put on false eyelashes and you'd no longer recognise them.'

'Try though. I'd take it as a favour.'

'Always glad to do a favour to one's friends. Tell you what, I'll try and find out. Make a phone call or two. Where could I get in touch, say an hour from now?'

'How about my friend's office?'

'That'd be a notion. People bring the oddest girls to parties.'

And with that he had to be content. He was so used to this childish rubbish that he took it as inevitable. These people were all moral imbeciles. On account of that they were dangerous: they knew no standard but expediency. Nothing interested them but a gold bar and even then they'd think it fake. Which was preferable?—this group that pretended the girl didn't exist, or those other idiots who were convinced she had never existed, but had been invented to gain leverage somewhere. They thought him a sad simpleton. And he thought nothing about them at all. Any more than a gardener wonders why weeds grow quicker than flowers.

He went back to the secret-service crowd and found his man still sitting where he had left him, finger still on the pulse of the nation's safety.

'I haven't tampered with anyone.' The man leaned back in a comfortable, well-padded leather chair. His desk was expensive too.

'Your people are holding this man La Touche?'

'That's what I've been told.'

'Who started this rumour about Israeli Intelligence?'

'Somebody wanting to make himself interesting.'

'There's nothing in it. Once more I say to you—don't meddle with what you don't understand. Now—what about this girl?'

'He's ringing me back at this number.'

'Less bad,' slightly mollified at finding Castang docile. 'Tell me,' in a more friendly voice, leaning forward again, 'do you think she's worth finding?'

'In the evidential sense, she'd probably serve only to confuse a simple matter. She might have something to add which clarifies this action of La Touche. Which is fairly unaccountable. She was at one time on heroin. If she still is she'll be useless, since they are interested in nothing but to satisfy their immediate needs. If you mean do I have a fancy notion that people got her laid alongside this painter Davids in order to keep tabs on his political activities—no, I don't believe a word of it. For a start, nobody on drugs would be the least reliable, or thought to be so by anyone remotely bright.'

'I'm glad to hear you speaking sensibly.'

'A girl of that sort, finding friends who seemed to satisfy her wilder aspirations, might get used as a tool at a very low level. Or for propaganda purposes, as leverage in an extreme case upon her family.'

'What do you know about these activities of La Touche?'

'Very little. Frankly they don't interest me. They may you.'

'Quite. If your judge has been reading spy stories and gets his

79

imagination over-heated, just be good enough to let me know. I'll handle it. There wouldn't be anything there for you. I make myself understood?'

'As long as it cuts both ways,' said Castang. 'I want to talk to this girl, about her father, and about this man Davids. On her personal relationships. Nothing more. If you don't like that then there's nothing I can do about it. If obstacles are put in my way then I will inform the judge. He can decide that for himself. The independence of magistrates is no part of my responsibilities.'

'That's quite all right,' said the man, soothingly.

The telephone rang. The voice was the same, light, merry.

'Monsieur Castang? . . . That little favour you asked. I've been glad to do what I could, but I can't manage it for you. No, you don't owe me a thing. It would have been a pleasure. . . . To tell the truth I thought I could have fixed that. Just on the spur of the moment, when you mentioned it, I imagined it shouldn't be too difficult. But to coin a phrase the model's out of stock. . . . No, there's no act being put on; the person you really want to meet just isn't in Paris. Left the country, I'm told. You know how erratic these people are. No motive at all that I can see, unless personal. You know—life is a bit of a bore, let's change the scene. Without being in the least rude, I'd hazard the guess that she thought meeting you would be complicated. To my mind it's as simple as that. Fault of the Press, I should imagine. Just couldn't bear to face the idea of a fuss being made. . . . I genuinely don't know. I'm told that England was mentioned, but I can't guarantee even that.'

'Thanks just the same,' said Castang. He put the phone down and said, 'Well, that disposes of your worries. They decided she was an embarrassment and pushed her out. Probably sitting in the airport waiting-room this minute. It wouldn't take her long to pack.'

The man behind the desk risked his first, very faint smile.

'My dear boy, they know very well that if she left now I could have her if I wanted her. England of all places, where there's a strict check at immigration.'

'So you mean she's still here but they've deliberately lost her.'

'No, I don't think that. They imagine I want her, and quite certainly they wouldn't want to irritate me for such a trivial motive, or if it were not trivial they would be tipping their hand, showing me that she had importance. No, it's probably true. She doesn't want to face the idea of being bothered by cops, and she just ducks it. That suits them. One thing they're really expert at is public relations and this is not a good terrain for them.'

'I love that,' said Castang grinning. 'Anarchists with a P.R. man.'

'But of course.' The man was unbending now, seeing that nobody was going to give him a troublesome moment. 'What else is it, over ninety per cent of the time? They plant a rumour, say, that they have a low-level Sam missile, and could fire it at one of these great lumbering planes from anywhere round an airport perimeter. A thought well designed to make a good headline. Whereas even if they had one . . .'

'Have they?' asked Castang, with some amusement: this man was proving that good public relations are never wasted.

'My dear boy, who cares whether they have or not? They know perfectly that I could make their lives such a misery, if I really thought they did.'

Not you, thought Castang. You're only a pen pusher.

'You mean you'd push a few of them under tube trains.'

'You ought to know better than that,' prudishly.

'No,' said Castang, 'you shoot them up quite blatantly. Two useful results: in the public eye they're just gangsters, and they get persecuted by the criminal brigade—me, for instance.'

'My dear boy—we'll have to get you transferred to Paris.'

Shit on that, thought Castang.

XIV

LOVE ME LITTLE, LOVE ME LONG

He got a late afternoon train, that would bring him home for a late, but still reasonable supper. To this pack of poisonous phoneys, a real woman like Vera was the only antidote. He had brought her a big bag of greengages: next to cherries—that Czech fruit—her favourites. She wasn't able any more to climb the hillsides and go down on her knees to get close to the ground—for it is only when close to the earth that you find the wild strawberries.

On the train he read a spy story, by a famous English writer, the specialist in moral imbeciles. It was of no interest. He scribbled in his notebook:

Monsieur le Juge,

I would be inclined to discount the whole political element, either as imaginary, or as being an exercise in public relations by DST.

2) the girl Patricia la Touche: enquiry among known associates met by timewasting tactics and a sense of embarrassment. Likeliest conclusion: this group, politically sensitive, feels compromised by the noisy rumour of political scandal in the Press. Information, probably reliable, is that she has crossed a frontier. Destination (unverifiable) England. Suggestion: warrant for interrogation via Interpol. DST unwilling and unlikely to act, their apparent policy being an agreed immobility failing act of terrorism on national soil.

3) Davids: no ground whatever for supposing him an Israeli agent, unless the emphatic assurances of DST are taken to mean

83

the opposite. From observation, such activities would be quite incompatible with character. Since the point is inconclusive, and in view of the strong obstructionism to be expected from other departments, my conclusion is that the entire political aspect should be excluded and treated as fictional, failing strong independent corroboration.

Respectfully,   H. Castang OPP.

He threw it aside with a sigh. He was going home to clean himself. His habit of taking a shower directly he got in was in a way symbolic. It wasn't just sweat that had to be scrubbed off.

The greengages, by a latter-day miracle, were not dry and juiceless from being picked unripe, but were full of blood, crisp even when bursting with ripeness, with a scent that filled the room, the bitter-sweet smell of her childhood; acid Slav scent of a little girl who could do with a wash, barefoot on a wooden ladder propped against the cherry tree. She sat eating them greedily, absorbed, immensely and simply happy. He sat opposite with his feet on another chair, propped on the bottom of his spine, where she had cracked hers, smoking a small Dutch cigar as a treat: rather heavy—they had mixed some dark Brazilian leaf in with the light Sumatra tobacco. More smokable though than the black things, skinny and knotted, that Richard affected and which knocked you down. He studied her: she was his balance wheel: without her he would be nothing but a bum.

The Cattleya, the papers had called her. Such a stupid name; she was nothing like an orchid. But a play on her name, and because the strongly-marked Slav features were exotic.

She hadn't changed much. The legs of course; they were wasted and there was nothing anybody could do about that. But the face and the upper half hardly at all. The one a trifle thinner, the other a scrap heavier, but still in essence the same as when he had first seen her, at the Antibes competition where he was on security duty.

Antibes was not one of the top international meetings, but was regarded by the trainers as a good proving ground for the tougher work to come, for seeing who was in form, and especially for developing the younger, less known gymnasts. That year all three of the Russian stars were there. Rumanova small and dark, the extraordinary jumper, amazing on the 'horse' and in the ground

84

movements. The very fair Liabuschinska, poetic and fragile, with beautiful arms and incomparable slow movements on the 'balance beam'. And the round-faced, doll-pretty Aronova, the reigning champion, not outstanding in any one exercise but unbeatable on average, so faultless and finished was her execution, her one handicap the slightly inexpressive features.

Castang had been a fair gymnast, in the military team during his army days, and watched with professional interest. Vera took his eye at once. She was far below the Russian girls, nowhere near accurate or inventive enough. Indeed she was only substituting on the national team for a girl with a pulled muscle, but in this the strongest rivalry she had faced she surpassed herself, and in her best exercise, the asymmetric bars, she had come equal second with a Russian prima donna, and the crowd applauded madly. Castang had been a bit unprofessional about making her acquaintance. Still, nobody more surprised than him when she ran away, suddenly, only three weeks later in Vienna. The Press had been quite positive that this was a romantic attachment to a Czech ice hockey star who had just done the same in Canada, and was disgusted when she married an obscure French policeman, neither photogenic nor likely to become so, and it promptly forgot her.

One day a year later she got again a brief headline. She was training a class at the local club; slack-muscled French sluts. Ironically, it was on the asymmetric bars that a hand slipped, perhaps insufficiently resined, and the big somersaulted jump-off had pulled to one side, so that she fell awkwardly just off the protective mat, and cracked pelvic vertebrae, or bust her arse, whichever you called it. Hadn't walked for nearly three years. Never would, in all likelihood, get much beyond the present hobble. He was the only person left who still retained, unmarked, the original cherry-eating Cattleya.

He had told her about Madame Davids. She apprehended and understood it all so much quicker than he did. She was not intelligent in the conventional way, the way he was 'a bright boy'. In many things painfully dense. And quite uneducated, never having paid attention at school, and shocking people by saying things like 'Where is the Panama Canal?'.

Now she was crying a little into the greengages, controlled as she always was. No noisy sobs and gulps or grimaces, only two white marks that came and went on the wings of her nose. Who was she crying for? It was not for the Cattleya, nor for the wretched fate of the two young girls. She wiped it off her face with her forefinger.

'You saw the papers?' he asked. The campaign had gathered momentum in a nastily antisemitic outcry. Photographs of Davids, oddly clever at disguising the broad and noble features, all sensual mouth and greedy eyes. La Touche photographed well with his distinguished, slightly pinched look of concavities below the high fine forehead.

'Dear sweet France, frightened again of offending the Arab pals and losing an arms contract . . . Justice!' with bitterness.

'It's just a storm,' he said. 'It'll pass. And say this for Szymanowski, he has integrity. He'll have no truck with this vulgar propaganda. Being a Pole he hates Poles, but since he dislikes Jews, for a Polish Jew he'll bend over backwards.'

'But in face of a deliberate Press campaign . . .'

'Pooh—yesterday's news wraps fish. He'll lie low for a while.'

'That man,' said Vera, 'why does he kill his wife, his child?'

'Forget all this political crap. What are you left with? Passion, a genuine crime of passion? Only one thing we know about that—no journalism, no trial, no nothing can bring that out. Either you're clinical, or you're sentimental. Best not try to understand.'

'But I want to.'

'Then go and see him. Talk to him. You might very well do better than me.'

'How?'

'You've a prison visitor's permit. I dare say the judge will give you an authorisation, if you ask him.'

'Did he love them?'

'I don't know. Not at all, perhaps, and then too much. The shrinks will be busy with it. These very controlled, rational men . . . How does one know?'

Vera finished the last greengage and looked at him desolately.

'Love me only a little,' she said, 'but love me a long time.'

Castang laughed and crushed his cigar out.

'Cattleya' he said teasingly; it always made her cross.

XV

TACTICS, AND TACT

'Funeral this morning,' said the judge, 'and I want you to keep an eye on it, Castang, from a discreet distance. I've told that man, the Viscount or whatever he is, there's to be no provocation. In the interests of justice, and in the name of decency and taste, I've laid down that it must be strictly private. He acted the horrorstruck, and assures me that it will be a purely family affair, out in the village where they have their country house, far enough out to discourage the vulgar, so that I don't suppose there'll be any demonstrations. But that infernal Dieudonné is clever at orchestrating a show: black veils and sobs and photographers, so you'll keep an eye open, and see that nothing gets out of hand. There might too be a possibility of this girl Patricia turning up.'

'Yes,' said Castang.

'Quite so, I've read your report. The wretched Press forces one's hand. They print all breathless that the girl is in hiding: she's only to pick up a paper to rush for cover. But there it is; I agree with you that she's a material witness and has got to be heard.'

'I can't see her turning up at a bourgeois family occasion like a funeral.'

'No. . . . I've put the usual telegraphic notification through to Interpol. Finding her would put a spoke in Dieudonné's wheel too: from what you tell me it's clear that Davids protected and cared for her. Damned Pole, but I don't like this systematic blackening.'

'The women egged him on. La Touche told me it had happened before.'

'Damned imbecile,' said the judge, meaning Poles. 'Should have had the sense to leave young girls alone. If it had been the wife alone—La Touche was indifferent to her games, and makes no bones about admitting it. . . . Difficult subject, with that irritating lacklustre manner. I'm not going to allow any blatant whitewashing: Master Dieudonné has overplayed his hand. I've ordered two experts whose objectivity will be beyond question. Definitely not from Paris—one from Bordeaux and one from Lyon and for heavens' sake see that neither of them are Jews . . .'

'Or Arabs.'

'Just so, that's exactly the way the Press twists one's arm; the swarthy complexion wouldn't do at all, and how does one go about asking for two psychiatrists please, and see that one is Norwegian and the other Canadian—exactly like these wretched United Nations soldiers who can't fight and impress nobody. Very well, Castang, off you go. They're due to begin at eleven, and it's twenty kilometres off.'

Castang, climbing into a stuffy police car that smelt vile, winding down all four windows, was unaware that Vera was disembarking outside the Palace of Justice, making heavy weather of those broad flights of steps in horrible sick-coloured marble. She did not know Monsieur Szymanowski at all. She was though quite close friends with the youngest of the panel of examining magistrates, Colette Delavigne, the children's judge, and through her had a prison visitor's card in her maiden name. One always encouraged prisoners with an interest in art. Those with literary aspirations less; there had been rather too many writing books about their experiences in prison. Vera made a good prison visitor, because she did not pity herself, and was curt with people who did.

In the country it was less hot. The city, in the broad river-valley, was notoriously hot. Out here it was still, officially, 'the plain' but since leaving the town he had been climbing imperceptibly, and the land rose here in a ridge, or more exactly a whaleback with a gentle approach from the city side, falling into an abrupt scarp on the other. The 'château' stood at the very top, commanding a magnificent view over to the foothills. A real château too; no gimcrack villa or false-classical pompery, but a simple, pretty country house in local stone with a slate roof.

The village was built up the whaleback, with cowsheds and farmyards up to the gate. Nothing but a slight widening of the unpaved street and two fine old lime trees marked the entrance: a wrought-

88

iron grille and a gravelled courtyard. There had been no room for the stables behind, where a paved terrace overhung the scarp, so that they were to the side behind a row of clipped acacias, and were converted to cottages. Nice, too, thought Castang, as a grace-and-favour residence. Wouldn't mind the château, either, come to that: cost a packet though to heat, in winter. Serfs bringing in the yule log would be the thing, and alas, he was a serf, but wasn't getting sentimental about it.

The gate was open and a dozen cars parked round the sundial. Castang had not been invited to drink sherry before the ceremony, nor to lunch after, and went to explore. Good village: château and houses had grown up together, taking each other for granted, and would bury one of themselves in simplicity and solidarity. The church was nice, with the cemetery next door; box hedges and a lych-gate. Lucky Hélène: no place here for urban yobboes or even earnest leftwing students cherishing their Arab brothers.

Everything smelt good: he wished Vera were with him to share it. Virtually everyone in France is a countryman by instinct if not by birth and he no exception. Even Hélène. She would be remembered and loved here as a pretty young girl. The local people had groomed and shod her pony, washed her clothes, put cobwebs on her cuts, fished her out when she fell in the brook and smacked her for disobedience. Even Charlotte, perhaps, with the more sophisticated urban upbringing, had come here to pick blackberries and mushrooms and been shouted at by village women for forgetting her sunbonnet.

Castang looked with appreciation at the 'dependencies', all properly there in their place: walled kitchen-garden, orchard, vineyard, turreted pigeoncote. These people—how was it possible that they had not known how to be happy? Would one ever get tired of that terrace (sheltered from the vulgar gaze by trees, but cops are good peekers)? The sun setting on the far plateau? To come out after spending the winter months and the opera season in the equally delicious town house, and stay through the summer till after the vintage . . . this was the earthly paradise. And Hélène looked for it in witty-tongued charlatans, and Patricia in heroin, and the young Charlotte in brushing her behind along the arm of La Touche's stiff financial colleagues, and he just didn't grasp it at all, and was glad not to be a psychiatrist.

The funeral procession had formed and was approaching. Quite a sprinkling of the older villagers had come to slip into the church, and about forty people were come from the house, and half of those would be relatives, with long black veils in the ancient style for the women, and the curé too had dived into the past to dig the old 'first-class' funeral trappings out of a musty cupboard: black and silver canopies and hangings. Castang lurked discreetly.

The chief personage was a stiff, thin man of fifty, presumably the judge's viscount, in whom dignity had become the sort of carriage the French call 'pète-sec'. Crack-fart?—the translation makes no sense but the type is universal. The usual amazing number of effaced female cousins. There would be absentees among the family friends. Some of the neighbourhood aristocracy were severe and militarily Catholic, and La Touche's colleagues had of course tactful prior engagements. But there was a fair sprinkling that lined up to shake hands at the end and murmur a bereaved word and depart with circumstantial expressions lasting till the car, and Castang looked at these, interested.

Among these, and striking enough to catch the eye in any company, was a tall man with silver hair and an unusually bleached or blanched expression, whose black suit and black eyebrows made him look like Dracula. Entertainingly so at first: Castang had no other reason to single him out. During the service in the cemetery he stood composed; one would say collected but that his eyes, like Castang's, flicked about with more than idle curiosity or boredom, and when as inevitably happened their eyes caught, Castang realised that he got a longer, cooler stare than the others. He was being examined, in fact, with a cop's eye except that this was no cop: too well dressed, and the long white hand wore a signet set with diamonds. Nobody Castang knew, and certainly not DST, had this subdued glitter, nor the elegant nonchalance with which this man walked to his car and paused to light a cigarette with the kind of lighter no crooked cop would buy—he wouldn't even know where to find it. Nor would anybody paid by the government risk a Maserati, let alone such a plain and hushed dark blue Maserati.

And yet the languid stroll was to let Castang catch up, and the performance with the lighter was to allow even a stranger to say a word in passing, such as two strangers might exchange when they belonged to the same club, and needed no formal introduction. Castang didn't take the offer up, but he felt no doubt: they did belong to the same club.

The man got into his Maserati with a supple movement of a tennis player and backed it out unhurriedly. Castang slid into the little Renault, anonymous but for its persistent police smell inside, and did the same. At an interval of thirty metres they pulled out of the traffic. They did not take the road to the town, but one leading further into the country. Castang wondered where the hell they were going, but was quite enjoying the idea of a tin-pot car tailing a Maserati, and an open tail at that.

The man made no effort to lead him a dance; stayed at an easy speed, signalled his turns in plenty of time, shepherding Castang along the way a destroyer on convoy might a rusty old bitch of a freighter that at anything over fifteen knots would burst its boiler.

They took country roads, and it was nearly thirty kilometres before they slowed to enter a village whose name was vaguely familiar, but Castang had no idea why until the Maserati turned languidly to park in front of a long building whose terrace was a great splendid mass of ivy-leaved geraniums. To be sure. 'Les Armes de France' was a restaurant with two Michelin stars and a red bird in a rocking-chair.

There were plenty of cars in the lot and most of them expensive. The Maserati, as though by right, got a slot right next the front door. Castang had to take the Renault right down to the end and plod humbly back. He found his man installed at a table for two on the terrace, and the service so rapid that the order for drinks had already been given. Two champagne flutes stood on the table, and as Castang walked diffidently up the steps the waiter came sailing up with a bucket. The man smiled politely and patted the chair next him. Castang sat down.

XVI

DIALOGUE

'With your permission I'm ordering lunch for the two of us.'

'Won't get a table in this place surely.'

'Oh, we will, you know. I hope that this will be all right. After a funeral, do you think?' The waiter had brought a 'Belle Epoque' bottle of Perrier-Jouet and settled it in the bucket, giving it two neat turns: unnecessarily for it was already cool.

'Cool,' said Castang. 'It, you, even me in a moment.'

'Don't eat any of that rubbish on little trays; it'll only spoil your appetite. Doctor Simon, Rainer Simon, at your service.'

'Castang, Henri Castang, S.R.P.J., equally.'

'Yes I know. A bad photo, there in the paper, but recognisable to a man with any eye.'

'Ear nose and throat?'

'No, law. Doctor is a slightly Germanic way of putting it.'

'What a lot of lawyers I keep meeting.'

'There are far too many to practise as lawyers. I have commercial activities. These menus are too large and time-wasting. Will you follow me or is that presumptuous?'

'You've already been presumptuous. Sensible anyway: I don't know what all this means.'

'Then I shall be guide in all these labyrinths. And another of these, waiter, and tell the sommelier the Margaux in a magnum.'

'I'll just phone my wife to tell her I'm lunching.'

'I'd rather you didn't. She won't be anxious.'

'It's a habit I have.'

'To be perfectly honest, I'd rather there was no trace of our meeting. I did not accost you at the funeral: sensibly, you left me free. I had been prepared to eat alone but I was much pleased at your joining me. I came down from Paris—no, not for the funeral although Gilbert is an old friend. Nor to meet you. But having met you—let's make a good lunch. I won't be mysterious, and strangely enough you can trust me. Equally, I will trust you. But I'd rather there were no phonecalls.'

'I'll be brushed with the angel's wing,' said Castang, drinking his champagne and signing to the waiter that they preferred to take their own second helpings. 'Discreet, this place,' approvingly.

He had never been before in a restaurant this grand. Vera would be interested. It was a disappointment to both of them later that he had no idea whatever what he had eaten, except that it had been good. As for Margaux in a magnum, he couldn't remember ever having seen one before. Next time, he'd ask for a jeroboam. Insist upon it.

'Well,' said Castang after they were at their table and his napkin had been unfolded for him and the second bottle of champagne arrived with the soup. 'Convey.'

'Yesterday I made the acquaintance of Madame Davids,' said Simon.

'So did I.'

'Yes, she told me. A good painter, you know.'

'Did you see the big nude?'

'I bought it,' said Simon, simply.

'The subject interested you?'

'You mean the nude, or the girl? I'm a collector. I have no interest in the girl whatever.'

'La Touche's daughter?'

'I know him, as I told you. I do not know his family. I went to the funeral, yes. For much the same reasons as yourself. I hope you like bone marrow.' It was a beef consommé, with tiny medallions of delicate things, that one must not allow to boil.

'What took you to see Madame Davids?'

'Once more, the same reason as yourself. We are not parallel—we have converged, gradually.' Red mullet in paper bags arrived, simplicity itself. The waiter spread the livers on morsels of toast and left them.

'I was curious,' said Simon, 'at this rumour of Gilbert dabbling in politics. It would be most unlike him. You see, not only do I know him well, but we are engaged in a similar business.'

'Oh, you advise Arabs about their investments?'

Simon did not answer, but concentrated on boning his fish with care.

'I know you to be intelligent: there is no need for you to waste any time upon stupidities.' Castang was irritated.

'Why not buy the judge lunch?'

'Ah. If I have not made myself plain, that is my fault.' The delicate, beautiful skeletons of the mullet were removed. The wine waiter pulled the cork of the Margaux, laid it on a napkin after sniffing it with deep pleasure, looked at the light through the first half-glass, and said, 'Solid as the bank. You prefer to help your- selves; just watch it towards the end.'

'And bright as a new pin,' said Simon. 'Good.'

'And there are few banks,' agreed Castang, 'that I trust my new pins to.'

'I'm sure you'll agree that Davids was not any sort of agent. Neither Zionist nor even Mormon.'

'It would surprise me very much.'

'And it would equally and absurdly complicate your position if my poor friend Gilbert were engaging in politics.'

'The judge wouldn't be happy.'

'I should make it clear that Gilbert's activities in no sense overlap—lapped—mine, and that his domestic troubles cause me grief, but cause me no embarrassment.'

'What business are you in?' asked Castang looking at his plate and wondering what was in it. Looked like beef. Was beef.

'I sell aircraft.'

'I see.'

'Quite right. These idiot rumours gather headway. I'm open with you when I remark that Zionist agents are more apt to find them- selves on my plate.'

'But not today.'

'No,' agreed Simon, eating.

'Do you have an axe to grind?'

'No other axe to grind. If I can convince you, and I hope that I can, it will enable you to see through things more clearly, and if this rumour can be scotched, why, Gilbert is a friend of mine. It will also make life easier for me. I don't act directly as a government agent, but it's natural that the Government is unhappy at these silly rumours. With any luck they'll die—if they're given no further nourishment.'

'Do you know Dieudonné?'

'Yes. He's quite an honest chap but he's a fool. I've told him so. I think he has the sense to stay told. That half-witted private army won't bother you any further.'

'I'm grateful,' said Castang. 'And I'll do my best.'

'Fine,' said Dracula. 'You like cheese?—or they do a thing here with prunes that's clever.'

'Let's stay clever.'

'I'm having both myself. There's a couple of glasses left in this bottle.'

'Nothing wrong with your metabolism.' That sounded like something the bishop said to the actress, thought Castang. He mustn't let this character put him in his pocket. Places like these did not make one drunk but they promoted euphoria. He had been picked up cleverly, steered adroitly, had his brains picked thoroughly. Tipsily grinning and saying things like 'let's stay clever' with sticky vanity. . . . Not to get self-satisfied, because this man was not taking the trouble and spending the money unless he was getting value. He lit a cigarette, sent the waiter for coffee, and said so.

'I like that,' said Simon. 'I count myself lucky. You see, telling the truth has become an unfashionable pursuit. This makes it a powerful tool. Most people are so dishonest that they are flabbergasted by a scrap of truth. Of course you're right. I lured you here with the notion of sealing off a lot of clumsy police meddling that would maybe handicap some business I have in mind. In certain circles I am known both as a friend and a business associate of Gilbert La Touche. We have given one another introductions to people who are very rich. And people who are very rich—am I boring you?—who eat in these restaurants and who frequent people like me suffer from over-simplifications. One easily gets infected by that attitude. They are neurotically suspicious: everything becomes a plot, everything gets done with ulterior motives, and being inordinately vain they think always of a ploy to separate them from their pathetic little millions. I'm speaking naturally of occidentals: orientals are completely different: we won't go into that. Sorry—were you about to speak?'

'Just to say you're right about the prunes.'

'Ah, I'm glad; I'm enjoying my own. You see, there's nothing a man like me dreads more than doing business with a man he can trust, and not realising it. I'm perfectly satisfied—are you?'

'Yes,' said Castang. 'I made a proposal to the judge that all this political stuff should be disregarded, and he wasn't happy. He'd be glad to have it confirmed.'

'You tell him,' seriously, 'that you got a good opinion. From a good doctor.'

'Less bad,' said Castang.

XVII

SCUFFLE

Get back from lunch late—but the businessmen are less concerned than policemen—and the rest of the day is gone in no time. Castang, going at a sober pace in the little Renault, took an hour getting back to the city.

Commissaire Richard, to whom an account had to be given of where he had been, listened to the story with an expression which could be called dampening, or sobering, or perhaps just deflating. Sympathetic in a sense, because being the divisional commissaire he held a certain position among the good bourgeois of his good city, and being the chief of the criminal brigade it had happened to him too to be given a lavish lunch and lots of patter, though as he had noticed—and now remarked—'The provincial bourgeois are mostly too mean to go beyond a one-star restaurant. Poor boys, they spoil the ship for a ha'porth of tar. Rather pathetic, but typical of that essential provincial pettiness, that they have never grasped the fact that a big bribe, a generous bribe, is more effective than a small mean grubby bribe. Have you drunk rather a lot?'

'If you mean did I fall asleep driving?—no. My wife wouldn't like it. Assuming we worked neck and neck, which was roughly the case, I've had one bottle of champ, rather fancy champ, and one bottle of very fancy bordeaux.'

'Are you pissed now?'

'No. Tacking to and fro in those country lanes I wouldn't have wanted to blow in any paper bags. But not now.'

'That's as well,' flipping his intercom switch and saying, 'Fausta dear, make some rather strong coffee. . . . I'll be seeing the judge this afternoon. I've a couple of jobs for you. Nothing very strenuous. You're to go and see the Israeli Consul. He's been fixing up a funeral for Davids, being rather nice about it. Davids loathed the State of Israel, and being the tactless sort of bugger you'd expect didn't mince his words about his opinion, and the Rabbi took a distinctly dim view. From there you're to go—you've an appointment at six this evening—to see Monsieur Jonas Meyer, who is a pillar of the local Jewish community and needs his ruffled feathers soothed, because he's not in the least pleased with the situation. Watch him; he draws a lot of water. You should be sober by then. Don't tell him any Jewish jokes; he doesn't appreciate them. Rather you than me, in fact, but that's your horrible luck. . . . Thank you Fausta, that's very nice. Does anybody invite you to restaurants with lots of stars?'

'Not unless they want to go to bed with me,' said Fausta.

The Israeli Consul wasn't like any consul Castang had ever met, being exceptionally good-looking, bronzed, muscled, and in general about to take the helm of a twelve-metre racing yacht, dressed too in a silk shirt and sandals, with longish hair that shook back in one piece and would never be tatty or ratty. He wasn't wearing a gun, and was unimpressed by demonstrators, who had, he said, suddenly galloped off behind the mesa like Hollywood Indians, waving their spears and catcalling, giving the defenders of the beleaguered wagon-laager time to comb their hair and get their noses powdered. He didn't want to talk about politics; nothing could be duller. Davids he had never met, but 'having had the job of getting him buried he had got interested'.

'We buried him this morning—I just got back from Paris by the afternoon plane. I rather liked the widow.'

'So did I.'

'I would have liked him too. We've plenty like that at home, but their energies are more easily channelled; can always go out and irrigate an orange tree.'

'Never did understand these Arabs,' said Castang. 'All they ever did was let the goats eat what vegetation there was, and sit scratching their own sores.'

'Marvellous thing the Press. Fellow pays a lot of money to print stories about dirty Davids screwing all these women. Wouldn't be at all difficult to print a lurid piece about bourgeois girls sold as white slaves in Beirut. Everybody's sick of being sorry for Jews, you see: they've done that for years. They'll be sick of being sorry for Arabs too, quite soon.'

'Tell me about Davids.'

'Not at all an uncommon type. A deeply believing man, to whom his religion meant a great deal, but who simply hated what he thought of as lip-service and excessive attachment to outward forms and letters. You know, curls and skullcaps and worries about eating lobster. The sight of what he called "good Jews" simply maddened him. To an artist, you see, all that seems ridiculously trivial. Ever heard of Ernst Toller?'

'No.'

The consul leapt up, prowled along a wall full of books, whipped one out of the shelf, turned pages rapidly.

'Quote from autobiography. "The words 'I am proud to be a German' or 'I am proud to be a Jew' sounded ineffably stupid to me. As well say 'I am proud to have brown eyes'. Must I then join the ranks of the bigoted and glorify my Jewish blood now, not my German? Pride and love are not the same thing, and if I were asked where I belonged I should answer that a Jewish mother had borne me, that Germany had nourished me, Europe had formed me, my home is the earth, and the world my fatherland." Now Davids felt like that.'

'Do you?'

A great shout of laughter.

'Man, my wages are paid by the Foreign Office, like yours are by the Ministry of the Interior. What does it matter what you or I feel?'

'Few people understand policemen.'

'The more reason why we should try and understand Davids.'

'I've got to see a man called Herr Jonas Meyer.'

'Yes, well, you'll find him rather different.'

You bet. Castang was received by the senior partner of Meyer and Sons in the senior partner's private office. The old gentleman was brusque, and had no high opinion of the Police Judiciaire.

'I ask you to get this rabble off the streets.'

'We aren't encouraging them, you know.'

'Yes yes yes, I know, I know,' with great impatience. Just the sort of thing that put one's back up, not against Jews necessarily, but against businessmen. So very much the French industrialist, and dynamic as all hell into the bargain. We export for you, don't we? We pay bloody high taxes, don't we? It's upon us that you depend for your balance of payments, isn't it? Which gave them the right, the absolute unquestioned godgiven right to put a three-hundred-per-cent mark up on their lousy shoddy products and grumble that the country was being run by plumbers' mates. One could go anywhere in Europe or America and hear the same phrase. 'Place is being run by niggers.' This one had got so French that he exaggerated his Jewishness, just the way some black men competed to see who's the niggermost.

'I know nothing about this man La Touche and couldn't care less. That's a matter for the magistrates. If they choose to make a great fuss about the villainies of this Davids in screwing his wife and his daughter that's all right, it concerns them. But to claim that this man was in any way whatever representative of the Jewish community in this city—that's overstepping it, that we won't have. I'm telling you this in private; that's correct procedure. You can tell your commissaire that I'm not going behind his back, not trying to cut his throat. Get this clear though. For the purposes of this meeting, which isn't designed as a basis for discussion, you can consider me as the spokesman of this community. You may or may not be aware yourself of the weight of what I'm saying. Your commissaire may—or should. The mayor does. The prefect does. The public prosecutor does. Paris does—I need only remind you that the aircraft industry is an extremely sensitive barometer to the prosperity of the country in the economic sense. And I'm not interested in who the aircraft get sold to, either, you follow?'

'Did you know Davids?'

Mr Meyer lit a very mild, rather perfumed Egyptian cigarette from the good old Arab firm of Dunhill.

'I knew him,' he said abruptly. 'I bought a picture from him. I thought it good. Now I'm obliged to put it in the cellar, treat it as a dodgy investment. Might go up, might go down. That's not a Jew, that's a Yid. I've no use for Yids; they're a liability. The state of Israel, let me remind you, wouldn't exist long if it wasn't for the likes of me.'

Castang, mindful of Monsieur Richard's instructions, wasn't telling any Jewish jokes. The consul had reminded him of the classic chestnut—when the tourists arrive in Jerusalem and ask to be shown the Wailing Wall, the natives bring them to the Ministry of Finance.

Ouf, the day had gone. Castang had wanted to see La Touche

there all peaceful and relaxed in his jail. He had wanted a few more things too, like a nice siesta after lunch. And now he had to sit here and be this old schmuck's whipping boy.

He didn't get back to the office till after six, and it was already twilight when he left the office. His shoulders were sagging; he was very tired indeed. All Richard had promised him was a couple of days off 'as soon as we've time to breathe'.

It should never have happened, he thought afterwards. Ordinarily I'd have been home a bit after six . . . well, before seven anyhow. It would still have been daylight. He'd have taken his bicycle, for ordinarily he kept his own car in the police garage, but he felt jaded, tonight.

The pavement along the canal bank opposite his home was used by the inhabitants as a car park: it was wide, and there was room for everyone between the thick old poplars.

Castang dragged the keys out of the ignition lock; hauled himself out, yawning. And there was just this much luck on his side, that he was looking in the right direction. The fellow came sidling out there from behind his tree done up in bogy-man style, stocking over the face and the head. And a bicycle chain. In a corridor between cars, there was precious little room for manoeuvre. Room for precious little anything, bar instinct. The instinct was not to draw his gun.

He would have had time, for the instinctive shot 'off hand' as the combat instructor calls it, at under ten feet, squeezing one off from the leather: he knew the jargon. He could even do the trick, for he had been to shooting school. At this range, when a man is coming at you full tilt with an offensive weapon, very, the thing is to have stopping power. Hence all the debates about the gun to carry: the instructor, who lives and breathes guns, goes boringly on about it. A forty-five will stop anything but is such a vast clumsy thing that only the more loony gangsters still use them. There is also a thing called a forty-four magnum, quite useful against tanks, and a three-fifty-seven magnum which will go through two Manhattan telephone directories and two innocent bystanders. Castang knew two cops who had this kind of armoury. One used a big Star, which is the Spanish version of the big Colt automatic; the other had been to America and come back with a Smith and Wesson heavy-duty, which is a thirty-eight on a forty-four frame. Castang disliked both men. A gun-shy cop is a danger to other cops, but a gun-happy cop is a danger to everybody. In these days the old seven-sixty-five which used to be carried by all European cops is frowned upon. It probably won't hit anything and wouldn't stop more than a stray cat. Most professionals, including Castang, carry a nine millimetre, like the Browning FN or the Walther. A few are more fancypants than this. Lugers are still made by the Mauser factory, mostly for boys who like looking at themselves in full length mirrors, and comb their hair before making with the parabellum. These guns stop anything Castang had met, but it was an academic debate here, because he didn't try, and it wasn't being gun-shy.

Be it a gun or a nail-file the thing is to be first: if you aren't, all the other rules are meaningless. Castang jumped towards the bogyman. Seeing a blob instead of a face he jabbed at it with his left hand. He had made himself small; the swung bicycle chain missed, thank God, his head. But it curls, it is flexible: some of it at least whipped through and fell upon his back and shoulder. He let out a short hoarse howl as it hit him, and gave the adversary, who was taller and thinner than he was, a short right-hand punch under the heart which hurt, as much as he could make it hurt, which was less than a bicycle chain. The bogy-man hit against a car, doubling up and falling off balance. As he sprawled Castang hit him with a knee in the lower belly. As he went down Castang kicked him in the face. He was not a man who enjoyed giving pain but his shoulder felt broken. The boy made a noise, and got another kick to make him quiet.

'Now,' said Castang with immense weariness, feeling the pain go down his arm and up into the top of his head, 'we'll look at you.'

He bent down and wrenched off the stocking mask and put it in his pocket. He decided not to bend down any more; it hurt too much. His vision was slightly clouded; he had a wish to be sick. He thought of taking this pretty boy by his long pretty hair and took his gun out instead.

'Get up,' he said. 'Do what you're told and quietly. Or I'll kill you. Pick up the chain. Hand it me. Now walk. Cross the road. We're going to have a tea-party.'

XVIII

TOBACCO ROAD

Holding the gun in his left hand while he used his right to twist
a door key made the sweat run down inside his socks: he felt he was
standing in a pool of blood. When he turned on the hallway light
and caught sight of himself in the glass he didn't like it: his eyes
were bloodshot and the facial muscles twitching. He opened the
kitchen door, said 'Go on', pulled a wooden chair from behind the
table, and said 'Sit down'. Vera appeared in the doorway, face white,
eyes enormous, saying nothing.

'In the bottom bureau drawer is a pair of handcuffs, with the gun
cleaning material, probably under a lot of junk. Bring them to me,
will you. And then get me a brandy and we've some codeine in the
bathroom.' Castang took a dishcloth, put it on the table, laid the
bicycle chain on it.

'This, manny, is going to send you up. For three years. First,
I'm going to re-educate you. . . . Put your hands behind you. Look
boy, I'll break your face with the gunbarrel and think nothing of it.
Make me a cup of tea, Vera, and then go knit socks, will you. I want
nothing to eat.'

'You'll eat,' said Vera, 'when I've called a cop and taken this off
your hands. First I can see your back's hurt.'

'It can wait.'

'Possibly but I won't. If you're going to make an interrogation,
you'll do so as well with your shirt off. Can you lift the arm a tiny
bit? I'll cut through it.'

'No,' said Castang, 'it's a good shirt.'

Facing him was a boy of about nineteen, fine-boned, the delicate features slightly marred by a slight nosebleed, where Castang had punched him, and a swelling bruise on the cheekbone, where he'd got a kick. From a soft moccasin, thought Castang; he's seen nothing yet. A pretty-boy Arab. A real little yid. Racist I'm getting, but I've had a day full of Jewish yids and all I needed was an Arab yid.

'Yid,' he said. 'Pretty yid.' It was to be saying something while his shirt came off, because it hurt and he wasn't saying so.

Stung, the boy spoke for the first time.

'I'm not a yid.'

'You think I can tell the difference between one semite and another?'

Behind him Vera gave a small liquid whistle and then a faint clucking noise.

'Is there a lot of blood? It feels like it.'

'No, that's all sweat. There's plenty of blood but what's the word: subcutaneous mostly. There'll be one hell of a bruise. But is there anything bust underneath? Apart from that it looks worse than it is. I want you to go and have an X-ray taken.'

'No.'

'Then I'm going to ring Rab. I've disinfected it, and I'm putting you on a cold compress. . . . Now let's just look at you,' to the boy. 'Keep your face still. A bit of cold water and you'll be as good as new.'

'Don't get him too clean; I might want him dirty,' reaching for a cigarette and wincing. Talk tough, he thought, knowing he wasn't going to hit this boy in front of Vera. She knew that. The boy didn't, though.

Castang had never yet hit a captive in cold blood . . . well, cooling. He'd seen it done several times. Twice he had seen a captive deliberately beaten up. Once after a cop had been shot, once a man who had hit a child: the child lost an eye. The tobacco road is now a rarity, not just because it is strictly forbidden, but because brutalised cops have got rarer, and the sadists have been diagnosed quicker. Castang wondered whether he would have slapped this boy's brain addled if he had him downtown. Here, in his own home, he wasn't going to do a thing. Vera knew this too. Behind him came a thudding noise of ice-cubes being turned out to make cold compresses.

He looked at the boy. There was no need to hit him. Being handcuffed to a kitchen chair behind your back feels first numb, then painful. He had made them tight, and by now they'd be biting.

'Tea,' he said, as the ice cold towel hit him, making him wince. The kettle whistled, answering him.

'I'm going to telephone,' said Vera. 'You still want a cop?'

'Yes,' he said, 'but no particular hurry.'

He sipped the tea boiling, feeling it doing him good. The boy stared at him unwinking, determined to be a man. He'd seen movies too. Vera changed the compress on Castang's back, and went out.

Brandy. Tea. Codeine. Towel wrung out in ice-slosh. All four, he supposed. He had turned back into a cop. He just sat there, smoking, feeling the codeine slowly getting a grip on the pain, saying nothing at all. He felt like some more brandy, and had a cup of tea instead. He put his gun back in the holster, took the belt off, and went and hung it in the bedroom. He came back, poured himself a second cup of tea, sat down. The boy hadn't budged, but the face had got sharper. Bones were sticking through the skin. Castang went on saying nothing till the doorbell rang.

It was a uniformed cop off a patrol wagon. In no hurry: a cop on a night patrol never is. One has to get through those hours, and the less fuss the better. He looked at Castang's closed face in the hall-way, said nothing, whistled slightly when he saw Castang's bare back, looked at the bicycle chain on the table, gave a long unwinking stare at the boy in the chair.

Castang went into the living-room for another chair. Vera was knitting. Socks, for all he knew. He brought back a fresh packet of cigarettes.

'Tea?' he asked the cop. Together they sat and stared at the Arab boy. Two are better than one. The cop refused a cigarette. In training, he said. Castang didn't ask what for.

Rabinowics arrived five minutes later. He was a professor at the University Hospital, not a 'real doctor', as he said himself, at all. He had been Vera's orthopaedic specialist after her crash, had become a friend. He had disclaimed all responsibility for her learning again to walk; said she'd done it by herself. He was rapid on his feet, made always an impression of displacing a lot of air in passage, and drove a Rolls-Royce to—or so he said—drive the neighbours into a frenzy. Castang's neighbours, who loathed having a cop in the building, were eaten up by envy and serve them right. Rab also teased cops, by parking the Rolls-Royce crooked, all over the place, and then pointing to the Aesculapius sticker with the twined snake on his windscreen and blandly defying them to prove it hadn't been an emergency.

He entered into the spirit of things straightaway—he never needed anything spelt out. He gave a long stare at the bicycle chain, another at the Arab boy, a glance at the handcuffs.

'Don't leave him too long like that.'

'Good for the soul.'

'But bad for the circulation.' He nodded to the cop as though it were an old friend, gave Vera an affectionate kiss and took the compress off Castang's back.

'Ow.'

'Yes,' said Rab, 'the humour of it escapes me too. Medieval sort of injury. Hence the invention of plate armour; less commodious than chain mail, but made for better insurance statistics.'

'Ow.'

'Lift. Lower. Lift. Lower. Tough little Gaulish skeleton. It's easier to make dints in a Frank. No displacement. Could be a hairline crack. You'd like an X-ray?'

'No.'

'Want a few days off?'

'No.'

'He wants to be tough,' said Rab to Vera. 'Very well, dear boy; the horse-liniment cure it shall be. It'll hurt for a while. Tickle for longer. What have you taken? Codeines, tut, they're illegal. Right, let's look at the boyfriend. Nothing wrong there. If he happens to fall off a truck at speed don't come to me for a certificate. All right, girl, hop in to the other room; I want to look at your leg.'

Silence fell, and lay.

'He's screwing your wife, in there,' said the Arab boy.

Castang said nothing. The cop changed the compress for him, not too unskilfully. The ice had melted but the water was still cold. Rab could be heard taking his departure. Vera, sensibly, had gone to bed with a book.

'Take the cuffs off him, would you?' said Castang quietly.

The boy sat, and rubbed his wrists, and flexed his arms. Finally he made his mind up and said 'Thank you' in a non-committal but well-brought-up voice.

'Yes,' said Castang. 'It seems like nothing much at first, but it hurts after a while. Circulation. . . . You're a student?'

No answer.

'I see your point,' conversationally. 'Try to see mine. A simple verification of your papers is all that is needed to know all about you. We're not going to hit you. I am sorry I hurt you: you'll understand that it was reflex action. We'll hold you.' He nodded at the chain on the table. 'There's no further proof needed, you see.' Still no answer.

'I'm not going to threaten you with a heavier punishment. And I'm not going to tell you either that if you co-operate you might get off easier. You take the responsibility for what you did. No more, no less. No martyrdom, no Press release, no nothing. Just a meaningless act. Nobody will be interested.'

The boy was a little taken aback. He thought for a while and said, 'It'll all come out at the trial.'

'There won't be any trial. That's right. Sure, we could charge you with half the book. Unlawful everything; loitering, nocturnal aggression, possession, wounds and injuries, aggravated attack, assault upon police officer. And we don't need to charge you with anything at all. Except the possession. Your student permit will be cancelled and the judge in lieu of punishment recommends your deportation within twenty-four hours. Everything wasted. Nothing to show for it. I'm asking you simply to think. There's no evidence at all. The doctor is a friend of mine. He'll say nothing. The man here found you in the street carrying a prohibited weapon. Recognised you as having taken part in an unauthorised manifestation yesterday in front of the Palace of Justice. Oh yes, I saw you there. Were you paid?' asked Castang suddenly, in a contemptuous tone.

'No,' stung.

'Dieudonné organised you?' indifferent.

'I had personal reasons,' indignant at the mercenary suggestion.

'Really?' incredulous. 'Member of a political group?'

'Personal, I tell you.'

'Who will believe that?' without any interest.

'Charlotte La Touche was my friend and I can prove it.'

'Oh, was she?' Lackadaisical. 'Why hit me? I didn't kill her.'

'You're protecting those who did.' Pointing a heated finger like a public prosecutor.

'Oh.' Puzzled. 'It was to protect La Touche, was it?'

'You know damned well. I knew Charlotte. She wouldn't have had anything to do with that Zionist spy.'

'I'm afraid you still have a lot to learn about Charlotte,' said Castang.

'Don't try to tell me lies.'

'Ah. You didn't believe the Press reports.'

'Everybody knows the Press here is run by Jews.' Castang raised his arms, and put them down quickly because the left one hurt him.

'Well, my boy,' he said slowly, 'this is going to hurt you a lot more than beating you up would.' One can't, thought Castang, really tell a lot from people's faces. It is an invention of fiction writers to talk about all the complicated things to be read in people's eyes. The eyes of most people are about as expressive as a bicycle lamp. This boy, though: lovely little lad with a bottom, no doubt, like a peach—dear oh dear, the things that will be happening to you in jug—is really the startled fawn. Apprehension, yes, that shows. The boy has been telling himself wonderful tales for the last three days. And is scared blind of evidence.

'Pass me the briefcase,' he said to the cop. Not an artist, that police photographer. But a careful, sound, painstaking technician who left no margin for error. Everything done three times, using a reflex camera that blew up prints to cabinet size with no distortion at all. Charlotte's naked body, hardly bloodstained at all, was not pornography, since whatever it was it was not titillating. It was hard, though, hard as granite. The boy didn't want to look and couldn't stop himself. The tears didn't mean anything to Castang. A lot of people cry, sooner or later, in the course of a police interrogation. It is themselves they cry for, generally. To be fair, there might have been tears for Charlotte too.

The boy would not be able to stop himself talking now, either. He wouldn't even want to. Perhaps, thought Castang, it comes easier too here in the kitchen than it would in the office. He wrote it down in shorthand. Tomorrow morning one would get it typed. There wouldn't be any need even to have the boy deported. He'd run home by himself. He'd had enough, of Europe.

It didn't add anything much to the central dossier. A calf love-affair. It would serve, though. It would help demolish the so-called 'political' angle. It helped demonstrate how a fact, any fact, could be made meaningless and even disregarded altogether. And it threw light on Charlotte. An unattractive little girl, who had had a pet dog. She might have grown attached to it, but it was still a pet dog, and the fidelity of pet dogs to basically unfeeling persons is always a good illustration of the fallacies of sentimentality. In defence of Charlotte—she had been very immature. Would Patricia, two years older and by account brighter, be the same? She had lived with Davids for six months. And that picture he had seen in Paris— there was a great deal more to that than there was to these horrible photographs. A step further, thought Castang, and—feeling his shoulder—a price paid.

XIX

THE TEDDY-BEARS' PICNIC

Even at eight in the morning there was no life in the air. As long as the sky stayed clear it had been tolerable. There was a haze after dawn, but it burned quickly off. Today it didn't burn off. The light was odd; the sky had a peculiar steely look. Castang had slept deeply but badly. He had hangover eyes. His back muscles were atrociously stiffened and painful. Vera did her best by massaging the back of his neck. She didn't want him to work.

'Rab told you. . . . It's a simple matter. . . . You don't need to have the X-ray if you don't want. . . . A certificate on demand just like that. . . . Only for twenty-four hours. . . . A day like this.'

'Going to be the father and mother of a thunderstorm.'

'Why won't you listen to me?'

'Look; it may seem complicated to you but it's in fact simple. I don't want any official notice taken of that business last night. This affair is quite complicated enough.'

'Oh . . . blow it,' said Vera, who strongly disliked swearing, loathed any sort of blasphemy, and 'When I say fuck I really mean it.'

'Don't worry. It'll be an easy day. Nobody'll do anything on a day like this.'

Since nobody would have dreamed of giving the police air-conditioning he plugged a small fan in over a file cabinet, which swept through ninety degrees and blew papers off his table, but for once nobody complained about the draught. The city sat under a smoggy pall. Fausta was in a bad mood. Even Richard, and it was rare, was in a bad mood. Around him hung a peculiar chemical perfume, something like abrasive scouring powder. Castang sniffed when he came in, not ostentatiously, but he was detected at once.

'It's these aerosols that stop one sweating. My idiot of a wife . . . this one is supposed to smell of green limes. Try Fausta; she smells delicious.'

'What is it you smell of, Fausta?'

'Bergamot,' complacently. 'But the real trouble is that Madame Richard thinks people will notice he smells like me and then they draw the wrong conclusions.'

'So I smell like the kitchen sink,' said Richard crossly.

'Don't make me laugh; it hurts my back.'

'What's wrong with your back?'

He explained: Richard got back into a good mood.

'Sensible of you. The last thing we want is the Press inventing terrorist gangs. You know they even make the hotel-school apprentices buy these aerosols now.'

'I'm very glad to hear it,' said Fausta. 'Who wants a waiter that smells of feet?'

'Yes, but even the cooks. This country isn't what it was. What have you charged this boy with?'

'Possession. Look; chain; stocking mask.'

'Have it sent to the lab. Prints and stuff, to tie it to him firmly if need be.'

'Yes, and my blood group,' said Castang nastily. Plainly, no work was going to get done: sitting around waiting for the storm to break and talking about cooks' feet, but the smell of bergamot came floating suddenly back, carrying a telex flimsy.

'You're going to enjoy this,' said Fausta. Sandwiched into the jumble-sale of prefixes and code-letters and all the electronic and administrative jargon was a message in English saying:

'we have possible identification of patricia la touche but appearance altered and carrying valid lebanese passport. cannot hold without court order and u.k. magistrate would certainly refuse to grant same without more positive identification. can maintain light surveillance but instruct rapidest and if possible send officer prepared to affirm. sorry but u.k. law exceedingly fussy about habeas-corpus 1066 and all that. please contact sergeant metcalfe message ends.'

'Blub-glub,' said Castang.

Richard turned a stony eye and said, 'You'll get on splendidly with Sergeant Metcalfe, so sharpen up your blub-glub. But what's 1066 and all that?'

'Some regulation or other. Deporting undesirable aliens, or words to that effect.'

'No no,' said Fausta who had a degree in history. 'It's the Norman Conquest. They used to own Aquitaine and have never forgiven us for wanting it back. Queen Aliénor they call Eleanor.'

'And she probably perfumed herself with bergamot—they didn't bother about little things like washing.'

'But not today for God's sake,' said Castang.

'No no, stop fussing. Find some photographs and stuff for identity, and I'll see the judge for a strong court order. No point in your going unless you can bring her back. Fausta, you get a telex off to this Metcalfe and leave out about Aquitaine, and book him plane tickets for the direct flight tomorrow morning. You can have the rest of the day free, Castang, but better go down to the clinic and get some physiotherapy, deep heat or whatever because you look a perfect wreck.'

There was a slow distant rumble of thunder.

'Here it comes,' they all said, looking out of the window. The sky had gone yellow and was darkening.

'Put the light on, Fausta.' Richard was lighting one of his thin cigars as a preliminary to business. 'Keep your pad; I'll dictate that message in a moment. I want to finish with Castang first. Can Lasalle read your shorthand?—no, well, if he can't, Fausta can. We have to hold on to this boy, but of course the judge will agree that he doesn't want the La Touche affair messed up by any more Jews or Arabs. Never mind, leave that to me. When he sees that chain and the mask the Proc will agree perhaps to deporting the boy with no further ado. Undesirable in every sense of the word.'

There was another, closer rumble of thunder. The lights cut out and the fan stopped. The lights flickered and went on again.

'I'll have Lasalle charge this boy—no no, better still, you had him picked up by a uniformed cop, we'll get it done by Fabre, and the P.J. is out of it altogether. Found carrying a concealed prohibited weapon.'

There was a really huge clap of thunder. The lights went out again and the telephone rang.

'Yes, Richard. What? . . . What? . . . This thing's going blub-glub, can you hear me? . . . No sir, I'll be over as soon as I can, I've some matters to discuss with you. The Metropolitan Police in London—damn this thing—no I said London . . . yes, Patricia La Touche but this line's hopeless . . . no, I have to come over anyway for your signature . . .

'Go get some infra-red or something,' he said to Castang, 'and make yourself extremely unwound, because dramas right and left, must be the storm has made everyone silly, or it's full moon. That La Touche has short-circuited: he's sacked his lawyers, is entering a plea of guilty, and the judge isn't happy at all. He's freezing the whole thing until the psychiatric reports are ready and he wants a new set of reports from us.'

Hailstones were bouncing off the sills. From everywhere in the building could be heard the sound of windows slamming shut.

'That'll strip a few vines,' said Richard, magnetised towards the window despite himself.

'If you go down in the woods today you're sure of a big surprise.'

'I'm not going outside in that,' said Richard.

XX

FRANCOPHILE BEHAVIOUR OF METROPOLITAN POLICEMEN

The knife, fork and spoon, from a cheap dolls' tea service, were plastic. The plane, inside if not out, was plastic. If one went by appearances so were the passengers. The stewardess had a strong resemblance to a rubber dolly bought from a sex shop. The food, naturally, was all by-products of the petroleum industry. Castang did not give any of these things attention or thought. If, as was always being threatened, there were suddenly no more oil, he supposed he would traverse Europe by bicycle and like it. As long as the aeroplane existed he would take it, and disliking it was whimsical. He did dislike it because it was a great waste of time: nine-tenths of these journeys were totally unnecessary and the people concerned would have done much better to write a letter. But if one gave way to this sort of thought one would do better being a municipal gardener, bedding out the calceolarias. I wish I were, said Castang, disciplined himself firmly, and thought: I'll only talk English, for the rest of the trip.

'I like—I want'—no—'May I have a box of matches, please?'

'What bus—which bus—goes to Aldwych?'

Which witch goes to Ipswich?

'Can I see Sergeant Metcahfe please, he expects me.' It would get better as he went along.

'No, miss, thank you not a drink but have you got some Evian water?'

'I don't know; I'll look.' Well, she'd understood, anyway, even if to judge by exteriors, and what else did a cop have to judge by, her mind was furnished with moisture cream and roll-on deodorant. His back hurt, but less than yesterday. He'd had needle sprays of electricity and water—they had more or less the same feeling—to break down the adhesions or whatever: the physiotherapist had been rather technical about it and he hadn't listened properly: in fact he'd successfully fallen asleep for twenty minutes at a stretch and dreamed with slight indecency that Fausta was tickling his shoulderblades with her hair.

'Sorry, ladies and gentlemen; slight panic in Heathrow. We're liable to be stacked for a while we hope will be short.' Windsor Castle, Slough railway-station, what might have been Virginia Water and was more likely the Hanwell Water-Filtration and Pumping Plant.

Rattle-te-tat on concrete full of puddles, and airlines belonging to countries where one would never want to go, and couldn't imagine anyone who would, and stewardesses with bared teeth and blue faces and their hats held on by scarves, and the huge dangling plastic sleeve leading to the grain elevator which instead of disgorging floods of rice to all the starving peoples ingurgitated Henri Castang and sent him on the long march to Immigration. Identity card scrutinised with the utmost attention, and his face stared at with a cop's blank unwinking gaze, and the 'Thank You' which sounded so much ruder than silence, and flow on, and change some money, Molière's face for the amazingly bland features of the Defender of the Realm, and then trundle trundle past innumerable factories making chewing gum and the thousand little gardens all identical, and then at last the plunge into the Inner Circle Tube smelling of synthetically-perfumed toffeepapers, and Victoria with the Sirocco blowing and posters inviting him to be whipped and massaged with 'Wank' written on them by fourth-form City gentlemen, and the smell everywhere of sweets which the English call Confectionery. So misleading to the European eye, to which confection means ready-made clothes, but not to the nose.

'Sergeant Metcalfe? Are you sure? What I mean is, did they say to ask for him? You see, I don't know really whether he's . . . oh I see . . . oh well, I'll phone . . . Metcalfe? I've a French gentleman here? do you . . . oh you do . . . well that's all right then. I mean, does he have to fill in a form? Oh . . . yes, I'll tell him. He says he'll be right down. If you like to sit down you'll find some magazines and things.'

But Sergeant Metcalfe was 'right down' before he'd had time to work out who Mr Punch was.

'Hallo. Delighted to see you. Now I wonder whether we should go upstairs, and you might like some coffee or something . . . no, no,' deciding this wouldn't do at all, 'that's all absolute nonsense, we'll go and have a drink; I've left my phone on automatic record, you've had a beastly journey, the pub will be nice and quiet.'

'I'm very obliged—no; much obliged.'

'Certainly not, you're not even just obliged: we are. Now this is quite a nice pub, would you like some wine?—it might not be very nice, would you rather a whisky?'

'Yes please with no water if I may.'

'Nor ice? Oh, do stop being so polite. And a gin and tonic. And cheers. And now,' in very good French, 'let's talk about lunch, that's very important.'

'You don't want to talk about business?'

'No no; lunch is much more urgent.'

Sergeant Metcalfe was all a policeman should be. He was very large, 'second row in the scrum', with a large smooth shaved face that shouted 'cop' a mile off, but not in the least bovine. He handled his big body very neatly. He was very extravagantly dressed, thought Castang at first—changing his mind quite soon—in a sports jacket of Prince-of-Wales check: poor old Edward has at least sartorial immortality. A silky white rollneck pullover. Nice trousers of Bedford cord which Castang, who was addicted to them, envied. Big well shaped hands, oddly white and very clean. Complicated but comfortable-looking cowboy boots, with chains and buckles and everything bar spurs. These English . . . Castang felt very small, meagre, and froggish in his havana-brown linen suit that had seemed so suitable at home and looked so pompously formal here. He had left his gun at home because of the hullabaloo it would cause on the aeroplane and because the English didn't wear any.

'I should be talking English,' relaxing rapidly.

'No no, man, hospitality. We talk French here, and when I come to see you then you can talk English, that's the way things go. You're looking miles happier already; do have another.' The gin and tonic got drained in one massive gulp.

'I thought you weren't supposed to drink on duty.' It was tactless but he couldn't stop himself.

'So we aren't. But shush. The Assistant Commander turns a blind eye, because he's read those awful Maigret books, and is quite convinced that French policemen will become exceptionally sharp after about four Pernods. And they ride everywhere in that lovely old folklore Citroën. All those English actors in *képis*—their heads are the wrong shape for *képis*. Quite pathetic. And now we're going to go Chez Solange and eat blanquette of veal—oh, don't worry, it won't be all that nasty.'

Castang felt much happier.

'So by that logic when you come to us I should find you one of those places where you can take away your curry.' Sergeant Metcalfe gave a great happy laugh.

'We're trying very hard. You know, this year there was the pistol shooting competition and you only just beat us. We're really working.'

Castang couldn't help it: this absolute refusal to talk about what he had come for was very sympathetic.

'I felt awful. The suit and the shoes—all wrong.'

'No, no, perfect; I could drive you straight out to the Teddington studios; they'd snap you up. You have you see that intellectual look. By definition the English policeman is bound to appear imbecile.'

'Don't go thinking you've the monopoly,' said Castang. 'It might be all right for us to look right, but God help us if we act it. What made us choose this lousy job anyway?'

'They had a good rugby team,' said Sergeant Metcalfe.

'Right. I was fair at gymnastics.'

'Oh yes—eleven boys balanced on one motorbike.'

'When they aren't wearing big white gauntlets, riding very slow and solemn in front of a politician in an open car.'

'Not worried at all about a hand-grenade, but living in mortal terror of a well-greased banana skin. It's very good really—the first lesson we have to learn is to accept the monumental stupidity. The only lesson, I sometimes think,' gazing sadly into his gin. 'You. You're lucky, over your side there's much more sense of reality.'

'But less humour. Is it true anyway, about the reality?'

'Oh, Lord yes. We're so hemmed in by myth. I'll give you just one example—the business about being unarmed. Supposed to be no guns in England—you know; every bloody airgun licensed by magistrates—whereas every little gas meter bandit has got one. And we're expected to go for him, presumably filled with courage by the vision of our widows getting given a medal by the Palace. Here, come on, you must be absolutely starving; let's go and eat.'

'I feel absolutely at home,' said Castang unfolding his napkin, 'except that the wine's far better than anything we ever get. Crafty old England.'

'You wouldn't say that if I took you to the police canteen and you were pressing down the spaghetti on toast. I think in fact you're right, though. There isn't any difference between us. The fear of foreigners, and particularly a dislike of the French, is a ridiculous and ignoble piece of folklore, assiduously fostered by politicians frightened of losing power.'

'Good phrase that,' said Castang admiringly.

'And we,' said Metcalfe with his big deadpan face, 'know that only the French can make a good phrase. There's a good one by the way about justice being meaningless. Pascal I think, or maybe Montaigne.'

'Of course,' said Castang. 'Learn it first week in law school. "Comic justice whose frontier is a brook; truth this side of the Pyrenees is heresy on the other." Pascal.'

'What did I tell you? "The bastards have a phrase for everything and worse still the bastards are always right." Raymond Chandler.'

Feeling delightfully euphoric, Castang drank a big glass of wine.

'Seriously, though—I've been saving this up till we were a bit mellowed—I've bad news for you. I haven't got Patricia.'

'Ah,' said Castang, turning back into cop. 'She slipped off, did she?'

'I hope you're not going to be angry. I blame myself, but it's no good saying I'd have done better if I'd been there myself instead of being stuck doing paperwork: I don't think I would. We're short on manpower of course—don't think I'm making excuses. One man seemed adequate. I wanted it to be unobtrusive. That's a mistake, I know: two or even three are much less obtrusive than one because he has to stay too close. I just didn't have another man. You see,' said Metcalfe sorrowfully, 'I wanted to keep this a criminal-police matter. The moment it's political, and Special Branch get into the act, the whole thing gets out of proportion.'

'I've had exactly the same problem,' said Castang. 'Look, don't give it another thought. Our judge at home will be cross, of course, because my coming back without her is a black eye, and this evasiveness leaves a big question-mark because the inference of course is that she knows more than she should and is unwilling to talk about it and why? Probably she knows nothing, of course: it's this irritating trick they have of drawing attention to themselves; making themselves important.'

'Oh yes,' said Metcalfe, 'it's familiar: slipping off to Spain hoping to get an evening-paper headline about the Missing Witness and maybe the *News of the World* will make a bid for the memoirs. But I'm afraid . . .'

'No notion where she's gone? Sweden, I dare say. I don't care: the judge won't bother following it up. Just, you see, she was daughter and sister to two of my victims, and ex-mistress of the third. And the assassin's surviving daughter—it isn't without interest, from the evidential point of view. It's all cut and dried: the whole thing's going to revolve round his state of mind.'

'Look,' said Metcalfe heavily. 'I'm misleading you. She's not in Sweden. She's in the bloody morgue. The Serious Crimes people have her. And they aren't optimistic.'

'*Merde*,' said Castang.

'Yes. *Merde* and *remerde*. Doubled, in spades.'

XXI

BREAKDOWN IN INTERNATIONAL
CO-OPERATION

'Fuck it,' said Metcalfe angrily. 'I'm only a pissing sergeant.'

They were back in the office. A grey cell in the big modern building. Lots of grey plastic, one wall nearly all window. Plenty of modern machinery which wasn't helping either of them. The cell was holding a high concentration of grey matter, but this wasn't helping them either. Metcalfe had played the tapes of his telephone calls back, and the result was a lemon.

'No, come,' said Castang. 'I'm an officer, good, and what does it mean? You have plenty of C.I.D. sergeants doing more important jobs on their own than I'd ever get a sniff of.'

'You don't understand,' said Metcalfe bitterly. 'Sure there are, you're right, there are sergeants who know their jobs better than most chief superintendents. But there are two factors you leave entirely out of your reckoning. First that you—I really envy that—have all a far stronger theoretical formation: one sees it in everything; doctors, engineers, pharmacists—you've all got degrees, you've all had that thorough intellectual training. We all have this pragmatic empirical formation, it's fine, I have no criticism, absolutely typical, take a Marshal of the Royal Air Force to train the cops, teach them to be self-reliant when the engine fails, good old Trenchard, keep the lip straight even when your parachute doesn't open, devotion is the thing. Christ,' furiously, 'the bloody inspector guarding the princess, nobody gave a fart that he was so badly trained his gun didn't work because the stupid clown had always left the magazine in and the mainspring had got fatally weakened. And I mean fatally—a Walther nine millimetre, beautiful well-made German gun, marvellous craftsmanship, and in the pinch it lets him down because he didn't know how to maintain it. Fellow just barely squeaks through with his life, and what does he get? A kiss from the Queen and a sodding medal, how incompetent can you get? And second this miserable stinking hierarchy: you're an officer if you talk nice. Otherwise you stay a sergeant; I ask you, Castang, how are you going to run a cop force on this mincing crapping difference between a grammar-school where they've grey matter and Stowe where they've architecture. So I have a fellow whose arse I have to wipe,' furiously, 'and he's an Inspector and I'm a sodding sergeant.' Castang was disconcerted. He was saved from agony by the door opening.

'Jesus, Metcalfe, what a stink in here, those filthy French cigarettes.'

'This is Inspector Treadwell of the Serious Crimes,' said Metcalfe in a majestic rolling period. 'And this is Commissaire Castang of the Police Judiciaire.' A curt nod.

'Do you speak English?'

'It'll do.'

'Well, what d'you know about this woman?'

'Nothing,' said Castang.

'Won't say, eh? Well, hereabouts we do our justice in public. Here's a woman dead of an overdose and you say "Nothing". Since I'm led to believe there's a warrant out for her and that an accident can be ruled out, I'm bound to investigate. I'd be inclined to see it as suicide if it weren't that some of these people she was frequenting might be more than small pushers to support a habit. May be a distribution network there. I look for you,' to the air somewhere between the two men, 'and you're out to lunch, while I'm left to sweep up the broken china. So now what about it?'

'If my English gets not good enough,' said Castang quietly, 'then I ask Sergeant Metcalfe to translate, all right? I say nothing because I know nothing. When you find out a thing, and when you tell me, perhaps I can make . . . link, yes thanks—and then I tell you. This woman was a witness to background, to character. Perhaps important, maybe, I don't know. But nothing suspected, nothing accused. I come here to try to talk to her, hoping for no drama, hoping no need for court order, to ask magistrate for extradition. About the drugs we know she has a small habit. Bit of pushing to support that habit, like you say, yes, likely. No evidence for anything else, as I am assured by our narcotic squad. If now you find differently, that is your enquiry, I don't interfere, I don't complain, I accept what your enquiry finds. Any co-operation I can give, I give, and I don't accept any contrary suggestion, all right?'

Inspector Treadwell had listened with no sign of impatience, unless it were brushing at his moustache with the nail of his forefinger, which might have been a tic.

'Very well. You give me that assurance, naturally I'm bound to accept it. I don't know how long you're staying, but I'll certainly see to it that a copy of my conclusions—when I reach them—is communicated to you. Since you tell me you know nothing about this woman's associates, or perhaps you mean that you simply aren't interested, then I see no point in your being associated with the enquiry, if I decide, that is, to pursue it. I'm not convinced either way. I'll ask you to excuse me now since I'm busy. I'd like a word with you please, Metcalfe. Nice to have met you, Mr Estang.'

Metcalfe looked anxiously to see if Castang were vexed, showed relief in a large wink—Treadwell was already in the passage—and got up leisurely.

'Forgive me a moment, Castang,' he said loudly. 'That's to say not longer than a small quarter of an hour, and I mean that. It'll be the quickest way out, for you. Here's some pornography to read; we've so much we're blowing our noses on it.'

He was as good as his word.

'Un vrai con,' he came back grinning.

'What's that in English?'

'Oh,' very blandly, 'I think we'd say a perfect prick. I got all we want; frightened him by hinting it could go to a higher level. Embassy makes a protest, question in the House of Commons. Is the Minister aware that there is reason to suppose a grave dereliction of duty on such a date, arising out of: he's picking his nose now. I'm sorry he was so rude. Nasty smell indeed. He's one of these people who do press-ups and admire General Montgomery: they think rudeness will excuse if not disguise their invincible ignorance. However, he's competent, I will say that for him. He didn't like the overdose at all; that's why he was vexed. What do you think?'

'I don't think it matters either way. I'm just feeling a bit sorry because the likelihood is I killed her. Nothing to do with my homicide, probably, though not provable. She'd no interest in her

125

parents, and the painter was an episode which she'd quite likely half forgotten. But mixed with these anarchists, who are fond of Arabs because there's lots of money there available, and money is always nice. She could have killed herself, and she could have been killed for a dozen reasons. She didn't have to know anything; she had just become an embarrassment or a liability, probably by the mere fact that the cops were after her. No, I'm mistaken, I didn't kill her, though I was the instrument. The Press killed her, simply by irresponsible suggestions that her father had a political motivation. We've been trying to deflate all that—you understand, that's why I had no enthusiasm for Special Branch.'

'Right. The drug-distribution stuff is bullshit by the way. Treadwell sees a headline in it for himself. Our active and ever-alert officer has again smashed a network. Bucking for a promotion. Bollocks to him. But is there anything at all I can do, still?'

'Turn into a plane and I'll fly you home,' sadly. 'I just wanted to talk to her. Poor little bitch. And La Touche, now . . . he's certainly made a clean sweep now, all around him.'

'We'll go somewhere nice and have tea,' said Metcalfe determinedly cheerful. 'I don't want that Treadwell to see me: I'm a living reproach.'

'Yes, it was embarrassing. I was going to open my mouth and tell you that you're talking nonsense when bingo, the door opens and in walks this chap who's been to Lancing or whatnot.'

'And he knows about as much law as a streetsweeper,' said Metcalfe happily.

'Why is it that the English have tea, when everyone else drinks it?'

'Now isn't that odd?' struck. 'I'd never noticed. In Jane Austen we all drank tea. I've no idea. But have you noticed too?—in England we have sex. It's exceptionally depressing. In France you say "Enjoy".'

'From time to time,' said Castang cautiously.

XXII

THE SCRUPLES OF THE PRISON VISITOR

'I'd like him to have a visitor,' said Monsieur Szymanowski, the Judge of Instruction. 'It would do him good. He's far too closed in upon himself. The psychiatrists won't pronounce, of course, until they have finished, but they tell me in confidence, without exception, that they're unhappy. I tell you in confidence, Madame,' shaking a finger.

'Monsieur le Juge,' said Vera, timid but obstinate. 'You know I wouldn't repeat your confidences. And I wouldn't repeat his, assuming he gave me any.'

'It's a case of conscience for both of us, Madame, and it worries me. In the old days a man on a murder charge was quite simply on the secret list. No access. Nowadays we take a less rigid view. What worries me is that if the defence were to find out you were a serving police officer's wife, and what is more the very man who was charged with the preliminary enquiry, they would shriek improper tampering at the top of their voice, which is loud.'

'There isn't any preliminary enquiry,' said Vera.

'Very true. And I would very badly like someone to break this last piece of unhappy news, which is that the surviving daughter has met a violent death in England—we probably never will know how or why. Brought by myself, I fear this news would only push him further into apathy. In short . . . well, you've done this job before; you know the dangers. . . . I'll overcome my reservations. Permission granted. If you infringe, be it ever so little, the private capacity—you do see that I'd be obliged to come down more than usually heavily. . . . All right, my girl. As long as you realise that I grant this request for strictly professional motives.'

'I accept that, Monsieur le Juge, knowing it not to be altogether true.'

'Off with you,' said the judge, shaking his paperknife at her.

She was extremely nervous, and it had little to do with the intimidating surroundings, for she had been here before, and things like having her handbag rummaged by the screws, or having a screw present (not really listening, but inevitably a wet blanket) did not worry her. She was frightened of La Touche, of whom she knew too much and not enough. Her fingers were trembling: she was glad to have a cigarette.

'How's the leg?' asked the screw in a friendly way. He knew her, but did not know she was a cop's wife.

'All right,' said Vera, 'but not very reliable. I find myself sitting down when I least expect to.' They had a laugh over that.

'I'll get your chap,' said the screw.

La Touche in his nicely pressed track suit was very polite and formal. Strangely enough, that stiff courtesy made it easier for her.

'This is Madame Spaniera,' said the screw. 'You'll get on well with her; everyone does.'

'Delighted,' said La Touche, kissing her hand. The light cool voice was as Castang had described it. 'What are you an expert in?'

'I'm not sure,' she said, not trembling at all any more, 'I think perhaps my dustpan and brush.'

'Ah. I've got pretty sharp with it myself. But d'you mean to say you've no doctorate in sociology? Or anthropology?'

'Nothing at all.'

'Then to what do I owe this pleasure?'

'Not even vulgar curiosity. I thought someone who wasn't anything at all might be a good idea, and slightly to my surprise the judge said yes.'

'He's a good honest fellow,' said La Touche. He might have been praising a conscientious subordinate, but Vera had been prepared for this.

'Well,' he went on, 'that's nice: I'm not anything either. You were quite right, Monsieur Morel; Madame is a light-bringer.'

128

'No, don't put me at a disadvantage,' said Vera. 'I'm nervous enough as it is.'

'I'm nervous too, and it makes me rude. I beg your pardon. I'm afraid I'm not yet clever at handling my new identity. Committing a violent crime changes one a good deal.'

'It doesn't change you for me at all.'

'I'm a corporal work of mercy? Has it a religious connotation?'

'Heaven, no, that would be horrid. If you mean am I Catholic and are you my brother, I'd have to say yes, but please, no self-conscious virtues. Going to cheer up poor old Charles because he's in hospital and it must be depressing for him isn't my idea at all. I don't know who I am. The secretary maybe; not very efficient but willing. A bridge to the outside world. Change your library books. Inform myself about anything you're interested in. Run errands. Fix any buttons the laundry tears off your shirts. Gossip. Conversation. I'm afraid my intellectual level's not very high but I'm interested in most things—as long as they aren't too abstract. Things like—oh you know, the foreign policy of the Chinese—I'm sadly uninformed about, I'm afraid.'

La Touche actually laughed. It was sufficiently unusual for Monsieur Morel, peacefully engaged upon *Reader's Digest*, to look up for a moment with a glance of astonishment.

'My dear girl, you're heaven-sent. I'm sorry, I would like now to be very informal. We can do better than the secretary. May I say Vera? My name is Gilbert. It would make the hospital bed softer, and be a kindness. It's true that I've always been an artificial person, evolving in artificial milieus, and here I'm more so than ever. This is a torrent of oxygen. May I ask you personal questions?'

'Please do.'

'Who are you? Will you tell me something about yourself?'

'Oh yes, though it's brief and boring. I'm Czech; it's written on my face rather, and I'm married to a functionary in the administration and I'm twenty-seven and I've no children I'm afraid which rather saddens me. I've not much use for being liberated which seems to me selfish and superficial and fundamentally self-defeating, and I had a baddish accident which left me hampered as you see, which is a bore, and I draw a bit, illustrations to various things, some children's books, and really I think that's about all: now you.'

'Ah. Well, to adopt your style, I come from a rich and narrow-minded family in the high bourgeoisie—what was your father by the way?'

'He made barrels.'

'Exactly. A craftsman, and useful. Mine was just the opposite but I thought him admirable.'

'Then he probably was.'

'Something to be said for that. Kind, anyway, and less rigid than I am. I am or was a servant of the State, which is a family tradition. I was trained to examine and verify state accounts. I am rich. I married money. To say that money doesn't mean much to me is no compliment: it's easy when one has always had it and is trained to use it. Poor Hélène—my wife—came from the ancient *noblesse*, rather God and Fatherland. She worried about her investments and of course they kept losing value, having been badly made. I've never been much good at enjoying life: I'm a dried stick. And dear oh dear, where do we go from there?'

'I'd say there were plenty of places to go. One starts again.'

'Like you. I disagree, but we won't go into that.'

'I only meant that one feels completely shattered. Without boasting I was a gymnast: quite a good one. I mean for years it was the centre of my existence, and when I bust my spine I thought it was the end. But I was just too young and stupid to realise. There are so many other centres.'

'Oh look,' pleaded La Touche, 'I'm enjoying you such a lot; don't be like those tedious psychiatrists.'

'I'm so sorry, I didn't mean to. But isn't there something to be said for them?'

'Probably there is and I don't want to sound irritatingly haughty. But they search, you see, for things they can measure. Mental health is a fact like another: well, I agree, and it's reasonable that they should look for the causes of an accident, a breakdown in myself quite similar to the neuro-physiological trauma you had. But to me you see this is quite irrelevant. I think that the breakdown was a moral one, and that the dried-out stick once snapped cannot be repaired.'

'I don't like metaphors,' she said. 'A human being isn't a stick.'

'I beg your pardon,' said La Touche. 'It is unforgiveable to be talking about oneself all the while. Prison makes one sadly egocentric. By the way, there are a few books I should like from my library:

do you think the judge would allow you to go to my house?'

'Yes of course; just give me a list. I can come twice a week, like the butcher's van.'

La Touche looked at her, as one looks at something beautiful that is going to disappear. Venice, perhaps.

'You are good.'

'Mm,' said Vera. 'You'll change your mind. I want now to say something I've been dreading. I'm afraid Patricia is dead.'

He appeared to shrink in upon himself that bit more. His face did not change much. He sighed a little.

'Very well. Tell me.'

'Not much is known. The judge heard today. He thought you'd prefer to learn it in private. It was in England. A cop,' she had come dangerously close to saying 'my husband', 'had gone over to talk to her. She was on dope, as you know. Apparently somehow she got an overdose,' gabbling it.

'Yes. . . . I suppose one can't be surprised at that,' he muttered. The eyes had gone absent; he wasn't looking at her.

'I'll go now, if you'd prefer,' said Vera timidly. She hadn't known what it would be like to bring a man news of his child's death. And when he himself had killed his other child. . . . She put that resolutely out of her mind. It was irrelevant. She wasn't a psychiatrist, thank heaven. 'If there's anything at all—no matter what—I can do, please please don't hesitate.'

She had not very much experience as a prison visitor, enough to know that 'feeling sorry' was a trap to be avoided at all costs. But there must be some sympathy, in its literal sense of suffering-with. There must be some solidarity. She was married to a cop, and was tra'ned to avoid sentiment. A prison is damn well not like a hospital. In her notions of justice she was very theological: very Czech, said Castang, laughing, very baroque-jesuit.

'I'm grateful,' said La Touche. 'That's a sign. There's nothing now to hold one.' The remark was not addressed to her and she decided to pay no attention. She waited patiently for him to come back, which he did at once.

'I said you were good. I repeat it. Now let's talk about you. Have you done this long?'

'Not very. It's not much. Three hours twice a week. There's a Yugoslav man—he learns Czech from me and I learn Yugoslav from him, by talking together. That's good, you see. I mean he's a poor man and uneducated and he's teaching me. And there's a man I teach drawing. He can't draw and I rather hate it, because he's getting an illusion that he can, but he enjoys it a lot and that must do good. And the director would like to give gymnastics lessons to the girls, but we've no equipment, and no money to buy any.'

'And what can I contribute? Not much. Hm. I'm rich. I'll talk to my imbecile lawyer. I think the judge would allow me to spend money on gymnastic equipment.'

'That would be nice, but don't do anything for the wrong motives.'

'Whose idea was it to come and see me? The judge? One of those damned psychologists? Tell the truth.'

'I will. Mine. But if I tell the truth it sounds so—so patronising.'

'Nevertheless.'

'I don't think things out much. I just thought it was awful for you—all right, I'll say it straight out—to have made such a hole in your family and perhaps it would be good if a woman came to see you—this was a very crude idea, you understand, so I asked the judge. What ideas he may have, of course, are no business of mine.'

'Well,' said La Touche, 'I think that very good. We won't talk about lessons. There's sadly little I could teach anyone. I'm a wretchedly sterile person. I've never done anything. Even elementary book-keeping or Latin would be beyond me. And it's too late for me to learn much. I haven't such a great deal of time.'

'Yes, you'll be out of here before much longer. Sometimes those instructions do take such ages, but I mean yours should be quite straightforward.'

'That's not quite what I meant, but no matter. I'd be content simply to see you come back.'

'Of course. Now the book list. Can I have the pencil and paper, Monsieur Morel?'

'Sure,' said the screw comfortably.

Vera was home in time to cook supper for Castang, cross, tired, and frustrated by his English experiences, but interested in hers.

'So the judge allowed it—never would have thought it. I was joking when I suggested it, and there she goes, trotting off solemnly to beard the lion in his den.'

'He wasn't a lion at all. All these judges are reasonable when you handle them right. He's very rigid, poor old Szymanowski, but he wasn't troublesome at all.'

'Crosscheck on the psychiatric opinions.'

'You know better than that. What do I know or care about psychiatric opinions?'

'They'll play a big role hereabouts. No law involved at all, hardly. This and no more—how far was he over?'

'He certainly isn't now. A difficult person, yes. Withdrawn, badly closed in upon himself, deeply embittered, a strong sense of inadequacy and a lot I'm afraid of bad melancholy—but not despair.'

'But was he off the rails at that moment?—that's the thing.'

'Oh yes, of course he was. Anybody is. But I'm perfectly aware that to claim so isn't law and isn't sense and isn't justice, and I have no interest in all that: to me it's perfectly irrelevant.'

'That's right. I'll be a witness. Won't budge off the facts. Luckily they're quite unshakeable. Everything depends on how the Proc is going to pitch his case. It's certain he'll go easy, because otherwise the court is on the hook. If this is sanity, the whole definition of an assassination plotted in cold blood is present. Opens the door most uncomfortably. But if the shrinks pick up a lot of stuff showing that this personality can become quite disabled by appalling vision— I mean fair enough, catching your wife and daughter together in bed with the same man is an appalling vision—then his actions are dictated and the cool and collected manner is just one indication the more. Did it like a sleepwalker.'

'I haven't any doubt but that this is so,' said Vera. 'He's under terrible strain all the time.'

'Then nobody has any worries. Not even me, as long as we keep this political stuff from getting out of control. Feel fairly safe about that now. You see, to admit a political element would now be an embarrassment to the English government as well. My chap Metcalfe is a very sensible fellow. He'll see to it that they remain quite happy with the notion of accounts settled in some drug gang. She was making off with the supplies or something, creating a private black market so they dealt out punishment. Perfectly plausible too. Or simply chopped her because of the extradition demand—attracting the attention of the cops, she's a liability: out. It would all be quite consequent.'

'This is horribly cynical.'

'Why? It doesn't affect La Touche. Look, what does it all boil down to?—I'll try and demonstrate. Forget this stuff about Israeli intelligence; it's crap. This painter happened to be Jewish, and was serious about it: I mean his Jewishness was essential to him. But as a painter: funny games in the state of Israel don't interest him. I feel sure of that, after talking to the wife.

'Now La Touche. He's an expert on finance, above all on financial management, on what's well run and what isn't. Pretty good choice for an investment consultant. Above all, knows everyone. Excellent contacts in all banks and insurance houses, hand in glove with all government spending and purchasing agencies, been at school with half the senior civil servants. Money, money, money, all this revolves around money. Semi-officially, some people are quietly asking him for advice about sponging up a bit of this vast pool of petro-dollars we hear about. Unofficially, he is used as a sounding board about governmental intentions. Some stuff pretty close to the bone there like aircraft and arms sales. But he isn't acting dishonestly, he isn't taking bribes—at least I don't think he is. Legitimate commissions on various things that aren't contrary to the "national interest" or disguised consultancy fees: it doesn't matter.

'Hereabouts I fall into guesswork. He liked this painter. Maybe he has secret Israeli sympathies. I know nothing and why should I ask? He saw, maybe, a man in the painter that was a good man as well as good painter. Better than himself, creative, uncorrupted— call it what you will. He's not worried about his wife; he's cynical about her. If the painter screws her, jolly good; keep her from doing sillier things. But about the daughters he had terrific guilt feelings, and I leave all that aside, it's for the shrinks. Finding the wife and the daughter together is just too much to swallow. He goes mataglap, takes the pistol, executes the lot, and then being a very serious person and determined not to embarrass the government nor the job nor the family he rings me up and says "I've killed; take me in". And that's really all there is to it. I've no doubt I'm over-simplifying.'

'And Patricia?'

'Ah, that's more coincidental than anything else, perhaps. Patricia is in total opposition. Nothing to do maybe with Jews or Arabs, but she's on dope, she is irresponsible, she gets the weird ideas they do get when on dope, and she's an active girl. Instead of just going off to be dimwitted and go Hare Krishna in a dirty yellow nightie she joins an anarchist group. Trouble with them is they're dodgier than her simple little mind can comprehend. Some

of these anarchists are genuinely dangerous. They link up with the
I.R.A., with those muttonfat *fedayin*, with Tupomaros and fanatic
armies of every sort. There's a parallel in that wretched child of the
newspaper magnate—Hearst, was it? Very troublesome, and all the
political police fair sweat blood over them.

'These people benefit from quite a large degree of toleration as a
consequence; too troublesome and expensive to do anything else.
In return they try to avoid being too flagrant, knowing as they do
that it's nice to have three regular large meals a day and a comfortable bed: they don't want to take to no *maquis*.'

He stopped: this was all useless, and a mistake into the bargain.
Vera had the look of extreme imbecility she wore when she wasn't
listening and didn't want to listen. It meant she couldn't cope, and
didn't intend to try.

How anyway to explain the inexplainable? How to say that a
cop, if he is to hold on to some sensitivity, retain an awareness of
integrity, goes white with black spots in order to avoid going grey
all over? There were areas in which he 'didn't want to know'.
There were one or two where he would say 'Find somebody else'.
Where a superior officer with any sense would not force him to obey
orders, because that would be the quickest way of losing a good
cop.

A bit of folklore concerning Basque separatists was one thing.
Rounding up a fellow and saying to him 'You're making too much
noise here in Bayonne: the government would like you to go and
live in Lille for a while' was fine. But mixing too much with the
complete moral anaesthesia of the hard core, the ones who would
smash anything, kill anybody—a classroom full of small children,
say—led to becoming morally imbecile yourself.

There were cops who were all black, all the way through. One
or two in every department. Castang knew two. He shook hands
with them in a corridor, murmured a meaningless cordiality—
'How goes it, vieux'—once or twice a year found himself having a
drink with them.

These were the ones used. To whom a senior commissaire, a
Richard, would say now and then in as few words as possible 'See
to that'. They would knock you off any way that was handy; a gun,
a knife, or a leaky gas main, with no hard feelings. Much worse:
with no feelings at all. If people were terrorists—real terrorists, not
just chatterboxes—you used terrorists against them. These people

were like the executioner and his assistants. You didn't see them very often, but they could always be found when needed.

This total moral insanity is one of the proofs of the existence of evil.

The ones who were really all black would not live very long. They would return to the master who sent them.

What kind of husband and father does a bad cop make? The ones that were just dingy grey, all the way through?

Castang switched the television on, and he and Vera watched a cowboy film, with an all-white hero, and a villain who was pretty black, but died bravely.

XXIII

PSYCHIATRIC OPINIONS

Commissaire Richard, running over a list prepared for him by the admirable Fausta of engagements for the coming month ranging from the unavoidable to the purely *protocolaire*, got past 'Prefect's reception and wine-of-honour for Mr George MacDermott' opposite which Fausta had pencilled 'An Assistant U.S. Attorney, s.s.o (some sort of) fact finding mission: heads of departments requested to attend.' American doubletalk, like Treasury meaning narcotics. F.B.I. or something. This was always complicated and tiresome: one had to look back to see how often one had skipped, in recent months, infernally boring functions of this sort, and how many one could skip in the near future without it being commented upon. One had to keep a few discards in hand: there would be people even more grindingly *protocolaire* than Mr George MacDermott.

'Date set Assize Court, trial Gilbert La Touche.' He picked up the internal telephone.

'Castang? Come in here.'

Castang was deep in bread-and-butter police work. That is to say nothing gaudy like homicides. Things pinched. With housebreaking, robbery. Without housebreaking, larceny. Complaints. The tide was swelling, of complaints, to the point where somebody—originating with Commissaire Fabre of the urban police force—would have to think-about-taking-measures, because there'd been too much mugging, and too many editorials in the local newspaper about Why Are Our Streets No Longer Safe? What were all these people doing, wandering about lonely streets at two in the morning, carrying, invariably, thick wallets ftuffed with banknotes? Why were they so stupid? Been running ater whores, nine out of ten. No patience with them. And they were always the ones who complained the loudest and most persistently, and always said they had brothers, highly-placed, in the Prime Minister's Office in Paris.

If only one could put a stop to the torrential sewer of hypocrisy. If only just once one could put a notice in the paper, saying 'Communiqué to the Public from the Police Judiciaire', saying Listen, grow up and have some elementary sense.

His phone rang. Richard. A concrete person. Vaguely phrased pep-talks were a rarity. If Richard wanted to give you the sack he invited you out to lunch.

Cigar going. Where did he get them from? Said to be Brazilian, but perhaps he grew them in his greenhouse between the orchids. Black tarry chewy things, knotty, as though made of vanilla. One always expected sputterings of saltpetre and then a blue flare, as carried by clippers in the eighteen-eighties, when collision at night appeared imminent. Economical anyhow: nobody in their senses would take one when offered.

'La Touche is coming up for trial. The instruction's finished; I forgot to tell you. You'll be wanted as witness. I'd like you to see what you can of this trial: you'll be called early on, so the observation part is easy. I won't be there at all, thank heaven. I've a lot of time-wasting rubbish anyway,' looking crossly at Fausta's list which was worse than usual, and his own diary beside it.

Castang was surprised.

'It's a snip, surely.'

'It's not that much of a snip. I don't mean there's anything wrong with your showing in the enquiry: that's all solid. You'll get the usual barrage from the defence. He sacked the Paris lawyers. Defended by a junior off the legal-aid list.'

'Good God.'

'That's by no means all. Fellow said, I quote, "I wish we had English law: I'd plead guilty: avoid all this flummery". Charming. Can you see the panic?'

'What would it mean?'

'I'm not quite sure—not a mandatory death sentence, I think, because the English have their hangman in abeyance still, I believe. Hanging by ᴄ thread.' Richard was quite good at gallows humour. 'Or did they reintroduce it for cop-killing?—it's of no consequence because of course the folklore won't do here, and they're hunting for a very severe President who'll stand no nonsense. Braunschwig would do nicely but this isn't the Paris jurisdiction, alas. But there's worse than that. Szymanowski much aghast: he's got all the psychiatric reports.'

'You don't mean . . . ?'

'Oh yes, I do. Perfectly sane in all respects and at all times. And La Touche said quite openly "Thank heaven for some shrinks with a little common sense".'

'What's this bugger preparing in the way of a nasty surprise?'

'Quite: that's the question everyone is asking. Before closing his dossier and declaring the instruction completed the judge wants to give himself a loophole.'

'Supplement of information?'

'If need be.'

'What the hell does he think further police work could dig up at this time of day?'

'None, I think. But when he starts like that, and I'm reduced to basing my own working time on "I-think-he-thinks-that-someone-else-may-be-thinking", the result is a fine shower of shit. So stay here for a moment—I'll tell you why in just a while—and I'll try and get light shed. Fausta,' into his phone, 'get me a line to Monsieur Szymanowski at the Palais . . . now about these muggings: Fabre's being tiresome. You remember the other day there was a party for that old imbecile Roupeyrolles.' This was a worthy but wooden-headed old inspector who had finally retired, much to Richard's relief, after forty years of devotedly mediocre police work. There had been an official 'apéritif' with a presentation of a medal and a chiming clock. Castang had congratulated himself upon finding a foolproof pretext for absence from these rollicking solemnities.

'The *sous-chef* appeared.' The big shot from Paris, Monsieur Marty, known as 'Eminenza' inevitably since there was a cardinal of that name, but the cardinal was a more amusing person than the *sous-directeur* of the whole P.J. apparatus. Castang knew vaguely that the occasion had been taken for a vast pep-talk involving Working in Harness Together.

'Well, he was very tiresome indeed.' The phone rang and 'Judge for you,' said Fausta.

'Good morning, sir. To come straight to the point I see that a

provisional date has been set for the La Touche trial . . . ah . . .
I see . . . yes . . . yes. . . . Castang's with me at present . . . quite . . .
this afternoon already: one moment till I look . . . very well . . . yes,
sir, I'll tell him . . . yes, I do realise . . . very good, I'll arrange
accordingly . . . it's understood, sir. . . .' Richard put the phone
down, and said blandly 'Do you know, in the course of Hitler's war
the Italians produced a phrase book to assist municipal functionaries
in their dealings with the occupying power, to wit American
sergeants. Among other masterpieces was the useful phrase "Permit
me to present to you the Count"—can't get anywhere without
counts. So there it was all nicely printed. "Posso presentare il
conte" and the English translation opposite. "Meet the Cunt".'
    'Ah, Sergeant Metcalfe would like that.'
    'You might bear it in mind too. There's going to be a conference
this afternoon in the judge's office. Fabre, myself, the brigade chief
of S.T.; likewise of Renseignements Généraux.' R.G., survival
from the old Sureté Nationale, another branch of parallel police.
It is like M.I.5, and the Special Branch: all these people have an
invented sound.
    'Another pep-talk,' said Castang with disgust. 'The judge this
time instead of Marty.'
    'And you instead of old Roupeyrolles.'
    'What have I to do with it?'
    'Your wife.'
    'What's she done now?' genuinely startled. There had been the
moment when Vera had 'chosen freedom' and been a slight
embarrassment, but what . . .
    'Do I have to spell it all out?' asked Richard irritably. 'Your wife
has got to know La Touche quite well in these last few weeks, but
that stays unofficial: the judge doesn't want it misinterpreted. Since
nobody grasps exactly what the man is up to, you will please
possess yourself over lunch of any lights your dear girl can
shed.'
    'She won't tell me.'
    'Be a bit serious, Castang. The judge wants a consensus of
opinion before he decides to close the dossier of the instruction.
What's La Touche playing at? Working up for a show trial?
Thinking with this precious lawyer of his of a grand denunciation
of government policies in the Middle East? The judge—and small
blame to him—doesn't care for the thought.'

'What would she know? They chat about Madame de Sévigné and her daughter.'

'You might just verify that.'

'It's ridiculous,' said Vera. 'Call for a psychiatric opinion on Richard, and that Polish bastard.'

'Spare me all that,' said Castang curtly. 'Be serious because this is. Three shrinks declare La Touche sane, so he goes forward to trial. He's not calling any experts in rebuttal. His lawyer is obliged to convey some notion of the defence, but before closing the instruction the judge would like to know what's coming.'

'Oh, why can they never understand?' said Vera angrily. 'I can say it all in about three words. If I'm visiting a detainee, as he's so prudishly described, I don't talk politics: I'm not that soppy: I'd have been sacked my first week. Nor do I encourage them to pour out grievances. La Touche is a highly intelligent and sensitive person who is most careful not to embarrass or bore me. He has lovely manners and it's a delight to see him. He's also a simple person. He trusts me, I think and hope. We talk about all sorts of things. Books mostly, which I haven't read and he has. It helps him, I believe, and even I'm damn well convinced. I'm not telling anything because it's all in confidence, his confidence, and I'm not doing any espionage for that Polish bastard. He's got to learn,' said Vera with Czech peasant wisdom, 'that if you try and hold a fart back it explodes the louder.'

'About three words,' said Castang mildly, 'and don't think I'm going to relay confidences; I won't. As you ought to know. Just one thing. Is La Touche planning some sort of political demonstration— to your knowledge? It's just that it could kick back. Richard will stand up for me, but bad police work will simply send us both to Madagascar to lecture on the penal code to natives. Mad dogs and Englishmen. Just try and give me something I can say at this grand reunion of counts.'

'He's not going to plead at all,' said Vera. 'He just wants to act, I'm quoting him directly, "like a man for once in his life".'

'Well,' irritated, 'what's his system of defence going to be? That lawyer the judge has designated is going to fall back on rhetoric. Sleeve effects.' It is the phrase, brief and graphic, for an advocate who has no argument, and who with a multiplicity of gesture (the lawyers' robes in the Republic have long wide sleeves) makes impassioned and emotional appeals to the jury.

'He doesn't talk about it,' said Vera. 'I can only say this much. He's good friends with the Protestant chaplain. Who is a young man not at all feeble-minded. I've met him. He said to me laughing that as a very young man he'd gone all ecumenical and decided to convert the Jews. He hadn't got very far with that because as he said, the Jews he'd succeeded in converting one wouldn't want as a gift. But he had learned something, he said, about how to convert Protestants to Protestantism.'

'La Touche gone all religious?' It was a familiar phenomenon among 'detainees'.

'It's not perhaps altogether imbecile,' said Vera rather nastily. 'When you lose faith in this world, put your trust in the next.'

XXIV

THE BOUNCE OF THE BALL

We're a funny lot, thought Castang. As the junior in this distinguished gathering—a mere inspector—he was keeping his mouth shut.

The rest were socialising. They were not friends in any sense of the word, and colleagues only in the most superficial. They had no particular liking for one another, and the professional cordialities they exchanged when they met were the thinnest of shiny chrome, peeling rapidly before corrosion, exposing the base metal below. Good enough metal in that these were all men of some quality. Good products of the system: intelligent, sensitive, quite cultured, of strong character, widely read, much travelled, deeply impregnated by all sorts of civilised values. But how little it all added up to. These metals were made brittle, as cast iron is brittle, by the almost pathological suspiciousness they suffered from. This went a good deal further than interdepartmental rivalry.

Having all met recently—at the apéritif for the retiring cop, where they had been summoned to hear the P.J. *sous-chef* deliver his famous lecture upon Working in Harness—they had upon that occasion exhausted the joviality which obtains among men of this type who do not see one another more than once a month: the jokes and the exchange of good stories. They had done their duty then, they all felt, upon an occasion they could none of them well dodge. Now they were all bored, because this was a waste of time. Each of them felt that he was not concerned by this small matter, and nobody among them wanted to become concerned, because nothing could come of that save 'emmerdements', that useful word which in

French conveys the abstract notion of being covered-in-a-shower-of-shit.

Monsieur Szymanowski, the present 'chairman', did not know any of them well. Richard he knew best. Richard, a quiet and exceptionally secret person—nobody present had ever met his wife or his two sons—was an unknown quantity to everyone. He had not much small talk, and was talking about golf. Since golf in Europe is a great deal more exclusive, expensive, and snobbish leisure-pursuit than it is in Anglo-Saxon countries, and the tax-inspector regards it like ownership of a yacht or a racehorse, the others were all thinking 'typical vice-squad performance. Typically P.J. Typically Richard.' Since they all knew that Richard did not take bribes, this made them cross. How does he do it on his salary? Monsieur Szymanowski, to whom a golf-club was a dangerous blunt instrument likely to cause grave injuries to the bystander, preferred to change the subject.

Commissaire Fabre of the urban police, the chief of all the municipal police brigades; criminal, moral, traffic, public order, and so on—he was what he had to be, a skilful reconciler of warring factions, soother of municipal councillors, good administrator, diplomat with mayors, prefects, and chambers of commerce—was a burly man with heavy muscles, now running to fat, and large, black-framed glasses. He campaigned assiduously to keep his weight trim, and was quite a sharp tennis-player in doubles. He also liked music, and went whenever he could to all the concerts and operas given rather grudgingly by the city to its public. When alone in his office he was notorious for a robust tum tum, half humming and half singing, recognisable to the initiate as barrel-organ Verdi. So jammy, so firmly constructed, so beautiful, so good. This trait was thoroughly attractive. But Fabre had an abrasive side. He was extraordinarily mean about small expenses, a perfect terror about postage-stamps and turning down the central heating, making everyone at his draughty gloomy headquarters replace their hundred-watt bulbs by forties.

Monsieur Frédéric-Alexandre Marre, brigade-chief of Surveillance de la Térritoire, was nearly as small as Castang, but broader and by some sleight of hand thicker. He cultivated a casual look, and was always seen in a Harris tweed jacket, a flannelette shirt with small checks, mysteriously a bow tie, and abdominal muscles like Charles Atlas—power springs from the pit of the stomach where the nervous centres are—decorated by an expensive belt in crocodile leather which did much more for him than holding his trousers up: he never wore a pullover. He had a furry teddy-bear voice and tiny shoe-button teddy-bear eyes, and the falsest smile Castang had ever seen. He had a slight resemblance to the secretary general of the big Communist trade-union. He enjoyed and cultivated this resemblance. He was an enthusiastic theatregoer.

Cardillac, Ambroise Edmond, was a complete contrast. He was best known to everybody for having been, a few years back, for thirteen whole weeks the champion of a complicated and esoteric television game, involving the identification of a movie's name— nine or ten of the damn things every week—from the meagre clues of the director, the supporting actors, and the script-writer. One was given each week a theme, of a star once famous and forgotten for the last thirty years save by people like Monsieur Cardillac who possessed all the back numbers of *Cahiers du Cinéma*. Perhaps it was part of Renseignements Généraux, translateable vaguely as Spying on Everybody, of which he was the local linchpin.

His morphological type was that described by the cliché 'cadaverous'. He was not very tall, not particularly thin, not even very bald, but his forehead was bumpy, his jaws concave, his neck strangely bony. His ears stuck out rather, and black fuzz grew out of them. He had extremely intelligent bright and mobile eyes. These for the television cameras had been masked by smoked glasses. Even now his lenses were tinted a rather horrible cold bluish colour, giving people in the same room a fear that a laser beam might come suddenly popping out to castrate you, or something equally nasty.

It is notoriously hard to say what it is that R.G. actually does. Surveying the Territory is a fairly transparent euphemism for counter-espionage, but what does General Information mean? Like 'Normal School' it means more than it seems but has a vaguely old-fashioned ring, connected with peculating financiers like Monsieur Stavisky, and Presidents of the Third Republic who got heart attacks while in bed with somebody's wife. This combination of vagueness and folklore is a puzzle to foreign journalists who are studying the institutions of the Republic. Suffice it that R.G. is minatory, muddled, and supposedly makes of the Minister of the Interior a mighty man, since he has access to all the dossiers involving dirty stories. Aha, Mister President-Director-General (of some boring textile factory in Roubaix), we know all about your filthy doings with tiny girls under age: always known, nobody knows why, as 'ballets roses', with all the implications of elderly and vicious but impotent voyeurism.

I'm the low man, the smallest and least fiercely-grimacing figure, on this totem-pole, thought Castang.

Isn't it strange? Supposedly, the company here present ought to have a dossier on every man, woman and child in say—put it in small, manageable figures—a hundred by a hundred; that's ten thousand square kilometres which is a lot. How is it that they miss so many notaries who whip off with the trust funds, wine merchants who have craftily mixed up the green tickets (controlled original appellation) and white tickets (limited superior quality—meaning largely undrinkable) or, to change scenery a bit, confirmed alcoholics who habitually torture their children?

How is it that the P.J. hasn't got the remotest notion who composes the gang that twice now has done such an extremely smooth job on major post offices and got away with the equivalent of sixty million pounds sterling?

How is it that R.G. have never found out that Millenium, that admirable and practically universal tranquilliser and happy-pill, is sold for seventy-five cents the dose costing one-third of a centime to produce. The difference, familiar to policemen, is between knowing a thing and being aware of it.

They had told—or had not told—the German Government quite a long time ago that the Chancellor's personal aide was a listening post. If they had told it might have appeared peculiar that nobody had paid the slightest notice. More likely that they hadn't told, being well aware that nobody would want to know.

In La Touche as a person . . . well, all policemen have the deformation of never seeing the people they deal with as persons. We all of us, thought Castang, probably know something about him but add us all together and it won't amount to anything recognisably human. The only person in all likelihood who would be the faintest use around here is Vera, and she has her trap firmly shut.

'Good,' said Szymanowski in a hurried indistinct voice, 'you are aware of my concern over this seemingly unimportant and stupid case. The facts are unsatisfactory and everything so far adduced leaves an atmosphere of confusion. Perfectly good system of defence and the man seems bent on ignoring it. Why? Between us and in confidence there might be some scraps of knowledge we can collate into some coherent whole. I ask you in turn to contribute what you can, and to examine the results informally. Monsieur Fabre?'

Fabre took his glasses off and closed his eyes.

'There was a brief flurry, at the beginning, of loud talk and slogan writing, which to my mind had no significance. It could have been in the interests of a variety of people to make us believe that this man was either being unfairly attacked—or improperly protected. Depending on which side you stand of opinion. Opinion is always polarised and some people seize every pretext for polarising it further. Accuse the Communists of Fascist activities. Conversely, use the same fact to claim that crypto-Fascists are seeking to split the unity of the workers. Classic, and anyway *post hoc propter hoc*. Aside from this, and for the rest, my services haven't been involved. I'm aware that an attack was made on Castang here, which could have made propaganda. It was the subject of a confidential report by myself to the magistrate. The young man in question was deported for carrying a concealed weapon. Since no charges were preferred, there was no prosecution. Further, nothing.'

'Castang acted sensibly, and with my approval,' said Richard. 'That Lebanese boy was inflamed by the girl Charlotte. Since she's dead we can't interrogate her. But it's clear—calf love, and she hung about with a group of Arab students. Tunisian, Moroccan—a type the girl found physically attractive. I had a couple interrogated by Lasalle, in his well-known babysitting manner'—nobody grinned— 'and there was nothing else to it. That man Dieudonné saw an opportunity for a little publicity, which he might have thought would distract us from more sensitive aspects, if there are any: Monsieur Marre as I then gathered was of opinion there weren't.'

'And still is.'

'One second just to say that while I wasn't concerned with the enquiry at its beginnings I am totally satisfied that Castang's handling of it was scrupulous in the extreme.'

'Nobody has queried that,' said the magistrate mildly.

'Just for the record, Monsieur le Juge. I won't be a witness at the trial—or not if I can help it.'

'Monsieur Marre?'

The teddy-bear had put a big long cigarette between his front teeth. Red and gold packet. So like them to smoke Dunhills. He spoke with his index fingers together on the point of his nose (his elbows on the table) and the second fingers on the dimple in his neatly shaved chin, forming a diamond through which his mouth spoke with the cigarette sticking straight out between. Witch-doctor, thought Castang, putting on grotesque mask to frighten natives. Me rain god; you ignorant niggers. No listen Tarzan: he white man's friend.

'And still is. Nothing that has happened here concerns me, since there isn't any threat to state security and never has been. I have received a report from a colleague in Paris, which I bring to your attention within the framework of confidentiality mentioned by Monsieur le Juge. The girl Patricia had some contact with an anarchist group. On as I understand a very casual basis: in other words she was seeking to make herself interesting. This lot aren't handling drugs . . . because doubtless . . . they'd be arrested by the police if they did. . . . As a known user of drugs, it's of course obvious that she would not be used as any sort of go-between: far too unreliable. She was not a source of information to our office: I make the point in order to dispel it.'

'Any idea why she was killed?' asked Richard. Castang knew he'd asked the same question in private. He'd said 'Alex' then.

'That I should imagine was the concern of the English. She may have compromised people in ways we know nothing of.'

'Which would seem to imply that she did have some knowledge it was thought worth suppressing.'

'Not necessarily. I make no criticism of Monsieur Castang here: he was doing his job. Somebody may have seen English cops standing around. Even if only an affair of illegal entry or a faked passport—the English are sensitive to such. People draw hasty conclusions. These groups are apt to meddle in what doesn't concern them, just to make money. They're vulnerable that way.'

'I can't make out what you're talking about.'

'I'm not talking about anything I don't know about,' said Marre. 'If the Channel ports are full of stateless Pakistanis that doesn't interest me in the slightest.'

A perfect smokescreen of confusion and innuendo, thought Castang. If she had a phony passport, and if somebody was making a lot of money selling them, and if there was a likelihood of her being interrogated, then quite adroitly Monsieur Marre was suggesting that Patricia being assassinated was all the fault of the English immigration officials.

Nobody wanted to pursue this, which was presumably what Marre intended.

'Monsieur Cardillac?'

'I'd better begin by saying that I will not entertain any suggestion whatever that the parties in this case, which I see as a clause in the penal code and nothing else, were manipulated for information purposes. A report of a certain conversation taking place between Castang here and a certain Doctor Simon was brought to my attention. I know Doctor Simon. I had a chat with him. As a selling agent for heavy industry, with I may add the perfect knowledge and approval of the authorities, he was interested in the contacts Monsieur La Touche possessed. I summarise these as people with money to invest in foreign securities: the connection is obvious. I am not aware that any serious suggestion has been made that La Touche used knowledge he may have possessed in an improper manner. In view of his access to confidential information in the fiscal area he had been subject from time to time to security checking. I go into no details: they are irrelevant.'

'Were the checks negative?' asked Marre amicably, dropping ash into his cupped hand and tipping it neatly into the ashtray.

'They were, my dear Alex. I repudiate totally any suggestion that this painter was an Israeli intelligence agent: it's preposterous. They don't work that way, outside bad fiction. Anybody with a grain of sense can see that in matters of finance Israel is not short of intelligence. I conclude: La Touche was of no interest to my services. It follows that none of his friends was, either.'

'This meeting, at least, serves its purpose,' said the judge. 'Any red herrings raised by the defence can be forestalled. Castang, I come to you last, for reasons you divine. Perhaps you'd like to sum them up yourself?'

'With respect, sir, I draw two conclusions. That since interrogating La Touche I have come to know a bit more about him and because of that I can make a shot at adding this up.'

'Yes.'

'And that on your instructions I pursued the investigation on a more personal level?'

'Very good.'

'Can I say that we'd all agree after listening that all these relationships were personal and no more?'

'That all these elements are fortuitous, and not causally connected? I think you could. You gentlemen agree? Go on.'

'That these different people have died—it may mean something to La Touche: it doesn't mean anything to me. I'm no wiser than when I began. On the purely personal level, pursuant to . . .'

'Yes yes,' irritably, 'we understand.'

'I've talked to the people, the prison officials and so on, who've been in contact with him. It overlaps the psychiatric reports, I believe. He's perfectly friendly and flexible, not unnaturally withdrawn or rigid, will talk about anything, but not on any subject concerning his family life or relationships. End of story.'

'Really?' said the judge. 'I'd been quite counting on that woman who's been visiting.'

'Yes, I got her to realise that. She was reticent, naturally.'

'It is to her credit. But you got her to see that it is genuinely in this man's interest . . .?'

'Yes, Monsieur le Juge. Her opinion is that quite simply, the man doesn't care a damn about his interests.'

'The man's abnormal,' said the judge, crossly, for him. 'He can't possibly not realise the gravity of the situation.'

'She hasn't any opinion to offer on that point,' said Castang.

Monsieur Marre took the dead cigarette butt out of his mouth and laid it tenderly in the ashtray. Monsieur Cardillac fidgeted as though his bladder were giving him trouble. Richard just sat and looked unemotional. Fabre still had his eyes shut.

'I don't know what the Advocate-General is going to make of this,' said Szymanowski, letting the file close with a snap.

XXV

UPHEAVALS OF THE PRISON VISITOR

La Touche had had his hair cut. Nobody expects prison haircuts to be dainty, but it startled Vera to find him crew-cut: greyer, harsher, the face seeming a lot thinner.

'Are you well?'

'In rude health, thank you,' smiling.

'It suits the shape of your head, but they've been a bit radical. I do my—' she bit it back; wasn't here to talk about her husband.

'I told them to be radical: I'll be entering the ring quite soon and I'm in training, so to speak.'

'So: what's the news then?'

'They're beginning to talk about a trial. The judge is rather mournful. Such a thin dossier. Good bureaucrats like it rich and complicated, like Christmas pudding; something that takes a lot of digesting.'

Vera knew this, having been given a law lesson by Castang.

'Instruction's finished,' he had said. 'Yes, "what, already?"— that's what every one's been saying.'

'I never quite grasp why it all takes so long as a rule.'

'Ho. Justice is inquisitorial, as opposed to the English system which is accusatorial. No—not an inquisition: an enquiry. The whole principle is to judge the person not the fact, the criminal not the crime. The examining magistrate is not a trial judge—total separation of functions. His role is to shed light upon the personality more than the mechanics, and to dig into all the background.'

'Building up the case against the unfortunate.'

'No, that's a common mistake. That is the prosecutor's role. An instruction is strictly neutral: 'à charge et à décharge' is the golden rule. Inclines actually towards the defence. Before every inter-rogation the defence counsel gets copies of all the papers—the day before—and a list of all the questions put. That's one reason why it all takes so long; assembling and organising the defence. Szymanowski's in despair because there isn't any bloody defence.'

'Keep still,' snipping carefully behind his ear. Castang was fussy about hair; it must be long but not ratty.

'And what happens then?' she asked now.

'Oh,' said La Touche, 'it's all very formal. Papers go to the Chamber of Accusation, which is a sort of judicial committee, and examines the dossier to ensure that the instruction has been correctly made and the legalities have been respected, and if every-thing is proper and absolutely ticketyboo, then they send you to trial. You are no longer a Presumed; you're an Accused.'

'Incredibly laborious.'

'My dear lady,' in a parody of his old stiff manner, 'you underestimate our passionate attachment to hairsplittingly precise formulae. What d'you want then—a Peoples' Court and barrelhead justice?—every hair on my head would prickle, if I had any. I'm not in the least impatient, having a long and profound experience of lawyers: only on the civil side so far, I'm bound to admit. This is my first acquaintance with the criminal courts, but the judges are the same. Naturally I've been trying to hurry them up, chiefly by not giving them vast amounts of paper to play with. By the way, they might not let me see you any more once I'm committed for trial.'

'Oh dear.' Second shock. 'I'm not sure; I'll ask the judge.'

'Are you disappointed?'

'I'm upset.'

'That touches me very much. I've become very attached to your visits. In fact if I may be allowed to use simple language, and you give me the only opportunity I have, I've grown extremely fond of you.'

Vera, angry with herself, blushed.

'Yes, it's bad, in a man who killed his wife and daughter in atrocious circumstances. I'm sorry; we'll speak no more of it. Can you—I'm alas obliged to fill out a shopping list in a hurry in case they remove you from contamination—get me do you think a Book of Hours?'

'You mean the psalms and things monks have?'

'Those prescribed for recital at given times, that's right. Lord thou knowest my downsitting and mine uprising—subject of scatological humour to schoolchildren.'

'I feel sure I can.'

'The chaplain will be puzzled but pleased at these upwellings of religious fervour in times of trial.'

'Is that what they are?'

'I've no idea. I'm simplifying, that's all. Continuing to simplify— my own existence, and if possible, other people's.'

'I've no earthly right to say it—but does the outcome of the thing —the trial—does it not worry you at all?'

'It would worry me a great deal if I thought it could go wrong.'

'I'm sure it won't, you know,' with some fervour. Vera indeed believed utterly that no murder could be committed by an amateur except labouring under temporary insanity, and was sure no reason-able person (assize-court judges were surely reasonable persons) would disagree.

'What's your definition of a professional, then?' Castang had asked.

'Well, committing a crime for interest: money, in the long run.'

'And when there's no evidence as to state of mind? Then there's technical guilt.'

'Oh, technical. The judge is a technician. That's what he's there for. They simply don't pass those ferocious sentences any more.'

'Hm.' Castang felt a little bothered sometimes about Vera's belief in persons of responsibility being essentially right-minded. It reminded him of Neville Chamberlain's belief that Herr Hitler would certainly be responsive to a handshake from his right-minded self.

La Touche was wearing the sort of expression described as whimsical.

'The English you know have a quaint medieval survival. A clerk gets up and says "How say you prisoner, are you guilty or not guilty?" I wonder whether anybody has ever said Oh all right, guilty, since you ask. Court quite relieved—get home early for lunch. They'd never allow that here; it wouldn't do at all. Incidentally, Madame, I've never known your name. Do you think our acquaintance has sufficiently progressed?'

'Vera. I do, rather.'

153

'You embolden me. I'd like to ask you something intensely personal, on a basis of strict impersonality. Not as paradoxical as it sounds. Assuming you were not a married woman, or shall I say rather assuming that you had no family or emotional ties. As you see that's very impersonal.'

'Not as much as all that. It's the way you describe your own situation, and I understand your viewpoint. At least I think I do, sometimes.'

'Then impersonal is the wrong word, but I'm looking for a technique. American lawyers use one called the hypothetical question. We hypothesize a situation in which both of us are in the situation as described. Would it be possible for the female person described to form an attachment to the male person described?'

Vera applied herself to this with the concentration she gave to every question seriously put; an anxious care that amused Castang, and for which he had much respect.

'The hypothesis I take it allows of a free man?'

'It would have to, I think,' said La Touche laughing, glancing at the stolid figure of Monsieur Morel, who was solemnly eating a sweet Vera had brought him.

'Then this relationship you describe would grow into a sexual relationship, don't you think?'

'I don't know. I suppose that's possible. Might it be platonic?'

'I've no experience of platonic relationships. I've no great faith in them.'

'Then accept the condition.'

'I think in that case your hypothesis seems reasonable, but I don't like it; it's divorced from reality.'

'It is, I'm sorry to say.'

'You're talking about you and me, aren't you?'

'I am.'

'It's a mistake, you know, to talk about myself. It's against my rule.'

'You're quite right. But will you take the risk?'

'Yes, I might,' she said after thinking. 'It might be good. But the consequences less good. All right. You see, I am a married woman of a basic sort. With complicated notions of honour, and conscience—all rather Spanish. I wouldn't—I mean I couldn't—start things I didn't know how to finish. And I have a real feeling for you. I refuse to let it get sentimentalised. Pretending that

Monsieur Morel wouldn't look and then imagining sleeping together is just mawkish.'

'I completely agree.'

'Oh dear. . . . You see I can't say I would, because I might, and I couldn't.' Losing all command of French, or Czech, or any other language. 'If I could—oh, damn. Then . . .'

'Don't cry,' said La Touche softly.

'No, of course I won't. But you see having said that, I can't come back any more. That is the consequence.'

'I understand.'

'I have to tell you something else. I've said to you that my husband was a civil servant. That wasn't quite true. He didn't know I came to see you. He does at present. He doesn't ask any questions. He wouldn't try to make—gain—anything from it. I don't betray anything you say, and I haven't, and I won't. You see, he's the cop who arrested you. My name is Castang.' She stood up and said, 'Monsieur Morel, let me out, would you?'

'Thank you for coming,' said La Touche. 'It gives me much happiness.'

'Me too,' she said. 'I'll look after the book.'

Monsieur Morel brought the book next day. She had written on the fly-leaf 'Coriolanus says "There is a world elsewhere" and this surely is not just quixotic'. He studied this for a time: the hand-writing interested him. One had lots of time in jail, as well as very little. It was quiet. The chief screw, sympathetic to his polite manners and to his never giving any trouble, as well as impressed by an 'intellectual', had given him a good table and chair, and was amiably lax over writing materials. For the greater part of the day it was not even noisy. For dinner there were lentils stewed with bits of bacon. The canteen provided virtually everything he needed, and he had lots of money; a great deal: far too much. He was though more grateful for far-too-much than he had ever been. In jail money has more value than anywhere else. By 'canteening' cigarettes, and a little extra fruit and soap, he got devoted service and friendship from the penniless, and a chess partner whenever he wanted one.

Prognosis about his 'case' was widespread: in a house of detention there are people serving short terms; a month or so 'confined to barracks', but the aristocracy are those who having committed felonies, or even crimes, are being 'instructed' and enjoy prolonging the instructions as long as possible: 'it all helps to pass the time' and will be subtracted from the eventual sentence. But they look forward too to their trials. It is interesting, exciting, there will be publicity. And once sentenced there is the move to a long-term prison, a 'centrale'.

'Properly organised, one is, then. Not like this pissy dump. Get a little camping stove, you can, and make a cup of coffee.' An earthly paradise . . .

'Psychiatric institute, that'll be you. Jammy. Do a little gardening for the screws, grow some fresh vegetables for them; they'll eat out of your hand.'

This trial was a bore. One would have to go through with it. He got that wretched Dieudonné to give him a list of his investments and goods both fixed and portable that could be realised. It was an agreeable surprise how much there was. That would do something, he hoped, for the poor, the ones who could not 'canteen'. In France, with money, you can do anything. 'Who are you telling it to?'

La Touche went back to a book he had been reading, one of those Vera had brought from his library, solid literature much respected by screws and all prisoners in for 'intellectual' crimes like fraud. This one was a re-discovery, forgotten since student days. A gem: Rudyard Kipling is a writer who has always been highly esteemed in France, and who translates well. A volume of short stories. One he was especially fond of, a fable and he enjoyed fables, called the 'Children of the Zodiac'. After looking at the 'Book of Hours', passing his hand over the binding the way a man who loves paper does, studying the little message Vera had written him, he went back to this story looking for a particular passage. When he found it he underlined it with pencil: he had been discovering the pleasures of annotation. If things go wrong, he told himself, I can make a 'commonplace book'.

'After Leo's death there sprang up a breed of little mean men, whimpering and flinching and howling because the Houses killed them and theirs, who wished to live forever without pain. They did not increase their lives, but they increased their own torments miserably.'

XXVI

DIPLOMATIC ILLNESS OF THE
MINISTRY-PUBLIC

Judicial mills turned, even when they had little to grind. Monsieur Szymanowski's 'instruction' dossier went to the Chambre d'Accusation, a particular type of tribunal which does not sit in public, which verifies that the instruction has been properly carried out, that all the defence rights have been correctly respected, and that there are no legal flaws in the case to be presented against Mr Thing. It works quite quickly, and after the occasionally interminable tergiversations of instruction the rhythm accelerates noticeably. The 'Proc'—or as he is known in legal jargon the 'Ministry-Public'—gets the dossier first, and within a strict time-schedule is obliged to present his conclusions to the tribunal. Precious little need here for time: the conclusions were simple and succinct.

'A triple homicide in circumstances allowing of no doubt, confusion, or mistaken identity.'

'A Police Judiciaire enquiry carried out strictly according to rule and with every respect for defence rights. Medical opinion both immediately and subsequently confirms clear-headed and consequent behaviour of the presumed. Experts of scrupulous independence and integrity agree upon total lucidity. A unanimous opinion that personality problems are minor in nature and adequately compensated.'

'Exhaustive enquiries reveal no political motivation or shading. No element herein could conceivably be held to compromise or embarrass any national interest. The sensitive and responsible position held by the presumed as a State Functionary, can in no sense be held relevant to the actions alleged against him.'

'The use of the word "allegations", while obligatory pending the decision of the Chamber to lay these informations at the door of the Assize Court, must be considered a legal fiction. At no moment during the preliminary enquiry by the P.J. or the instruction subsequently set afoot has the presumed departed from full and free admission of his entire responsibility. The rarity of this circumstance can in no terms be accepted as an indication of mental instability.'

'In view of the detached, dispassionate, and disillusioned attitude of the presumed towards his wife and daughter, the Ministry-Public sees no alternative to a prosecution based upon culpable, deliberate, and wilful homicide.'

The Chambre d'Accusation, to nobody's surprise, marked the dossier with the republican equivalent of 'Le Roi le Veult'. It is only the third stage in the six different phases of a condemnation for a major crime, and the most impersonally formal. It is roughly equivalent to, say, a Grand Jury of the Commonwealth of Massachusetts bringing in a true bill against Thing. We the People consider that Thing must be brought to answer for his disturbances of the public tranquillity.

Behind this sedate affixing of seals to parchments there was a sense of scurry. An Assize Court sits every three months, except— as in Paris—where there is too much crime to cope with at this leisurely interval. It is a serious affair. There are three judges, who must all be Counsellors to the Appeal Court. The Advocate-General, presenting the prosecution case on behalf of the Ministry-Public, is likewise a person of much weight and substance. As counterbalance, in major criminal trials, there is traditionally a formidable array of defence talent. Half a dozen names, of advocates whose reputation in criminal pleading is worldwide, crop up over and over again. Unless one or more of these names is present, the authorities feel uneasy. Without them, it is felt, the jury can feel itself browbeaten by the thunders of the Proc and the authoritative, sometimes haughty airs of certain Presidents—and the President of an Assize Court has very wide discretionary powers.

It happens, occasionally, that a relatively young and unknown defence counsel by his skill, brilliance and determination can make himself a mighty reputation, and enter the ranks of the great operatic tenors (all pleaders are actors, but not all overact). But without a good strong cast, the public, and the Press, may make nasty remarks about justice being seen to be done. Hereabouts La Touche, tiresome in many ways, had been unusually tiresome.

In a way (said the Proc, in private) that imbecile Dieudonné was at the bottom of it. One didn't understand how a sound lawyer, albeit no pleader and with no experience whatever of courts, could lose his head to this extent. Ten thousand advocates never go near a courtroom, and are the harder-headed for it.

Perhaps in secret a sympathiser with the extreme right wing?—vague appellation containing a multitude of oddities. Certain it was that he had approached a Paris advocate of notoriously extreme views.

It could be something more personal and more deeply buried, a hankering for theatrical behaviour in a man who had never done anything in his entire existence but write legal safeguards into contracts. However—said the Proc—we aren't trying Dieudonné.

Directly he had heard the name proposed, La Touche had flatly refused even to see him. Various people at this point had taken Dieudonné aside for a word in his ear. Trying to give a political complexion to an affair of this sort is a perversion of justice. A sound trial lawyer would see that it wouldn't wash. La Touche at this time had appeared to oscillate between apathy and cynicism, going as far as to say to the judge that he 'washed his hands of the whole business' at a moment when he was much annoyed at the appearance of the psychiatrists. Since he had nobody but Dieudonné to represent him at the sessions of instruction the judge had asked crossly for somebody for heavens' sake from a big criminal practice with experience of trial procedure. And when, after all this trouble, a really big gun had been persuaded that it wouldn't be a wasps' nest, and came down in person to see his client, accompanied by his bright young man who would do the donkey-work during instruction-sessions, he had been extremely vexed. La Touche, suddenly coming out of his mantle of mute disinterest, had said politely that sorry, but he didn't want this simple affair dramatised by a Parisian pleader whose presence alone in a courtroom would be a honeypot to journalists. Even more vexed at a session of asking reasonable questions and getting obstructive answers, the judge suspended the instruction and sent for Commissaire Richard.

'It doesn't matter what we call it—say a supplement of information. I want to find out what lies behind all this.'

Richard said nothing and went away wondering what he was supposed to do.

'Castang, look, they're so tangled up in lawyers that Szymanowski's becoming highly fractious. Nothing to do with us, but he doesn't want to use coercion, so a negotiator is needed and that's you; you've always got on well with him.' And dragging his feet, Castang had gone to the 'parlour'. The P.J. can interview a 'detainee' with nobody else present.

'At least you've got no axe to grind,' said La Touche. 'One can't talk to lawyers, who are incapable of understanding anything.'

'I'm a passive instrument. My work is done and I've no further role to play. If I can do anything unofficially to help you I will.'

'Help,' said La Touche. 'I hadn't thought, in my arrogance, I would need help. But I've been wondering how to extricate myself from an impossible situation. The judge fusses about defence: I can't make him grasp that I neither want nor need any.' And I'm not going to be a witness to your insanity pleas, thought Castang.

'I can't do anything with lawyers,' he said tactfully. 'All these judges and procs are my hierarchical superiors.'

'I realise that. . . . I'll trust to your discretion,' suddenly. 'Between us then in all simplicity.'

'Your experience ought to tell you that they're only trying to respect form.'

'Having respected form all my life, which is too long, I wish to get this back into a human context. I'm resolved on that. I'm stubborn on this point.'

'You can, I think, go along with them without hypocrisy. What were you intending—to stand mute?'

'More or less.'

'It doesn't work—they go over your head and behave as though you weren't there, and the position is falser than ever. The judge commits a lawyer off the legal-aid list, and he is regarded as your mouthpiece. That he hasn't the remotest clue about your thinking doesn't worry them: the forms are obeyed: you are defended. You simply make a farce of the entire proceeding—it seems unlike you to approve of waste and stupidity. It makes no difference to me. I'm a witness, but neither for nor against you, a witness on procedure and not on the heart. I think I'm genuinely unprejudiced, and that you can trust me if you want to. If you don't want to, all right. The passive instrument will go back and tell the judge to shove it. But I remark that here there is no lawyer or screw present. You can speak, and freely.'

La Touche looked at him queerly.

'Logically, my whole position lies in being illogical. You won't be offended if I say that to put trust in a cop sounds illogical.'

'But you must put trust in somebody. Not lawyers. Not cops because they've a secret tiny taperecorder and will play it all back to the judge. Who, then?'

'Very well, tell me.'

'In this affair I've only met one,' said Castang seriously. 'The painter's wife. She impressed me. I suppose she's Jewish—she doesn't have a funny nose or wear a wig or anything. Jews have that intransigence that forces one's respect.'

'Ah,' interested. 'This is the party to which I should like to belong. *Los intransigentes.* The extreme republicans. Nothing political about that—do you understand? Nothing left-wing.'

'Sure,' said Castang. 'My wife is too.'

'Tell me about the painter's wife.'

'He was intransigent too. As I understand. About art, I mean.'

'Yes, indeed. In fact that is at the root of this affair.'

'I see . . . at least very dimly I think I glimpse. All right. She refused to make any complaint against you. No court action, no appeal for damages, nothing either civil or criminal. She was too young to have been in a camp, but I've met this attitude in a woman who'd lived through Ravensbrück.'

'Yes. I hadn't made the bridge. I know nothing of camps. I have not, you see, lived at all. I simply want to end as a man.'

Strange, thought Castang, how these lawyers—for this is just another lawyer—adopt weirdly sentimental attitudes. A few weeks in jail, and he starts throwing heroics.

'Reduced to essentials, she doesn't bother about forgiveness, or justice, or any of this crap. Nothing to forgive. What justice? Belongs to God, huh?'

'We won't indulge in theology,' said La Touche dryly. 'Stick to this world.'

'By all means. Compromise with it. Go with the punch. Since they want you to have a lawyer, take one. Tell him what you please. As long as he can talk, at the trial . . . you have to go through with

161

the trial, you know. As long as the shrink doesn't pronounce you unfit to plead.' As dryly as La Touche.

'Over my dead body.'

'Good then, I've done my best. Given you I hope good advice. Do something with it.'

La Touche was polite to the judge at his next session, and Richard was pleased with Castang.

'That's fixed up. Fellow off the legal-aid panel. Bright, too. Delighted with this. Name's Weber. They were a bit fussed lest it sound Jewish. Looks a bit swarthy too. We're getting like Heinrich Himmler around here, worrying about the physiognomies.'

'All that's needed now,' said Castang, 'is to make sure that none of the jurors are called Abdul.'

'The Proc,' said Richard, swinging his swivel chair and stretching his long legs out, 'is going to have a sudden attack of a virus infection. Oh, no worries, nothing to put him in hospital. It won't last above a week or so. But an acute laryngitis, depriving him of vocal cords.'

'Has he Arab blood?' asked Castang with an innocent look.

'You may well ask. He can disqualify himself on grounds of personal friendship with a Counsellor to the Accounts Tribunal, meaning they've both got money invested in the same concerns. Odd, by the way—did you know that if you're a civil servant in the Accounts Tribunal you're exempt from jury service?'

'La Touche says continually that he's lived his entire life divorced from reality. On the other hand, so is a cop exempt from jury service.'

'I should bloody well hope so,' said Richard. 'How did you find him, by the way?—without going into any details.'

'The shrinks say he's sane and who am I to contradict? A bit spiritually illuminated—one often finds that in intellectuals serving a spell in jug. The monastery syndrome.'

'Ah yes, devote ourselves henceforward to prayer and good works: it's all that peace and quiet.'

'Opting out.'

'Shave your head. Wear sandals. The Hare Krishna performance.'

'They're selling stuff on the street called Spiritual Sky Incense,' said Castang. 'Doesn't half stink. Jasmine and all.'

'Sounds like that stuff Lasalle puts on his hair,' said Richard. An unusual piece of disloyalty, from him, but they both disliked the oleaginous commissaire who was officially Richard's second, but who preferred his office to the street. 'All right—just thought I'd let you know. Now we've work to do; where's Fausta?'

'Is this Weber German or what?'

'Oh, Alsatian or something. Safe, anyhow.'

'Who's going to be President? Not that old anti-semite Mirecourt?'

'I don't know, but rest assured, he'll be stricken with laryngitis too at the crucial moment.'

'It'll be even more of a farce than at present seems likely unless they've someone good.'

'Where have you been then?' asked Richard, as the door opened.

'Changing the typewriter ribbon. One has, you know, to wash one's hands,' said Fausta blandly.

XXVII

THE WITNESSES

The life of an officer in the Police Judiciaire has lengthy stretches of monotony and wearisome bureaucratic routine. He forgets the paradox of his vocation, which is its ambivalence. When engaged upon an enquiry he is an officer of the law, part—and supposedly the sharp point—of the judicial apparatus, armed with great powers as well as a technical bag of tricks and a gun, restrained with powerful safeguards from becoming a petty Hitler through the arbitrary exercise of these powers. In the different stages of his enquiry, he is directly responsible to the Procureur of the Republic, the Judge of Instruction (who possesses such strong legal instruments that Napoleon remarked that he was the most powerful man in France) or the President of the Tribunal. It would seem thus logical that the P.J., executor in penal matters of this legal grip, should depend from the Ministry of Justice. In fact, in nearly all countries he belongs to the Ministry of the Interior. One is reminded of the comic cross-talk in the English farce, between the Home Office and the Foreign Office.

'They're aliens. Consequently your department.'

'No no, my boy. These are Undesirable aliens. Consequently your department.'

For about nine months of the year the average P.J. officer uses his gun to stir cups of tea with. His life is that of any civil servant, translating reams of statistics into more statistics, to feed the voracious appetite of other civil servants for nice, neat, manageable figures which look well on the page. And like every government functionary in the world he is always a year or two behindhand.

Talleyrand, it is now universally agreed, was a very great man, and never more than in his notorious, abominable, appallingly intelligent instruction to his civil servants. 'Not too much zeal.'

In France there is a long and amiable tradition of exciting, sometimes brilliant cinema, the French equivalent of the 'Western', concerning the conflict between a bandit, mostly heroic, and a cop who is a cynical bastard and a baddy. The baddy has to win, a type of masochism much enjoyed by audiences, who are put on the rack and love it. In this tale, Commissaire Richard would be a cynical Mephisto, manipulating everything because he's a raging psychopath, Castang would be shot—he might show some gallantly futile courage—and . . . but the reality is, as Vera is rather relieved to find out, a little less catatonic. Most of the time, Castang is unzealous, and comes home in time for meals. A typewriter basher, using his gun as nailfile, pipecleaner, or paperclip, he forgets all about being an officer of the law, and consigns people like La Touche (administrative equivalent of the rough end of a pineapple upon the digestive tract) to oblivion. Vera, concerned if unzealous about soot on window-sills, the health of the trees opposite, the ridiculous price, doubled in twelve months, of a small tin of tomato-concassée, and the nagging need for doing-something-about-that-ghastly-bathroom, does the same. When La Touche actually came up for trial it was a shock.

Vera wasn't a witness to anything. She had gone back to the judge, after her last interview with La Touche.

'You gave me a hard task, and I'm not really up to it. I don't think I can reconcile my conscience to any more.' Monsieur Szymanowski had been nice about it.

'I wish a few more people would act according to the dictates of their conscience. Very well, I won't ask you. I take note that the man has become more co-operative, and there are small but healthy signs—he's more in touch with reality, less catastrophically apathetic. I don't know how much you have contributed to that, but certainly your influence has been a good one.'

To Castang she said nothing, simply that she found La Touche 'too complex: I didn't feel firm ground under the feet. I do better to stick to fraudulent managers. Assassins are like eating giraffe; it might taste good but one feels so bloody guilty.' Castang just said, 'It's for you to decide—did you remember to buy blackcurrant juice?'

Castang was a witness. He sought an interview with Commissaire Richard, who said he didn't know but Fausta would; she always did. Fausta had it all written down: her memory was exceptional, but like a judge of instruction only the written word was valid.

'I had a long girlish chat on the phone with the Proc's secretary —you know?—she has red hair and smells rather peculiar, but she's perfectly human with women. I know you'll say she's a bit les, but it's not true at all: I can tell, believe me. The one Lasalle fancies, but he never got anywhere. Good, after this brief but telling sketch, 'the President will be Monsieur Ziegler.'

'God, another Alsatian.'

'Next best thing to Monsieur Braunschwig who can't be produced because the Seine Tribunal is over its ears.'

'Good; next.'

'The assessors are Monsieur Tatin.'

'Oh God, Demoiselle.' Poor man, he suffered from his name. There is a sort of French dessert, an upside-down affair of apples and caramelised sugar, most delicious when properly done, called Tarte Tatin. Who the Demoiselles-Tatin were is a piece of folklore long lost in the mists of gastronomic myth, but alack, Judge Tatin had an old-maidish way with him.

'And—this is very good news—Madame Marie-Laure Rampollion.'

'Hurrah.' Marie-Laure was a perfect sweety, and by far the prettiest judge in France, and at forty-seven her figure aroused the fierce jealousy of Colette Delavigne, the Children's Judge, who was twenty-eight.

'Those lovely gentle eyes,' said the men, sentimentally.

'That great huge sexy mouth,' said the men, even more so.

'Sensitive,' said Fausta. 'And I know about her throat, so please . . .'

'Next.'

'The Proc is going on leave.'

'Aha.'

'Not—I quote textually—on holiday. Nor is he ill. But on medical advice, at a good time of year, he is taking the thermal cure at Contrexéville, for nervous strain.'

'Oh, that's absolutely brilliant.'

'Occupying, consequently, the seat of the Ministry-Public will be the senior substitute, Monsieur Mars.'

'I don't know him,' said Castang.

'I do,' said Richard. 'Blond hair in waves as though lacquered. A piss-vinegar expression. Very quiet and controlled. And extremely, frighteningly bright.'

'Oh dear.'

'In this instance, an unknown quantity.'

'Oh dear, pity the poor policeman. I have nervous strain.'

'You can go to Contrex for the cure when the Proc is back. Can't risk meeting him there, wrapped in his little towel with his navel sticking out.'

'Can't I go to the Pyrenees?'

'No no,' said Fausta, 'that's only for women with gynaecological troubles.'

'But that's me,' said Castang despairingly.

'Keep your eyes firmly fixed on Marie-Laure.'

'Yes, that's something. But what will the jury be?'

'Artisans, housewives, respectable craftsmen. And no Jews or Arabs.'

The intercom phone rang.

'Castang, a lady would like to see you.'

'Does the lady give a name?'

'A Madame Davids.'

'Tell the lady I'll be right down.' He found her more than handsome, in gay and pretty clothes, and asked her out for a cup of coffee.

'I'm not wearing mourning or anything,' catching the approving eye. 'I've got to be a witness, and since you're the only person I know I ask for a bit of guidance in this labyrinth, which is frightening.' She sounded joyous, and he felt some embarrassment.

'I'm afraid that the defence may try to blacken your husband.'

'No,' calmly. 'I'm a defence witness.'

'Oh . . .'

'Maître Weber wrote me a very nice letter. He's going to plead insanity.'

'Naturally. He may have a hard row to hoe; the experts seem against him. He could have asked for a further check before the instruction closed—too late now. I imagine he thought it unlikely to find any more favourable conclusions. It's his only way out, of course.'

'Psychiatrists don't know everything. Yes, thank you, I think I will have some cake. The man's spring is broken. He has let himself die. It is a phenomenon similar to what was seen in the camps a lot. The Musselmen they were called. They refused everything progressively, and simply died of inanition. But I think he can be brought back, and I want to do my best. I'm sure it's irregular, and improper, and everything else, but I want to appeal to you. If you can reconcile it with your conscience—not to be too severe. I must add,' hastily, 'I'm not an emissary from the lawyer, and I'm not trying to tamper with you.'

'The lawyer wouldn't have tried,' said Castang, smiling. 'I'm a piece of colourless glass; the light goes straight through. I'm only a technical witness. I haven't any real opinion about his state of mind—and if I had it would be inadmissible. I'll certainly not be hostile, but I'm only allowed to testify on procedure. You on the other hand will be much more valuable. You could have asked for civil damages, and you haven't.'

'Monsieur La Touche's civil lawyer offered me a large sum. I have refused. To do him justice, he wasn't trying to buy me.'

'But the suggestion might have been made.'

'Yes,' turning her candid eyes upon him. 'And I would have refuted it.'

'I suppose yes, it is improper. I'm a bit on your side, but I can't show it. A word if I may of completely private advice—don't pitch it too strong—the court might think "oh, emotional appeals", and react against you.'

'Yes, I understand. And thank you very much. You give me the courage I needed.'

'You won't quote me to the lawyer? I'd be obliged as well, you see, to react against him.'

'I won't. And he's a sensitive man. Which is perhaps better than clever. He's clever too—I think he'd see that it wouldn't do.'

He reported the meeting to Vera, who listened with her face held carefully reserved.

'I've changed my mind,' she said afterwards. 'I think after all I'd like to come to this trial. Do you think there'll be a great squash?'

'Yes and no. The political stuff has been so carefully and elaborately defused that there isn't any whipped-up manifestation. There'll be inevitably the morbid—hoping for sexy details.'

'Revolting.'

'Justice is public, girl. They can't put too severe a filter on who gets in—defeat their own ends. Be a lot of Pressmen, inevitably—

it's undoubtedly going to be more interesting than seemed likely. No trouble where you're concerned—the police have a few methods of polite bribery. I can get the doorkeeper to hold you a place, and keep it quite anonymous.'

'I won't arise theatrically in denunciation.'

'I should sincerely hope not. Ziegler has anyway the reputation for standing no nonsense from anyone.'

'I don't agree in the least that La Touche is a Musselman. It's interesting though that she should take that attitude.'

XXVIII

THE PRESIDENT OF THE COURT OF ASSIZE

'Gentlemen, the Court,' said the doorkeeper in one of his moments of glory, unnecessarily loud. Everyone stood up, Vera hoisting herself.

She had never seen La Touche in ordinary clothes. In a grey business suit with an unexpectedly gay tie he was impressive. The prison pallor did not show up; the prison haircut suited the austere face. The haggard look she had last seen had been replaced by composure, serenity. The two cops, on either side, with their habitual hangdog look, were simply footmen: he took their presence for granted.

The President, and despite his extraordinary clothes—all those robes and a funny hat—was even more impressive. Vera was unprejudiced, being unused to courts and to the paternalistic, slightly silly look, as of a playing-card king, of many magistrates. A noble face, which she could draw, and did: several newspapermen were doing the same. A bulky man, but not fat. A face with a great deal of bone in it. Caricaturists could seize upon the nose, which prolonged the big forehead with hardly any interval. This Greek look went round the courtroom like the beam of a lighthouse.

The assessors (noticed the experienced onlookers) were both less effaced and less probably-somnolent than usual. Beneath the greying curls and the roly-poly features Monsieur Tatin's brightness of eye belied the 'demoiselle' nickname. Madame Rampollion's celebrated columnar throat and amazingly wide mouth were more than just statuesque. All the journalists wrote down 'good court' in unison.

Monsieur Mars, wrapped in the fearsome robe of the Ministry-Public, and on the *estrade* with the judges (the term 'parquet' comes from the older times when the prosecutor was on 'the floor'), had a closed face giving nothing away. He looked strangely and if it is possible appealingly young. Certainly he was not attempting to project an artificial severity. He looked like La Touche; calm and self-confident. This resemblance—they had almost the look of twins —gave added pleasure to the gentlemen of the Press.

Maître Weber, alone and the more impressive on his bench usually full of black crows shaking their sleeves behind the accused and his cops, looked well up to his job. The variety of people who had muttered 'looks semitic' were now squashed—it was the same group who had muttered about the President's nose. Monsieur Weber was a young man, and quite unknown, having been picked off the 'legal-aid list'. It didn't worry him at all to be alone where ordinarily *le prime-donne* of the Paris Bar would be sitting. He was fat, curly, comfortable, with a blue chin and library horn-rims. He sat admirably still and unwound, with no nervous fidgeting, his sleeves left in peace. Vera felt obscurely comforted.

The public, despite a high proportion of Chelsea buns and steamed suet-puddings, seemed reasonably well-behaved. Vera's neighbour, who appeared to be a hardened trial-goer, smelt of peppermints and muttered wise comments to himself, but inoffensively. Like the technically minded at a football match, who count the number of touches or corners, and write it down. In technical terms of course, as when the two teams scrum down, and one succeeds in 'hooking against the head'.

The President's voice was ideal; quiet without being soft, perfectly audible over coughing.

'The Court sits. Only one preliminary remark. As most but not all here present are aware, the discretionary powers given me are great. I remind you that I will rigorously enforce the rule that no signs of approbation or disapprobation will be permitted. Any person giving vent to such will simply be put outside. Furthermore I intend that this tribunal shall proceed with sobriety and courtesy—and where possible, brevity. May we have the jury, please? . . . I inform the public—those who are not hardened rogues—that the prosecution may without explanation challenge four members of this jury chosen by lottery from the list, and that the defence may refuse five. . . . Very good. Monsieur Robert Abdessalem is excused.

Let us please have no shuffling or muttering. Madame Angèle Wirth is excused. . . . Monsieur Gabriel Hautbois, we pray you to excuse us. There is absolutely no aspersion cast upon your character or judgment. . . . Admirable. We are now assembled. I ask the public to take note; there are nine members of this jury chosen from among yourselves, the public, making twelve when completed by the Court. Good. Ladies, gentlemen. I ask each and every one, solemnly, whether you are in any way, even remotely, related to any party in this case? Any previous acquaintance, social, professional or personal? Have you been in the service of the accused or any other party? . . . Admirable. The Court will swear the jury. We will all stand up. We take off our hats. I remind the public that this is not folklore. This is a profoundly grave and solemn instant: we are not just paying lip service to Armistice Day. Members of the jury, each and every one, this is an ancient and beautiful formula, none the less alive and vivid from being embodied in Article Three Hundred and Four of the Code of Criminal Procedure. You do swear and promise before God and before men, to examine with the most scrupulous attention the charges which shall be preferred against the man named to you. You will betray neither the interests of this accused man, nor those of society which accuses him: you shall communicate with no person until after the declaration of your judgment: you shall listen with no hatred or wickedness, with neither fear nor affection: you shall decide following the conclusions of the prosecution and from every means of defence, in obedience to your conscience and your innermost conviction, with the impartiality and the firmness belonging to free and upright men, and solemnly to keep the secret of your deliberations, even after judgment is passed and your functions have ceased. . . . This solemn oath I now administer: you will each upon the calling of your name raise your hand and repeat distinctly "I do swear it". . . . I thank you.'

Slipping back into his conversational manner.

'Monsieur La Touche, will you have the goodness to stand up? This I may say is formal. The Court establishes your identity. We ask you to confirm your name, place and date of birth, your *curriculum vitae*, your background and circumstances, your past career. . . . Thank you, that is clear. I address a remark to the jury and the public. The accused's high place in the public administration, his eminent qualifications, his notable services rendered to the

State, have a place here in this trial. Under strict limitations. In the eyes of the Penal Code, Monsieur La Touche could have spent his life pushing a wheelbarrow—oh yes, the Code has eyes.' It got the first laugh, a mild one. The President let the laugh go.

'The law dictates that the judges—you, the jury—should have, and I quote, personal experience of human realities. For this reason the debates in this Court are oral. During the process of instruction, the law recognises only the written word. Here in the Court of Assize, the opposite holds good. It is the spoken word to which you will listen. The witnesses will be asked to narrate. They may be interrupted and questioned, but it is essentially their words—their own words—to which you will pay attention. The Ministry-Public, by tradition, may pose direct questions to witnesses. It is the usage that the defence puts queries through my mouth. This has been known to create an impression that the Court is biased in favour of the prosecution. I wish it to be known that under my powers I give counsel permission to question witnesses directly. With the sobriety, courtesy, and where possible brevity I have previously insisted upon.

'Shall we have the witnesses? . . . Have the kindness to place yourselves in line. . . . You are the witnesses. Some of you are experts, and one of you is an agent of the administration, that is to say the police. Those have previously sworn, upon their honour and conscience. There is normally no need for you to swear again. In fact—again under my discretionary powers—I do ask you to swear again, and I hope you agree.' And the formula which has suddenly ceased to be one. Without hatred or fear. . . . We've a long way to go, thought Castang. When we say it we mean it.

'The witnesses will retire, to be called each in due turn.' Vera had a mad impulse to get up and follow them.

'Monsieur La Touche, I ask you to listen attentively to the act of accusation, which the clerk of the court will read. In accordance with the terms of Article 327 I enjoin him to use an audible and intelligible diction.' Even the two cops were infected by the ripple of laughter.

'I understand the laugh. But why did the legislator take pains to include such an injunction? So that you should all understand that the assize court does not try a man until every condition attaching to the pursuit of this man by society, and his examination by the instructing judge, shall have been fulfilled. We do not do this lightly.'

No, thought Vera, he isn't just being theatrical. This care taken to inform the public (about technicalities which easily become meaningless) is good. And it *is* like a theatre. They have played these roles over and over. To make it come fresh each time . . .

'We are trying this man for taking away life. No man may do this in peacetime without being called to account. The law prescribes that the State may take away life, after precise and strictly controlled deliberations.'

There was a quiver, as of antennae, among the journalists. For the first time something crucial had been touched upon.

'This sanction, in our time, is almost unheard-of. But it exists. If the situation arises, in our deeply-felt respect for life, we examine it with very great gravity. Monsieur La Touche, I proceed now to interrogating you upon these facts, the fundamentals of the case against you.'

XXIX

EXAMINATION

'Would you prefer to speak from where you are?' in the easy, conversational tone. 'It is the normal procedure, but you could come closer. The law states that you should be free from constraint.'

Maître Weber, for the first time.

'With respect, might that not be rather increasing the constraint? Psychologically.'

'He is at liberty to say, and you to advise him.'

'I'm quite happy here,' said La Touche, in his social-occasion voice, which Vera had never heard. Oh, I beg of you, she said silently, don't let him treat it as a joke.

'Good. Then I ask only that you pitch your voice just a little higher. I hear you very well, but I wish the members of the public sitting at the back to hear you too. If it does not inconvenience you,' courteously.

'Not at all.' Very much the visiting lecturer: a slight problem with the local acoustics.

'I shall be repeating, broadly, the questions put to you by the judge of instruction. You are free, naturally, to add to or take away from the answers you then made. The accused,' in one of his punctilious asides, 'is of course not on oath, unlike the other witnesses. He may be questioned by any member of the court, as well as the advocates. If in the course of questioning a member of the jury feels he wants further enlightenment upon a point, he may ask to put a question, and I shall allow it.'

'Would you like me to narrate?' asked La Touche simply. 'Would it make the procedure less laborious?—I mean no sarcasm there.'

'By all means narrate if you prefer. I may have to pull you up—to elucidate a detail for the court. Or possibly even to protect you from faulty interpretations.'

Weber had folded his arms, and appeared made of stone. Monsieur Mars adopted the air of the intelligent listener in the first row, who will animate the lecture by asking a question.

'I will only prompt you in case of your memory lapsing,' said the President, with the ghost of a smile in the voice, but none on the face.

'As you have heard I am a functionary in a senior position. I keep—I am using the present tense to make this more vivid—office hours, but these are flexible. I try to keep my work as far as is possible up to the date and even the minute. This allows me occasionally to leave my office early. Such was the position on the date in question. I add that it was a very hot day—nobody felt like working, much. I reached home, thus, in midafternoon. This happened, I should say, sufficiently rarely for the event to be unexpected.

'At my home—I skip the geography which can be shown with plans and photographs—I knew that Monsieur Davids was working. He was a painter, engaged upon a portrait of my wife. He worked there every afternoon about that time. I took an interest in this picture, and wished to take an hour to study and discuss its progress. I greatly admired and respected this painter, who was a man of the highest talent and a most interesting personality. Is it allowable and relevant to say a word about the painter?'

'It is.'

'I made his acquaintance under strange circumstances. I had at that time a daughter, my elder daughter, a student in Paris. She got into bad company and was taking drugs. This circumstance was largely my fault. Suffice it that she was in circumstances of want, poverty, and misery, and that I did little to help her. There was a gap between us and a lack of communication. This is not irrelevant. The painter, Monsieur Davids, found her vulgarly but graphically in the gutter. He took her in, sheltered her, fed, clothed and warmed her. He also painted her, as I subsequently learned. He succeeded in stopping, or at least arresting, her dependence on drugs. When she was as he judged restored to health, some few months after, he brought her back to me, explaining what he had done and asking me to show her the affection and confidence she lacked. This act struck me very forcibly.'

'We are given to understand,' said the President, 'that he also seduced her. Is that so, or did you so understand the situation?'

'I don't know about seduced. That he slept with her?—he didn't tell me as much.' A small, timid laugh amidst the public. 'I suppose I am man of the world enough to realise that the probability was overwhelming.'

'We cannot,' colourless, 'hear Mademoiselle La Touche as a witness, alas. She has since died. The event has nothing to do with the jurisdiction of this court.'

'Nothing to do with the painter?' interjected Mars, casually. His voice was light, without the resonance of the President's, and more metallic than that of La Touche.

'The fact was the subject of judicial enquiry, under a commission of interrogation issued by the judge of instruction,' making the ponderous phrase sound manageable: one of Monsieur Ziegler's gifts. 'The investigating officers were satisfied that her death had nothing to do with any party in this case—a fortuitous occurrence. She had relapsed into renewed dependence on drugs, and may have taken an overdose.'

'I am satisfied,' said Mars. 'I beg your pardon, Monsieur La Touche.'

'I beg it of you'—*je vous en prie*, that handy, untranslatable phrase used in doorways and lifts; universal expression of courtesy and consideration. 'I wish only to let it be understood that Monsieur Davids brought with him unusual recommendations to his high qualities.'

'We will hear Madame Davids as a witness to this episode. Continue,' said the President.

'I asked him to stay, and to paint a portrait of my wife.'

'With your permission.' The soft, deep voice of Weber. Not elaborately measured—as conversational as the others.

'Maître.'

'To stay—as a house guest? So that he had your full confidence.'

'Certainly.'

'I need not ask whether your wife had your full confidence?—it is rhetorical.'

'She had—naturally. I knew of course that she was occasionally —sometimes habitually—unfaithful to me.'

Two or three voices began phrases.

'Monsieur the President,' boomed Weber. 'Since you give me the latitude—one moment, Monsieur the Procureur. Let's get this clear. First, whatever your wife's habits or attitudes, and whatever your overt or suppressed knowledge and suspicions—this man was a house guest. Face the fact; he abused that privilege.'

'Yes, he did.'

'And may I say this?—as a man of the world you may have had suspicions, or knowledge, of your wife's divagations.' Wanderings from the path, thought Vera. Good word. 'In the interest of family harmony and marital unity, you behaved as though they did not exist.'

'That is correct.'

'Until such moment as you could not avoid seeing, realising, acting.'

'We're not quite that far yet, Maître,' said the President, almost apologetically.

'If the word is too harsh,' said Mars, softly, 'correct me. You showed yourself a complaisant father, where your daughter's virtue was concerned. I think that here you showed yourself a complaisant husband.'

'That is also correct.'

'Do please continue.'

La Touche did. He had walked in, found nobody, walked upstairs, 'I have light feet' apologetically: walked into a bedroom, found—in a defensively ironic voice—'a debauch'.

Clamour. The President, while as light-handed as La Touche was light-footed, wasn't having any. A debauch!

Yes, a real debauch. What else would one call it? He had stood studying the situation. Thought about it. If you could call it thought. Said to himself, you know, 'What does one do?' Had made his mind up. Wasn't having that. Gone to the bedroom cupboard, a little nook, you know, built in. Little pistol. His wife's. A toy, given by him: she'd asked for it as a present. He knew how it worked. Certainly not loaded—dangerous toy. . . . He'd loaded it. Well, yes, they were all a bit paralysed. Taken aback. Anyone would be. Hadn't taken this seriously? Well, he was not a melodramatic man—ordinarily. And then he'd shot the three. The little pistol held six shots. He'd fired all six. Yes, quite calmly and deliberately.

The questions fired in from all sides. La Touche remained calm, both unhurried and unworried.

It was the President—Monsieur Mars, continuing colourless, was careful not to ask it—who had to put it.

'Monsieur La Touche—are you seriously saying you gave this thought and consideration?'

'I can think of no other way of putting the truth.'

'Now think carefully—I've noticed you don't use words or legal terms loosely, and you have had, of course, legal training.'

'You're asking about premeditation. Oh yes, I thought.'

The antennae rippled like a cornfield.

'Why?' The bald word was delivered quietly, with deliberation.

'I have given that much thought. I have to admit that I still really don't know. To free myself? To simplify? To avenge? To act as a man, at last? As to that, the time has come now.'

'The advocates will interpret your answers. The Court will appreciate—but not prematurely. Tell me, Monsieur La Touche, are you aware that this answer may be damaging to you?'

'Perfectly.'

Vera thought that everybody must be holding their breath. Certainly she was. The President made a slow movement, draggingly, with his hand.

He picked up a little red book, something like the Thoughts of some chairman or other.

'I am going to read to the Court . . . Section First of the First Chapter, of Part Two of the Penal Code, concerning crimes and felonies against the person.' There it is, thought Vera. Literature is full of the voice of doom. Nobody need put on any black caps. The voice was uninflected.

'Article 295. "Homicide committed voluntarily is qualified as murder." Article 296. "A murder committed with premeditation or ambush is qualified as assassination." Article 297. "Premeditation consists in the design formed, before the action, to attack a particular person, or such person as may be found or met upon the way, even when such design may depend upon circumstances or conditions." Article 298. "Ambush consists in waiting for a space of time either great or small, in one or more places, while lying in wait for an individual with the intention either of giving death, or of inflicting violence." ' A change of tone.

'Articles 299 to 301, concerning parricide, infanticide, and poisoning, do not fall within the province of this court. I pass to article 302. "Every person found guilty of assassination, parricide or poisoning, shall be punished with death." You appreciate, Monsieur La Touche, that we shall be obliged to consider narrow and exact definitions of the law.'

'I appreciate,' said La Touche bleakly.

'Monsieur the President . . .' said Weber, enormous in his black robe.

'You will have plenty of time, Maître, and opportunity. I think that we can now hear the witnesses.'

And all of a sudden there was Castang, small, businesslike, and unemotional, standing on the 'parquet' in front of the judges.

XXX

THE WITNESSES (2)

'I call you first, because you were, as we understand, the first person on the scene after the event. You are an officer of Police Judiciaire. Your qualifications and experience are admitted. You will please narrate in your own words the events of that afternoon.'

Castang did so. It sounded painfully bald, but he was asked to be no more than factual.

'No more than factual, Inspector,' said Monsieur Mars dryly.

'I have nothing to add.'

'Maître Weber,' said the President.

'While I quite agree that a police witness is not a technical expert on state of mind, he was the first person on the scene. His professional training and experience give weight to his personal viewpoint.'

'That is reasonable,' said the President.

'This collected and calm demeanour, Monsieur Castang—it's fairly usual in such circumstances?'

'As far as my experience goes. One sees it in road accidents.'

'So without diagnosing where you are not qualified, or using terminology inexactly, physiological shock or something akin? Yes? And you asked for a doctor straight away, and that wasn't for the victims—they were plainly dead? Two purposes, you'd agree. Both sound—to help you know whether you could question this man, and to bring him rapid treatment in the event of his needing it—agreed?'

'It is always desirable to have a medical opinion rapidly.'

'An opinion on state of mind—he wasn't ill otherwise. My

question is quite straightforward and simple—did his behaviour seem natural and normal?'

'To me, no, it didn't.'

'Have you experience of a coldblooded assassination?—of a man coolly planning and carrying out a triple murder?'

'No.'

'Have you ever seen behaviour you would call callous or unfeeling, as opposed to this unnatural calm, in crimes of violence?'

'I've seen apparent indifference in a professional criminal after beating a man up. Some time later.'

'No, your professional or hardened criminal wouldn't hang about waiting to be arrested, would he?' Both joining in the laugh.

'This occasion did not resemble that other at all?'

'No, not in any sense.'

'This man expressed both pity and remorse?'

'According to my notes made an hour or so after, he felt and expressed pity, and said that he wished to feel remorse. I don't pretend to have the wording absolutely exact. That was the sense.'

'And by then he was showing signs of regaining his equilibrium?'

'Yes, I think he was.'

'Factual enough for you, Monsieur le Procureur?' asked the judge smiling. 'All right, Monsieur Castang, you're excused; take a place.' Vera felt quite legitimate pride.

Medical witnesses in courts are generally only too aware of the possible embarrassments inherent in giving a clear yes or no to anything much. Better to be over-prudent, and the prose sound woozy, than imprudently go out on branches when there are woodcutters about. The wooziness of the prose gets worse as the technicalities designed to mask it fly thicker. As Mrs Gradgrind, a woman who suffered all her life from Ologies, remarked when dying, 'there's a pain somewhere in the room, but I'm not certain I have it'.

The doctor Castang had called was hopeless, but the judge of instruction had noticed that too, and the President did now.

The three psychiatrists—two of them, anyhow—made efforts to be comprehensible, were patently honest, and one at least showed courage. But temporary insanity is a very thorny affair. You see, said the one who got talkative, with a man like this you must be very cautious. Highly intelligent, extremely sensitive, trained to debate abstractions. . . . Oh yes, most courteous; outwardly co-operative but in fact obstructive. Habits of scepticism, self-control. A whole series of public and private personages. Neuroses, undoubtedly, some crippling. But nothing psychotic, nothing disabling. Both centrifugal and centripetal patterns. My dear man, you're paranoid, I'm paranoid; everyone is, more or less: the question is, how well do we handle it? People have rigidities, hankerings for authority, reinforce their fears and uncertainties in a liking for rules and regulations. Is this psychotic? Then the whole Ministry of Finance had better get packed off to Sainte-Anne. I realise that this man sought relief from stress, and a wound, and pain. Certainly it all appeared as a betrayal. Yes, he had deep respect for his wife's family milieu and trusted her to observe form. Yes, he was most disappointed in his daughters and blamed himself for their failings, and sought to punish himself. Yes, the painter was a man he greatly admired and respected, and this weakness— more than the betrayal of hospitality or friendship, though both these loyalties were sacred—was a fierce blow. But I'm very sorry, I'm not prepared to use the term insanity. Monsieur La Touche, as his whole life and career shows, is powerfully structured and has unusual command. Like Mr Kipling's shipwrecked sailor, he is a man of infinite resource and sagacity. He behaves well in tight spots. The etiology of these patterns . . . well, etiology is the assignment of a cause; the philosophy of causation. In medicine the science of the causes of disease. . . . Now the ethology . . . damn it, it's the science of character formation. . . . Look, this is not physics: we can't express these things as an algebraic equation.

And that awful word 'para'. Parapsychology, and paranormal . . .

Madame Davids did better at first, because so refreshingly not paranatural. Worse as she went on, because she got angry with Monsieur Mars. The President, hideously watchful for any accusations of antisemitism, began to be a little chiding. She did a lot of good, thought Castang, but she also did harm. She was too much on La Touche's side. Her simplicities, and simplifications, were too much like those paradoxical Yiddish jokes, an offence to French Cartesianism. Castang, listening, was too often reminded of the classic 'If the rich could hire the poor to die for them—what a living the poor would make!' Davids in Paris had just got frustrated. Perhaps in New York a La Touche would have been simply delighted. 'Those two frightful women—Lord, man, I make you a present of them.' La Touche had had such peculiar notions of personal honour. And so had Davids . . .

Once the doctors had been got rid of it sailed ahead faster. There were few witnesses. Maître Weber had assembled a couple of distinguished gentlemen who explained the extreme integrity of La Touche's professional and personal life, and said that an assault upon this integrity would be a thing he would react against. With violence? If the threat appeared violent.

The President appeared encouraged. La Touche, re-examined after the witnesses, was brief and colourless.

'We will break for lunch. Since this trial is notably free from irrelevancies and since there is no civil pleading on behalf of injured parties, I will ask the Ministry-Public to present his requisition after lunch. If the pleadings are not lengthy, there is no reason why deliberations should not take place today.' This briskness startled the journalists. Good law though, thought Castang. As long as he doesn't appear to be hurrying things unnaturally. A trial of one day only is almost unheard-of, in an Assize Court.

Lunch—Castang like a good cop had reserved a table in the local pub a day before—was silent. He ferried Vera. They ate beef à la mode which was the 'plat du jour': the less prudent only got sandwiches.

'La Touche has been pretty good. He only did one silly thing— that idiot remark about acting like a man. Self-dramatisation, and self-pity.'

'I don't know what to say,' said Vera, 'so I'm saying nothing.'

'Ziegler's good. Weber's doing well.'

'You did well.'

'I won't get into trouble,' said Castang shrugging. In a way, he wished he had.

XXXI

PLEADINGS

The formal phrase is 'The word is with . . .'

'La parole est au Ministre Public.' And this remark, brief and sober, launches the formal speech of the prosecution.

Monsieur Mars rose to his feet, taking off his glasses, arranging his robe, placing his notes exactly where he wanted them, with no rhetorical gesture. His voice was very well pitched, his tone dry and unemotional, his command of himself and his material total. Once more, Vera was struck at the uncanny resemblance between him and La Touche; they might have been twins. A very dangerous man.

He would not be lengthy. The President's appeal for brevity and sobriety was one to which he could respond with, he hoped, exactitude. Courtesy—certainly. That was an indispensable attribute of society. And so was severity. He was here to represent society. An unpopular role in certain quarters. Today, society suffered grievous and insidious attack from every quarter. And above all, its essential basic unit—the family. He would not embroider. Nothing here was on the borderline. No issue here was shadowy. No trial here of abortionist or drunken driver, no homicide by imprudence or motivated by social conscience. This was basic. By admission, by legal proof, by realisation and acceptance at the earliest stage, this was homicide with premeditation. No witness queried that. Everything now rested upon responsibility. That this responsibility existed was likewise admitted by all, save by Madame Davids, whom he respected and admired, and whose ethics—he would make a brief quotation from Hannah Arendt—were based upon the necessity for total forgiveness. Society, alas, could not accept that. Charity—yes. But the notions of charity and justice cannot be confused.

A diminished responsibility? He could and did accept such a concept. In practically all cases, save hardened, professional crime for venal motives. Here—he wished he could. Monsieur La Touche had not acted basely, ignobly. But he had acted coolly, with calculation, and in full knowledge, accepting the responsibility. He had with perfect deliberation chosen to put himself outside society. He would have to accept the consequences. Not natural? Not normal? No. But deliberate. By so doing, he renounced the protection of society. He was an outlaw. No society, even in epochs when the rules for its preservation are held sacred, has ever been able to tolerate the outlaw. He who flouts the basic rule 'thou shalt not kill'. Anarchist is an emotional word. But it means 'he who denies the existence of law'.

The prosecutor did not attack the individual. He was the defender of society. The defender of the individual, left with no defence, would launch an attack upon society. The Court would hear. The Court would appreciate. Society would be accused of being fascist; he, its defender, would be painted a Hitler. The jury would decide. The jury was society.

Of guilt or innocence there is no question. Every effort has been made. The experts have strained the resources of scientific explanation. But in their conscience they cannot say that responsibility is not present.

Punishment. He had given this much thought. Prisons he disliked, but until the legislator found other means of rehabilitation—and this was a most thorny subject—one would have to reckon with them. But for La Touche? In the case of a homicide with premeditation, a triple homicide, he could—the law admitted no less—ask for nothing less than imprisonment for life. And this was—according to his conscience—a cruel and unusual punishment. Could it help? It could not. It would be the accelerated ruin of a man who had been noble and upright. It could benefit neither society, nor the individual.

Some form of rehabilitation through psychiatric treatment? A facile, seductive solution. It could and did work in numerous cases. Here it was pure hypocrisy, an evasion of responsibility. La Touche was neither insane nor even psychotic, nor likely to become so. It is excluded.

188

The recourse to extreme mildness, falsely equated with 'comprehension'. Such measures as a prison sentence suspended, the placing of the person under strict measures of surveillance and control? He was a strong believer in these. The person who has failed in an ordeal of life, which is cruel, who has fallen on stony ground—yes, wherever possible he would attempt this. The weak, the humble, the misled, the uneducated, those who have suffered long and patiently before collapse—here justice was mercy. Here in this court, a day or two previously, he had asked for such measures to be taken, and the court had agreed. To reiterate the circumstances would be emotional, rhetorical. A woman who had killed her alcoholic husband and her handicapped child, in the extremity of her despair.

Can we speak of despair, here?

'I would, here, be false to the role I have claimed were I to renounce the gravest of my responsibilities. The accused has left himself no way out, and I see no way out for him. It is for these cases that the legislator has—in wisdom—left a loophole. There is a temptation here to metaphor. The body, in its wisdom, when threatened by infection gathers its resources. Antibodies, complex immunological processes, given the body to protect it from septicaemia. These defences cannot, upon occasion, cope with a grave infection that has been neglected. The result is gangrene— death. The only recourse left is to surgery, to amputation. Members of the Court, in my soul and conscience, I do not ask you for a death penalty. I require it of you.'

With nothing visible upon his large face the President brought himself out of his attitude, the attitude of complete concentration with which the music lover listens to a very well-known piece. Even the best-known of pieces—say the Seventh Symphony of Beethoven.

'The word is with the advocate for the defence.'

Weber, thought Vera, is not unequal. A good man comes up to scratch, like a boxer at the bell.

What, she wondered, is 'scratch'?

He's equal to it, whatever it is. Massive, large, courageous.

'I will try to be even briefer than the Ministry-Public. The learned and skilful, eloquent and concise Advocate-General has left me, you may think, little ground for manoeuvre. I do not want it. He has left me few ways out, loopholes, boltholes. I do not want

189

them. I am a young and inexperienced advocate, chosen at my client's express desire from the legal-aid list, designated by the leader of this Bar. That would be an excuse for my failure to rise to these heights of eloquence. I do not want it. I want nothing, members of this Court and jury, and you the public, but the simplest and most obvious justice. No charity, no rehabilitation. Neither high-flown ethics concealing the most barbarous and primitive of society's sanctions, nor sobbings over our gangrenes; and abortion or alcoholism, however much the Advocate-General may pretend not to use emotional frames of reference—these are emotional, polarised, irrelevant words. The truth is that the Advocate-General does not know how to grasp what has happened here, and in his confusion clutches at the most emotional of all concepts—eye for eye, tooth for tooth. The most primitive, the least efficient and the most senseless of all.

'You will ask me to avoid rhetoric, and you will be quite right. The death penalty is simply beneath contempt, and you will not consider it for a single instant. It is disgusting, nauseating, revolting to every honest man. The legislator has kept it among our statutes.

'You may think, as I do, as thank God an increasing number of persons do, when they make the effort to think and that is your duty, that the legislator knows very well that there is no good government without a corresponding degree of cant and hypocrisy.

'The Prosecution tells you—I might be permitted to say, arrogantly —that there is no question of guilt. Guilt? Who is going to judge of fire, who has not been through it? Some of you may have felt the heat of the fire, in your lives, and drawn back, pretended it did not exist.

'Insanity? Do you know what insanity is? Does anyone? The three eminent specialists we have heard do not. Are you going to arrogate to yourselves a superior knowledge?

'I ask you to recall the words of the other expert witness—the experienced and honourable officer of police, who replied to questions with truth, without fear or hatred. He was guarded, and he is quite right: he is an agent of the administration, and he was seeking to ensure that his professional conduct be found blameless. This cool and impartial witness to the crucial moments after the dreadful and irrevocable act did not wish to condemn, to blame, to pass judgment.

'Shall we, all these months after? The experts know nothing, and

190

take refuge in learned ologies. We know nothing. We do not understand. We have, up till now, made little effort to understand. We might very well conclude together with the wife of one of the victims that there is no understanding but in total forgiveness, but more is asked of us. We are asked to judge; the law insists upon it.

'Technically—technically!—guilty, no doubt of it. This alleviates and simplifies our task. There is no claim for civil redress—another blindfold the less. Nothing prevents our looking at this case with honesty and loyalty, both to ourselves and to society.

'The man is sane now; a child could see that. The man was not sane then, and a man—or woman—can see that. He acted, within the honour and integrity which nobody has questioned, for what he thought to be right. That he was mistaken, we will agree. In the grip of forces at that second stronger than his training, his skill, his intelligence, character, experience and comprehension, I am convinced we agree. Psychiatric treatment—I am in agreement with the Ministry-Public—would be futile. Prison—again—senseless, stupid, utterly negative and cowardly; a denial of all our responsibility to society.

'I now ask you to consider. The man has already suffered. How much? A few months of prison and is that so very terrible? These defence advocates invariably dramatise and sentimentalise. Do I do so, in asking you to go just a little further? What of a man who loses everything in one blink? His family, his honour, and home. His position, livelihood, and the universal respect and esteem. He has nothing now: he is stripped naked. This is a greater punishment than any you could mete out. Greater even than the death sentence you have heard demanded by the gentleman who claims to embody all the rights and privileges of society. Those are not contained in him but in you. The man in the seat of the Ministry-Public has an essential and noble function, but you must not forget that he is the prisoner of that function.

'You can do better, and you will. Since we are dealing here with a matter of technical guilt, which this man has never denied or sought to evade, the law requires of you a technical condemnation. You may pass a prison sentence, and you will suspend it. That will be one more reminder, to rest with him every day of his life, of that dreadful day.

'This will be justice. I have not asked for mercy, for that comes too late. Mercy was a thing to ask for him before it was the thing to ask of him. At the moment when he walked up the staircase of his home, unaware of the dreadful spectacle awaiting him. At the moment before he was subjected to an intolerable strain and something in him snapped. At that instant, members of the jury, he had two, three seconds for deliberation. You have all the time you ask for.

'I have done.'

The shuffle that fluttered through the public; the sighing, coughing and muttering that can suddenly swell into a 'mark of approbation' was quelled on the instant by the President.

'The Court,' he said in a loud clear voice, 'is fully appreciative of, and grateful for, the scruple and moderation shown by these pleadings.' The flutter subsided slowly to silence, quelled by the eye commanding the courtroom.

'Monsieur La Touche. Before entering upon the final phase, that of deliberation, it is customary in our Courts to ask the defendant whether he has something to add to the conclusions of the pleaders.'

'Monsieur the President,' slowly and uncertainly, 'I—I beg your pardon.'

'Do not hurry,' kindly.

'Monsieur the President, and my judges,' his self-command was impressive, 'I believe that it is customary for the defendant to say that he associates himself with the words of his defender, and to throw himself upon the mercy of the Court. Yes, of course . . . I mean, I do so. But the conclusions of the Advocate-General . . .'

'Monsieur La Touche,' kindly, 'the Court has not yet deliberated.'

'But with these conclusions I have much . . .'

Oh sit down, Vera longed to shout. Weber's face had gone back to stone. Monsieur Mars had an expression of serene expectance, that of a man waiting to be insulted and armed against it.

'Sympathy . . .'

'You need not say now what you feel under stress. Other opportunities will be given you.'

'You are right. I am given to errors of judgment. I will say nothing.'

'Very well,' gathering up the courtroom between his hands, open before him on the desk; switching back, perhaps with relief, to formal language, 'I now pronounce the debates closed. I order the deposit of the dossier with the Clerk, who will close and seal it according to law. We will read the list of the questions to which the Court must answer. These concern, as the law dictates, not only the question of eventual guilt, but all the circumstances attendant upon the acts of the accused, which may be held to attenuate, or in certain cases to aggravate guilt if guilt be found.'

We've had a few bad moments, thought Castang. What was that imbecile about to say? That he thought yes, a death sentence is a splendid idea? Pretty clever tactics of Mars, to show 'severity' by an exercise in logic which lets him pretty neatly off his hook. It might almost have been a speech for the defence! Leave them no loophole, really, but to let the fellow go right this minute. Weber did nicely to show quickness of mind, but the Proc had done his spadework for him!

'Before retiring,' said the President, 'the Court has yet another vital duty. This is that I read to you Article 353 of the Code of Criminal Procedure, the text of which is also as the law demands exhibited in large and readable type in the place where we deliberate.

' "The law does not demand an account from the judges of the means whereby they reach decision, and prescribes no rule wherefrom particularly depends the fullness and sufficiency of a proof. It prescribes that they should ask themselves in silence and recollection, seeking in the sincerity of their conscience, what impression has been made upon their reasoning by the proofs afforded against the accused, and by the means employed for his defence. The law asks of the judges one question and one only, summing up the full measure of their duties: 'Have you an intimate conviction?' "

'I terminate by recalling to you Article 365, which states that the replies made by the court of assize to the questions posed are irrevocable.

'The accused will stand down. The doorkeeper will guard the entrance to the jury-room, to which no person is granted access without my express permission.

'The hearings are provisionally suspended.'

XXXII

DELIBERATIONS

The public had plenty to occupy it, for some time at least. Excited voices echoed in the corridor, on the stairs, and in the vast hallway known as the 'Salle des Pas Perdus'. There was a queue for lavatories, telephones, and to get one's word in first. The journalists shrugged furiously, and the concierge collected various small bribes.

The professionals had all made their little arrangements. Castang's were to bring Vera down the stairs and along the passage leading to the offices of the Judges of Instruction. Not to Monsieur Szymanowski, who since finishing his task had withdrawn officially from all outward sign of interest, wrapped in the cloud of detachment that expresses the strict legal separation between instruction and judgment.

They slipped in to Colette Delavigne's office: she had arranged to pass this time with them, in quiet, and at least relative comfort. Her clerk and her secretary made coffee in the outside office: Colette, finger on lips, produced a brandy bottle: needed.

'Already? . . . Ziegler was quick; is he good?'

'Very.'

'Demoiselle?'

'Didn't utter, bar associating himself with the sentiments expressed by more or less everyone.'

'Super. And Marie-Laure?'

'Uttered briefly and well, to the effect that whatever opinion one might possess as to the role of the female sex in modern society, here the law recognised no distinctions whatever. Particularly in a sex case. Naked adulterous wives slaughtered by husbands avenging their honour were strictly for the birdy-birdies.'

'Marie-Laure,' said Colette who did not like the lady all that much, 'is always particularly strong on everything concerning bottom-talk.' The phrase, 'histoires de cul', switched them all skilfully into objectivity.

'Well?' she asked.

'Well what? La Touche is bonkers. Provided a variety of slight but telling demonstrations. Weber succinct, suspended sentence. Mars succinct, this won't do, that won't do, so all we're left with is death penalty. Since, plainly, that won't do, and in view of La Touche's odd behaviour, Ziegler will steer them to the nervous breakdown formula. Which is what both Mars and Weber want, and so say all of us. Jolly good.'

'Was that what it was?' asked innocent Vera. 'I couldn't understand. Mars frightened me out of my wits.'

'Just explaining that prisons are no earthly use, either in perp or for a fortnight, once one has meditated upon one's sins. We're lovely and early—four-thirty.' Vera wondered whether La Touche was reading Vespers.

'They won't take long in that case,' said Colettte.

'What happens exactly?' asked Vera timidly.

'Oh my darling . . .'

'I spare you the section on judgments,' said Colette, grimacing at the little red book which she too had on the desk. 'Briefly they mayn't come out. There is chat. Ziegler puts himself in the background and makes the others talk, bringing them out. They vote after a while to get the mood and general feeling. Then bit by bit get the voting more precise and exact. As often as they like. Secret of course, in writing, and the Pres burns the bulletins after reading them aloud. Much like electing a Pope.'

'But he must have a huge influence upon them,' voicing an objection often made.

'Not as much as you'd think and even a bad judge can't budge them—they've seen how bad he is, in Court.'

'Have you done it?'

'God, no. I'm only allowed in felonies at the worst, with two others, and no jury. Even for children the assize is special—must be appeal-court judges. I could be an assessor, for children's assize.'

'But if he was set, say, on getting a conviction . . . he must have such overwhelming moral authority.'

'Takes at least eight to four for conviction. A seven-to-five is an acquittal.'

'Ziegler,' said Castang, with conviction, 'isn't a convicting judge.'

'What are they going to do then?' It was a well-known trick of Vera's to get things explained three times, very simply and slowly as to a backward child. People who did not know her, watching the explanations being examined carefully for signs of speciousness, sophistry, or cant, mistook the obstinate scepticism for impenetrable stupidity.

'Jail is a good place for a nervous breakdown. Now we're all nicely rested we can face the psychiatric clinic with equanimity. Suspended sentence is even better, as Mars was careful to point out, once rid of the alcoholic husband.'

'But he said just the opposite.'

'Oh, Vera—always takes everyone literally.'

'Certainly. As he said there's all the difference. This is a man with trained, formed decisions and judgments, not a poor wishy-wash carried helplessly along on the tide of events. With all the sophistication of several generations of leisured, cultivated up-bringing.'

'Which did not equip him to handle domestic crises,' said Castang patiently.

'But will the jury agree with all that?'

'Hence the deliberations,' remarked Colette.

'Even if there are a few fanatics on the jury,' said Castang, 'Ziegler will quieten them. And remember Marie-Laure. She's not going to allow sobstuff over that abominable Hélène.'

'This is all very well,' said Colette, 'but juries are very odd. It's true that since the judges sit with them there are fewer of those idiotic sympathy votes. But it's also true—and any judge who has sat on a jury will tell you—that they're unpredictable and have the oddest fixations one can never quite get rid of.'

'Certainly, if the trial's been bad. This one's been exemplary.'

'Plenty of things about justice are exemplary,' said Colette gloomily. 'Even the Code can appear a monument of generous common-sense instead of just dimwitted industry. I do agree that Ziegler is a good judge. But the rarity of that strange animal may lead one to overestimate its significance. A judge without prejudices is like an honest cop. Tends not to rise in his profession.'

'What kind of prejudices?' Vera, still patiently puzzling away.

'Anything you like. Racial, political, sexual, religious. Or just plain personal. Judges being people, you see—it's the good thing and the bad about them.'

'As far as that goes,' said Castang, 'everyone was exemplary. And we never heard a whisper about politics.'

'I have never really understood why there ever should have been a whisper about politics,' said Vera.

Colette shushed Castang.

'You're much too impatient. You live in a world where every sort of sordid little pretext is used as a possible stepping-stone in the rat race. She doesn't and you persist in being ungrateful. All those things like unselfishness and loyalty and simplicity, and you always tend to treat her as though she were divorced from reality. Whereas you know perfectly well that without her . . .'

'I'd just be another crooked cop. It's just that I detest feeling ashamed of myself. Like judges.'

'You'd better keep quiet now,' said Vera chillingly.

'Look,' said Colette, 'you are perfectly right; there isn't anything political about this and never was. But being a senior government functionary, La Touche is judged—no that's not the right word; opinions are formed about him—by hypocritical standards. In some way or another he was friendly—and it doesn't bother me—with a lot of these Arabs who have so much money. It still doesn't bother me.'

'It bothers me and I think it deplorable that these people who go canting on about their oppressed brothers don't spend a penny to step in when the rice crop fails.'

'Now you are over-simplifying. La Touche may have been most concerned about the rice crop, and been working away quietly on it. These people seem always to have one thing in common and that is their morbid, pathological suspiciousness. By alleviating that he could be doing a useful job. Meanwhile he's bound to a large extent by governmental policies. All right so far? Isn't it just the same as being a cop? If a diplomat is not dishonest in his attitudes how will he ever do a job?'

'Jesuitical.'

'That's the word for every one of us,' said Colette, taking one of Castang's cigarettes. 'Let's leave that. La Touche makes friends with a painter who happens to be Jewish. He doesn't care. What importance has it? That the man is a good painter. Just as the other man is a capitalist with money to invest, a long way before he is an Arab. But people have these facile, superficial little attitudes learned from television.'

'The great big lying cant machine.'

'My dear friend,' said Colette. 'Easy on. Just a machine, manned if you like by bands of posturing monkeys, giving a little information, and inevitably people think they get a lot. So you can't blame them, can you, when the wiseacres say that La Touche was either using or being used. Either way, because of his senior position and all his pals, a threat. That's all. Nobody would believe he liked Davids for picking that girl up and cherishing her, which shows he's a nice person. A nasty person, which most of us are, would have loathed Davids for just that reason.'

'Maybe La Touche did loathe him,' said Castang, 'and worked him deliberately into a position where he could treat him as hateful and contemptible. The psychs have been on about it no end.'

'I don't care,' said Colette. 'I'm not judging this, thank heaven. I've only learned one thing judging children, and that is that the adults, so-called, behave very much the same way. Aphorism, there are awfully few adults.'

'Surely you can shut the office,' said Castang. The secretary and the clerk had gone home. 'Let's go have a jar, and think about supper.'

'I want to hear the verdict,' said Vera.

'So do I but if we take some pizza or something we don't have to worry about the soup getting cold.'

They went out to the pub called 'A l'Ecoute du Palais'—the Listening Post. Most of the journalists were there having a jar too. Beginning to get fractious at its taking too long, feeling peckish, worrying about whether the pizza would be edible.

'Starve those buggers into submission.'

'Can't deprive a judge of dinner.'

'Big chap like Ziegler, looks like a strong man with a knife and fork.'

'Alsatian, isn't he? Give him a bloody great sandwich stuffed with sauerkraut.'

'Phone's ringing.'

'Bugles are sounding recall, boys,' shouted the barmaid. 'Will everybody settle up, please? We've no shortage of change.'

'Gentlemen,' said the doorkeeper. 'The Court.'

The President looked much more tired than La Touche.

'The Court sits to announce its verdict,' in a dulled voice with no ring to it.

'I have here the list of questions drawn up for the consideration of the jury, with the answers duly apposed, signed as the law requires by myself as President and by a member of the jury designated by lot.'

He's furious, thought Castang. It's gone wrong.

'I remind the assembly that a clear vote of two-thirds or over is needed to produce conviction, and that spoiled or blank votes count invariably in favour of the accused. The vote is guilty.'

No reaction: none of the pundits had considered anything else.

'In the vote upon attenuating or aggravating circumstances, none have been found.'

First sensation.

'Silence,' said Ziegler.

Silence was restored.

'In the vote upon punishment, subsequent to consideration of the personality of the accused as the law directs, the options open to the jury depend upon attenuating circumstances having been found.'

'Politics,' said the peppermints man next to Vera, loudly. 'Fellow too friendly to the Jews.'

'Silence,' said the President, departing for the very first time from his serenity.

Silence was imposed.

'In the event of attenuating circumstances not being found the choices of the jury are restricted, exceptionally, to the fixed pains recognised by the Code.'

'But they always find attenuating circumstances,' said the lady on Vera's right, puzzled.

'Attenuating circumstances!' said the peppermints man with contempt. 'Hypocrites!'

Silence imposed itself.

'The fixed pains recognised are criminal reclusion in perpetuity, and death. The Court has refused to accept the first. The penalty has therefore been adopted in accordance with the recommendations of the Ministry-Public.'

'I didn't catch properly,' said the lady. 'What does he mean?'

'Motivations,' went on Ziegler remorselessly. 'The public may not be aware that contrary to the judgments of other courts, the Court of Assize is not bound to give the motives for its decision. This is because of the decision given by a jury as opposed to a bench of judges.

'The decisions of the jury,' Ziegler was ploughing on, 'proceed by positive and negative answers, and from their decisions there is no appeal.'

'I don't understand,' said Vera to the peppermints man, who seemed something of a legal expert, 'there's always an appeal surely?'

'No Appeal Court,' he said angrily. 'Only Supreme Court of Repeal. And they don't judge on fact. Only on law. They quash the decision only if the law is bad.'

'And is it?'

'Bad?' breathing at her fiercely. 'It's the best farce that ever was.'

'Sorry dear,' said the lady on the right, 'but I haven't quite caught on: he talks so with the points of his teeth.'

'Monsieur La Touche,' said the President, now quite in command of himself. La Touche, certainly, appeared more so than ever. He made a formal kind of bow.

'Monsieur the President, I beg you to accept on behalf of the Court my thanks.'

'Nothing further?'

'I welcome the verdict.'

'Nothing further?'

'No.'

'Very well.'

'I wish I could understand,' said the lady on the right, exasperated, 'whether he's guilty or he isn't: I can't make the old bugger out.'

Vera surprised herself, by not feeling surprised.

XXXIII

MONSIEUR THE MINISTER'S HOSPITALITY

The Officer of Police Henri Castang went about his business. The cop's guide, philosopher and friend, the Code of Criminal Procedure, has nothing to say about death penalties, save that when legal means are exhausted, the condemned has still the right to the prerogative of clemency, exercised by the President of the Republic. Since the time when General de Gaulle showed a disinclination to put people to death this has become something of a formality. Subsequent presidents have maintained a reputation for liberalism in this domain.

Since it was a novelty—he had never before been associated with a case ending in a capital condemnation—he had the curiosity to look up one or two of Vera's Ology books: when she had first asked to be a prison visitor she had read up Crim and Pen. Here he found only laconic footnotes. The condemned is removed to the departmental prison, where he is placed in a special cell, under continuous surveillance. He may smoke, read and write without restriction. Food is of a liberal nature. Visits are controlled in a 'rather more strict' fashion: details are lacking. Such barbarous relics of medieval times as leg irons have long been abolished. A prudish silence surrounds the subject of the guillotine—is that a medieval relic? It has no doubt benefited by all the very latest technological improvements, but there again there aren't many. Like improving that other barbarous relic the knife and fork. One supposes that the blade is kept sharp. Maybe they now have an instant-reaction quick-release system, though cops still talk about 'pulling the string'. Anyway all that tedious muscular effort is now spared the operator, and the executioner is not over-worked: he won't be going on strike or anything. Various other pruderies have been thought up by humane persons. You don't even catch a glimpse of the nasty thing till the last possible instant. The premedication department, that famous old glass of rum, seems a bit crude still, but it is hard to think of a local anaesthetic that will do better. Even the pharmaceutical industry research teams, who are full of enterprise, cudgel their brains as the saying goes, in vain on this point.

Commissaire Richard had little more to say than Colette: a mumble to the effect that juries were very odd, but if one were to make a sweep of all the medieval survivals, there'd be no law left at all. What would we do then? Sociologists (remarked Richard in his occasional portentous moments) were like bad playwrights: they have no third act.

Vera knew little more. She had lunch one day with Colette (Castang, much bored, was investigating a supermarket hold-up) but even inside the Palace of Justice there had not been much gossip: it had been a seven-hour wonder.

'It went nine to three, I think. Ziegler and Marie-Laure held out, and so did a juror. But that old Tatin stayed hard. And the body of the jury seem to have been resolute from the start. I don't know why. La Touche hadn't made a good impression, and then there's his background—oh, queer little things. It just added up wrong. Nobody wants to talk about it.' And neither did Vera.

Time passed. The Court of Repeal, while slightly unhappy about a few of the procedural points, found nothing bad in law. So, well, it was up to the Chief Magistrate of the Republic. He'd commute, of course—he always did. And then one could arrange oneself comfortably. Find the fellow a nice job in the prison hospital or something. Parole him after a decent interval. People would forget about it all: they always did. Probably already had.

It came as something of a shock. The administration, like juries, was unpredictable, and the message was very curt. Telex messages often are, but Commissaire Richard read it three times before sending for Castang.

'Don't ask me, because I don't know. Truly I don't. You are simply told to take a plane—expenses authorised—and present yourself at the Ministry—the central office in the Place Beauvau— at this time exactly which you will observe to the minute. Slightly weird. Sorry; can't help you. Guessing is futile. Go, and doubtless you'll be told.' Castang put on his best suit, to be on the safe side.

'Will you be back this evening?' asked Vera.

'I wish I knew. Disconcerting. Perhaps I'm getting James Bond's job. We'll be moving into one of those very smart flats, the sort with closed-circuit TV in the elevator.'

'I'd hate that.'

'So would I. We'll cross that bridge when we come to it.'

Nervousness; a rubbery condition in the thighs. Henri Castang, not being in form, is dropped from the ski-team for today's slalom. Up steps. Pompous portal. Terrifying concierge person, controlling all the little pink permit-slips.

'Yes?'

'Castang. I have an appointment. Don't know who with.'

'I do,' already bored. 'Wait there.' Not over five minutes passed.

'You're Castang?' said a quiet, chilly voice. He looked up. Recognisable without trouble, from Press photographs and television appearances, the Minister of the Interior. Quite handsome, classical features. A slim figure, a bit round-shouldered but well tailored. Nothing much remarkable about him, bar the eyes, a blazing blue. Blue is generally considered a cold colour, but these were hot, fierce, apt to strike terror. Castang wasn't impressed enough by ministers to be terrorstruck. He just wondered what the hell went on. How often did one see ministers busying themselves with obscure provincial cops?

Not much bloody hospitality round here. No glad-to-see-you-old-boy. The Minister just stood there with his hands in his pockets and didn't even look at him.

'Where's that wretched car?' he enquired of nobody.

'Coming up now, sir.'

'About time. Else we're late. Come on,' taking Castang by the upper arm, like a cop. The Cardinal's Guards will escort James Bond forthwith to the Bastille. He will remain there at His Majesty's pleasure. Signed: Richelieu. The Minister waved a cop aside, wrenched the back door of the car open, made an abrupt hand movement, jumped in beside him.

'Sorry sir, but . . .'

'We're just crossing the road. Don't ask questions.'

Two cops at the gate leapt to attention and saluted. A third, racing out into the road, blew a screaming whistle-blast. The black DS came on to the Rue Saint Honoré like the wrath of Jehovah, and before Castang had realised that 'across the road' from the Place Beauvau means the Palace of the Elysée there were two more cops saluting, the door was being whisked open, the Minister was running athletically up another flight of steps, and he was stumbling incompetently under the disdainful bored look of Paris cops. Inside the hallway a thin still man in black clothes was inclining his head to listen attentively to the Minister talk. He beckoned to Castang with a calm, affable expression.

Double doors. Anteroom, vaguely green and gold. Style of some Louis or other, or maybe some Empire or another: he neither knew nor cared. The Minister was whisking through another pair of doors, but under Castang's nose there was suddenly a young man with a smiling, pleasant face, an easy, open palm outspread, and unmistakeable cop eyes.

'Moment. You're Monsieur Castang, that right? Just the identity if you don't mind. Ah, good. A cop. I daresay you might be wearing a gun?'

'Well, I didn't know I was coming here.'

'Quite all right,' receiving the gun on his open palm, 'no need to excuse yourself. A tiny moment.' A second pair of hands slid from behind under his arms. With automatic ticklishness Castang jerked his chest out, understood, held still while the hands slid downward and the eyes kept smiling peacefully into his. 'Lovely. So sorry. Go ahead.' The door was opened for him. The décor here was grey and gold; quiet, a little faded. Some velvet, some brocade, some white stucco, some pictures in gilded wood frames. The Minister, hands again in pockets, was talking silently to a portrait of somebody. One of his predecessors possibly. Maybe the Duc de Choiseul?

Castang just stood there like a great clod of soil, but he didn't have time to get any wetter. The third pair of double doors opened —the brocade on the far side was a dull ruby flash—and the President of the Republic walked in, shut the door quietly behind him, gave a quick sweeping look across the whole room.

'Good morning, Roger,' shaking hands briefly with his Minister. 'And you'll be Monsieur Castang, correct?'

'Yes, Monsieur the P—'

'You just say sir. Very good. Sit down. You don't know why I've sent for you?'

'No sir' fighting down James Bond once and for all. Nor was it just the sack!

'No. I didn't want you to know, that's why. No previous con-fabulations or cooked-up stories. You're no good to me mortally embarrassed, either. Relax. Roger, just push two of the buttons, the white and the green, will you? I want to get acquainted with you, Monsieur Castang, and it may take half an hour or more.' The two sets of doors opened. Two menial persons stood obedient. The President looked at neither of them.

'The justice dossier,' to the secretary behind him. 'A glass of champagne,' to the footman behind Castang. The Minister, sitting with his legs stuck out, went on looking at portraits.

The service here was something like. The President, instantly, had a dossier and his reading glasses. Castang, almost as instantly, had a small silver tray by his elbow, holding a half bottle of bedewed cold Krug, a little crystal jug of orange juice, two Baccarat glasses, and a saucer with six canapés.

'I want you at your ease,' said the President, not looking up from his dossier. 'If you smoke, there are cigarettes beside you on the little table. Take what you like and do not be intimidated.'

There was a little match-book, white and gold, saying 'Elysée'. Castang put it in his pocket. Nobody will believe this, otherwise. Cop: one material proof. He moistened his lips, as the saying goes, thought the hell with it, took a big swallow, instantly felt fine.

'That's exactly what I wanted,' taking off his glasses. 'All right, Castang; you're a state servant, you seem a good one. Forget now your regulations for a few instants, and answer my questions. Be concise, yes. Be precise, yes. Be detached, yes. That is all pro-fessional. The reason why you're now sitting opposite me swigging that stuff is that I want you to be personal.'

The Minister didn't say anything, right to the end. He wasn't asked for any reminders, or any opinions. Castang never learned what he was there for. Presumably they had a little chat afterwards on the phone. He himself got thanked at the end, and got his hand shaken, but there are any number of obscure people in crowds who shake hands with Presidents during what the French call 'crowd-baths'. There was a recurrence of the previous act: steps, black DS, cops, whistles, suspended traffic, salutes. And all Castang would ever be able to say was 'Once, children, a very long time ago, the traffic got held up for me to cross the Rue Saint Honoré'. Even this was not the pleasure it should have been. While in the car, with the

Minister, the two piercing blue eyes were suddenly swivelled and plunged in like poniards.

'You understand the meaning of the word "secret", do you? I hope that for your sake you do. Because if you don't, you'll lose skin.'

Decidedly, the hospitality of the President was better than the Minister's.

XXXIV

THE REASONS OF THE STATE

'I've had a very high and mighty memorandum,' said Richard. 'Exceedingly, ingly, peremptory. So we're all going to obliterate this from our obedient and disciplined recollections. I hope, by the way, that your recollections were a bit disciplined.'

'I think so. You'll never believe this, but I got a half of champ. Krug, too.'

'No!'

'Wasn't enough to get me pissed.'

'How fortunate.'

One could get trussed up with official secrets, singed and gutted and plucked until one was just a goose in the market, but one's wife was oneself: one was talking in one's sleep.

'Coo,' said Vera, much impressed.

'Yes, coo. Likewise holy cow. Moo.'

'Is he bright?'

'Very. Had the dossier at the fingertip. Likewise knows how to use tools.'

'Calling you like that proves it. In the long run, nobody knows more of it than you.'

'I know very little about La Touche. I suppose nobody does. Even you. He's pretty odd, you know. Wants to die. Wrote to Pop saying so.'

So had another complex character: a gangster who condemned to life imprisonment for murder had got hold of a gun, taken hostages in the prison pharmacy, killed a woman nurse and a prison officer before being overpowered, been tried for this new crime, sentenced to death—hardly surprising—and caused some worry to the then President. His wish to die had, finally, been given him. One could say that the Presidential Grace had been accorded, not refused.

'Did he say anything interesting?'

'He quoted a few people. That old gag from Pascal about the Pyrenees and justice being contingent. Then he went over my head a little. Something from Simone Weil about nations never going to war for essentials but always for prestige. And some geezer who was a martyr in Roman times. Big shot, local Prefect, millionaire, owned half Aquitaine, offered himself as a slave to the Visigoths or some folk similar. Wrote all about it to a writer called Ausonius, who didn't understand and was most indignant about it all.'

'And who did you quote?'

'Nobody much. Madame Davids, a scrap. She has two sorts of Jewish story—besides the funny ones, I mean. One called a *hagada*, which means roughly a legend or a parable, and one called a *halaha*, meaning action or law: that's this: I must say she pinned my ears back with her damned stories, but this one did stick. Apparently it's Jewish law that a man declared unanimously guilty has to be acquitted. That is highly complex and technical, to do with there being twenty-three judges in a criminal case. But there's no Proc, and no defending counsel. So strictly only ten members of the tribunal are judges, the others being prosecution or defence, and if the whole court condemns, the argument runs that the man hasn't had a proper defence.'

'None of that is the case here. And the jury wasn't unanimous.'

'Doesn't matter. The modern version would be along the lines of God intervening in the debate, saying "You have condemned. But Me, I pardon." '

'And did God tell you what he thought of that?'

'He didn't even tell the Minister.'

'So still nobody knows.'

'He reflects.'

'Who was the man who wrote to Ausonius? He sounds interesting.'

'Somebody called Paulinus. But quotations made by Presidents aren't necessarily a guide to what they really think.'

'No,' said Vera sadly. 'I learned that back in Czechoslovakia.'

XXXV

WHAT MAKES THAT REAR RANK BREATHE SO HARD?

La Touche had taken up smoking, and seemed to find pleasure in it. He read a good deal, and wrote quite a lot. Most of it went into the wastepaper basket he had asked for, which the guards emptied without curiosity. Sometimes he tore a page out of his exercise book and put it in a manila envelope, whose privacy nobody peeked into.

'What do we need anyway—an art of living or an art of dying? What on earth is the use of a life one does not know how to leave?'

'Always this anxiety. A passion for "survival" at any cost. Our admiration is reserved for those who "fight back". Reasonable and legitimate, as long as exaggeration does not give rise to cant. Survival can be ignoble. We admire, rightly, the Uruguayan rugby players who ate their dead companions when the plane crashed in the high mountains: that was a noble survival.'

'The men who know how to die have been sentimentalised. Charles the First was a despicable person, who realised some important truths about being a king. The Carmelites, who went up the steps singing, attached no importance to death. Find an example in the bourgeois class.'

'Better . . . the English soldier who said "I am just going outside, and may be a little time". Snow gives an easy death, it is said: one slips off comfortably to sleep. But it is the readiness which counts. There are certainly innumerable condemned criminals. I acquire no merit whatever. Less ignoble than survival, that is all.'

'By all means abolish this penalty if it can be done without cant.

But a condemned man must be allowed to choose it if he wishes. As long as this hypocrite snivelling about "respect for life" stops.'

'Those who fail their tests should be given a chance to try again. And this does not mean prison, which is nothing but despair.'

'I say to myself "I will be brave on Tuesday fortnight". That always seems such a very long way off. But Tuesday fortnight always comes.'

So it did. Commissaire Richard got an official letter.

'Well, the appeal has been refused: they're pulling the string on La Touche.'

'It's what he wanted. I'm no longer surprised. Anyway, one never knows why governments do things. Quite likely that some imbecile somewhere has quacked that firmness must be shown.'

'You're being imaginative again, my boy,' said Richard.

'All right, I know,' answered Castang sulkily. 'Bourgeois government can't be caught showing tenderness to one of their own and severity to Johnny, and I'm not paid to say that. I know.'

'We'll just stick to the point at issue,' said Richard. 'As you know there's a long list of people obliged to attend executions and the commissaire of police gets his little invitation card, just like a town hall reception.'

'Wouldn't be in your shoes.'

'I've news for you: you are. La Touche has asked for you to be present: d'you want to refuse?'

'Yes. Rot the silly bastard: he's never been anything but trouble. Oh hell, I have to say yes, don't I.'

'You do. You've never been, of course.'

'Have you?'

'No,' said Richard seriously, 'it's the first time it's arisen. I don't like it any more than you do, and also it's not altogether bad. There are too many cops who say blithely they'd pull the string their bloody selves. And if a cop's been killed one understands. But mostly they're desk cops. This is a lesson.'

'For you?'

'Yes.' Richard's moments of humanity were rare and sudden, and did not last long. 'To be honest, I'll be grateful for your support.'

'When?'

'Day after tomorrow.' Castang did not tell Vera.

A lot of people got invitations to the government's dawn cocktail party. The President of the tribunal, who read his with a face of stone: the Judge of Instruction, who made his worst face and was tart towards policemen. The Proc, who to do him justice said he'd go. Monsieur Mars, however, said bleakly that he had foreseen the event, although he had not expected it. Having taken one half of the responsibility, one could not evade the rest. I've done it before, said the Proc, and you haven't . . . well, I'll say no more.

The defence advocate, Maître Weber, who felt very sick.

Inside the prison, the director talked to screws, doctors, chaplains.

'There's a rather horrible ritual—this stuff with a white shirt and processional solemnities. There's no use talking about being simple or human, but for the love of Christ let's make sure we're efficient.'

The Protestant chaplain asked his colleagues for a whisky.

'This man's officially a Huguenot, so I'm on the line. He says he doesn't belong to any church at all, and maintained that even before, but he agrees he's a believer. Well now, we're all grown up. None of that ecumenical bullshit need apply. I'm just asking you for professional solidarity.'

'Well yes, of course,' said the colleagues.

'It'll be a new story about the Prot, the Papist and the Yid,' said the Catholic chaplain helping himself to more whisky. 'Will he take Holy Communion?'

'He says he will, and I'm convinced it's with a true heart. So I thought both of us . . .?'

'Sure, but what about old Finklestein here?'

'No bother at all,' comfortably. 'The Youps will be there. In fact I hadn't known quite how to tell you but he sent for me and said he'd killed a Jew and how did one go about asking forgiveness. We have edifying texts for the occasion; do you both no end of good.'

'And what about our esteemed Moslem brother? They're very good when it comes to capital punishment.'

'And one small offence against charity, Father.'

'I only confess nowadays to my analyst.'

'We must certainly ask him; I know he has a special blessing. There was that Arab boy a year ago who got commuted but it did look for a while as though. And we Semites, you know . . . I know too that it would please La Touche.'

'Right,' said the reverend gentlemen.

'I have an awful sinking feeling. I know it's only death, but they suffer, you know. That stuff about it's only knee-jerks is crap.'

'So did Christ suffer,' said the Rabbi briskly.

'I'm certainly not saying gas is more humane. Just that as a military man, I have a prejudice in favour of bullet wounds.'

'I'm all for lung cancer, myself. An unreconstructed pacifist.'

'You'll be turning vegetarian next. It's just I'm a bit frightened about cold sweat and vertigo.'

'So are we all. So is he.'

'No; we can't let him be braver than we are.'

XXXVI

WHAT MAKES THAT FRONT-RANK MAN FALL DOWN?

'A touch of sun,' said La Touche, changing shirts.

Castang had been cowardly. He hadn't gone home at all, and told Vera he would be out all night, but nothing to worry about: nothing unsafe.

'An Englishman,' said Richard unexpectedly, 'called Ralee or is it Ralay, asked for a second shirt. I could do with one.'

Stand outside it, Castang told himself quietly. Everyone here could do with a second shirt. There is, also, a strong smell of whisky.

'I'm not very keen on the taste of rum,' La Touche had said to the director, 'I'd rather have a brandy if it's all the same to you.'

'I put a hell of a Mickey Finn in it,' admitted the doctor afterwards. 'Strung up like that one can't tell how quick it will work. But some muscular relaxation anyhow.'

'I'm glad I took up smoking,' said La Touche.

'I never thought,' said the chief screw afterwards to the director, 'I'd ever live to see a civil servant make like Bogart.' They were both connoisseurs of last-reels.

'You know what he said in reality?' delighted. 'Throat cancer, you know. Hurts to swallow.'

'All right, skip that part.'

'"I knew I never should have switched from Scotch to Martinis."'

'Oh boy.'

La Touche passed in front of Castang and his eyelids wrinkled with pleasure.

'Good. By the way, there's an envelope in my cell. You'll look after that?'

'Of course.'

'Kiss of peace?'

'Thank you,' idiotically.

'And incidentally?'

'Yes.'

'Give my love to your wife,' said La Touche.

'Go in peace,' said the four chaplains. 'Go with God.'

'Shalom,' said La Touche.

That was all.

'Ho, the young recruits are shaking, and they'll want
       their beer today,
After hanging Danny Deever in the morning.'